# CLASS REUNION

*Class Reunion* is a deeply nostalgic story charting the rites of passage and changing fortunes of three convent school friends, their lives forever influenced by the confines of their Catholicism. Clare is pretty, clever, privileged and a conformist. She marries well, and is sure to lead a happy, successful life. But does she? Pippa is fey, artistic and a dreamer. Devout yet unconventional, even though she embraces the religious life she wants to do her own thing in an increasingly tolerant age. But can she? Eleanor, the sceptic, abandons her religion. More ambitious than her two friends, she becomes a media star. But a fatal mistake at the beginning of her adult life costs her dear. She wants happiness—but will it elude her? Linked by a series of class reunions, Nicola Thorne plots the story of three very different girls who, as they progress through womanhood, remain strongly influenced by the past.

# CLASS REUNION

## Nicola Thorne

CHIVERS PRESS
BATH

First published 1999
by
HarperCollins*Publishers*
This Large Print edition published by
Chivers Press
by arrangement with
HarperCollins*Publishers* Ltd
2000

ISBN 0 7540 1439 8

British Library Cataloguing in Publication Data available

Printed and bound in Great Britain by
REDWOOD BOOKS, Trowbridge, Wiltshire

*For Stefan and Rebecca with love*

# CONTENTS

PROLOGUE

# JUNE 1998

We were known as the three musketeers, Pippa, Clare and I. Our friendship began at junior school, strengthened as we grew older and in the sixth form we were practically inseparable. It seems very strange to think that such strong bonds made in our formative years could ever be broken. But they were, and eventually we lost touch.

We were all born in 1946—the year after our fathers returned from the war. I remember most of the girls in my class, but none better than Pippa and Clare.

Only interludes of my school life come back to me now. I remember the day I arrived at St Catherine's Convent, aged nine. Although I have only a hazy recollection of my last day there, I remember the summer of that year, 1964; the lazy days after the exams ended, and the sense of expectation about the future.

For some reason too I remember the Dog roses that cascaded over the tall convent walls, the smell of flowering currant on the path leading to the lake, and the tall scarlet and purple rhododendrons that lined each side.

All this I recalled so clearly the day I went back to the convent for the first time after

1

more than thirty years. The occasion was the annual reunion marking the hundredth anniversary of the foundation of the school.

The nuns had now gone, and the convent was in the process of becoming an institute for higher education, part of the town's new university.

When I was a pupil, the grounds had been beautifully kept. There had also been swans on the lake, and a boat. There had been well-maintained tennis courts and several acres of meadow leading down from the main house and which, in my mind, I always associate with tall grass interspersed with buttercups, clover and cow parsley, and endless summer. The chestnut tree at the bottom of the meadow was heavy with pink blooms; but above all I recall, so vividly that I can almost smell it now, the pungent aroma of incense wafting from numerous thurifers as the annual Corpus Christi procession wended its way through the grounds. We all wore white dresses and veils; parents came; the clergy from the diocese took part and the bishop—heaven knows how he did it—carried the monstrance above his head until Benediction, which was celebrated at an altar constructed at the far end of the grounds. Our childish voices, accompanied by the adults, rose to the heavens in a paean of praise as with the greatest enthusiasm and fervour we belted out the processional hymns.

As I walked round the by now neglected and

2

depleted grounds, the lake bereft of swans and the ruined hull of what must have been our boat projecting from the water, it was difficult but not impossible to recall the days of my youth, and the friends I made then.

I'd arrived early to have the opportunity to wander round before confronting the party of old girls assembling on the lawn. I was anxious to see Pippa, Clare and all the others again, but I felt apprehensive too, and I hurried along the path by the main gate to collect my thoughts before anyone would see me.

*    *    *

Clare Pearson was one of those girls who excelled at everything. She also became more attractive as she grew older. She had dark wavy hair, alert and intelligent brown eyes, a fetching smile and a dimpled chin. She always avoided getting into trouble whereas, invariably when I was younger, I was caught and sent to bed straight after supper without any recreation; or kept in after school and not allowed games. Not that I minded (games were never my forte) but Clare, being good at everything, was captain of netball and a star on the tennis court. She also excelled academically; everything came to her easily. By the time we were in the sixth form I had stopped misbehaving. We were both school prefects, Children of Mary, but she was Head

3

girl. Yet, despite her astonishing versatility, Clare was popular, and lots of girls had crushes on her.

As they had on Pippa Sidgwick who was a most unusual girl because, although she appeared unassuming, she was a person you noticed. The impression she made was of someone fey, a dreamer, impractical, enigmatic yet fun-loving, which seemed to sum up the contradictions in her personality. She was fine-boned, with skin like porcelain, wispy golden hair and azure-blue eyes. Yet she had a toughness and robustness which her air of fragility cleverly concealed. I think this was what made her such a puzzle, so hard for others to understand. Though not as clever as Clare, she was academically sound, had a good voice, drew and painted beautifully.

Some of her mystery was expressed in the fact that, although not a Roman Catholic she was more religious than either Clare or I. She went to Mass every day and used to stay behind afterwards to pray. I know she wanted to become a Catholic but her mother wouldn't let her. She said she had to wait until she was old enough to know her own mind.

I don't know what drew us together. We were very different. I was neither good at games nor academic. I was good at acting, though, and liked to play a part. I was rather rebellious, a bit of a show-off and ambitious. That ambition never really left me.

4

I think what we shared was a great sense of the absurd; we were iconoclasts in a world where conformity was drilled into you. At that time we didn't question our faith, but we questioned everything else.

*      *      *

For some years after we left school we kept in touch. Pippa and Clare went to university. I didn't even apply. I was anxious to earn a living and be independent from my parents who were perpetually hard-up. There was a touch of Mr Micawber in Father who was always hatching unsuccessful business schemes unrelated to anything he'd done before; so it was not surprising that they failed. Besides, he had a poor opinion of educated women, thought university a waste of time and, as I was unlikely to get a scholarship, he could never have supported me. So I took a secretarial course and got a job on a local paper.

Eventually Clare, Pippa and I stopped meeting; correspondence ceased, even Christmas cards, and we lost touch. To my regret now I never even attended one class reunion.

This was the first one, and after such a long time I wondered how would they view me and how would I find them?

Reaching the bottom of the hill, lost in dreamy reminiscences about the past, I sat on the bank by the side of the lake. It was a sunny, tranquil day, very like the kind of day so many years ago when we three girls would lie in the tall grass, surrounded by the sights and sounds of summer—Pippa usually with a pad in front of her, sketching—and dream about our future.

Oh, what dreams.

# PART I

*A Start in Life*

CHAPTER ONE

# JULY 1964

Every morning after Mass, when most of the congregation had left, Clare used to walk slowly along the side aisle and quietly open the chapel windows, one by one, to let in the fresh air. In the winter she might open only a couple, and then she'd hurry out to the warmth of the corridor. But on a summer's day she lingered by each opened window, taking in the sight below her. It was so cherished and familiar, yet always new and fresh with each seasonal mood: the meadow stretching down to the lake where swans glided majestically and, in a corner, the row boat with its oars drawn up, ready for someone to step aboard.

This morning Clare stood by each window for a moment longer than usual. The sky was a deep blue and the pink blooms of the chestnut tree swayed to and fro in the gentle breeze that rippled the waters of the lake and ruffled the feathers of the swans.

Today was a special day because it was the last one of her life at school.

By lunch time they would all be gone, taken to the railway station in the school bus or collected by parents. All round there was bustle and excitement. Through the half-open door of the chapel she could hear a medley of voices coming from the dormitory nearby, as lockers were cleared and bed linen dispersed into large bags ready for the laundry. In the holidays the dormitory would be cleaned and possibly repainted, ready for the new influx of pupils the following term.

Nine years earlier they had included Clare, Pippa and Eleanor.

'Let's be friends,' they had said, meeting in the corridor outside the dormitory, new and lonely and rather timid. They bonded then, and friends they had remained. It was terrible now to think of that final parting.

Clare knew that she would be back. Her family came from the town; there would be reunions and visits to the school, but that camaraderie of buddies who had shared so many things, so many confidences and moments of intimacy from girlhood through adolescence would be at an end. No going back. Time to grow up. But if she felt sadness as she opened the last window, she felt excited too.

One or two of the more pious nuns always stayed on after Mass, deep in meditation, but now only one person remained, kneeling in a pew near the front, head partly covered by a short black veil, hands joined in prayer.

Pippa was sometimes teased about her piety. She was always the last to leave the chapel, sometimes creeping late into breakfast.

She was extremely devout, although she was not a Catholic. She never missed Mass and came top of the form in religious knowledge. Clare edged along the pew towards her, reached out and took her arm.

'We'd better go or we'll be late.'

Slowly Pippa raised her head and Clare saw that her cheeks were tear-stained.

'It's not the end,' Clare squeezed her hand encouragingly. Pippa nodded. She took a handkerchief from her pocket and blew her nose.

'I know, but I'm afraid.'

'There's nothing to be afraid of.' Clare looked anxiously at the chapel clock. 'Hurry, or we'll miss breakfast.'

\*      \*      \*

In the refectory grace had already been said, and a buzz of sound greeted them as they entered. They apologised to Mother Brendan, the mistress of the boarders, for being late— she was indulgent on the last day—and took their seats next to each other at the sixth form table.

Eleanor had already started eating.

'What kept you?' she asked, looking up.

'Sadness, nostalgia,' Clare removed her napkin from its ring and spread it on her lap. 'I felt as though I was taking my last look round at the grounds from the chapel window.'

11

'Oh you'll look again, I'm sure, plenty more times.'

'We'll all be back,' Pippa said, recovered now from her tears, 'for the reunion.'

Eleanor grimaced. Everyone looked so *old* at reunion days. She couldn't imagine wearing a hat and gloves and carrying a handbag and chatting about one's family and children. But maybe one would when one got that old.

But Eleanor too felt sad, although she was probably more apprehensive about leaving school than the other two. Pippa and Clare had places at university, subject to good A level results, but she was going straight to secretarial college. It was her choice, her decision. Sometimes she regretted it, though she was never as good academically as the other two. She would probably just scrape through her As.

The group of sixth formers sitting at the table, together as schoolgirls for the last time, included many she was sure she'd never see again: Mary Barlow, Joan Dixon, Kathleen Lonsdale, Jennifer Cuthbert, Ruth Brown, Margaret Potter. But what of Pippa and Clare? For so long they'd been inseparable. It was a bond like no other.

They always stood a little apart from the others—Pippa, Eleanor and Clare. Some people made unkind remarks about the closeness of their friendship, others felt excluded. Most, however, envied them because

12

in that small slightly claustrophobic world they were a rather splendid trio, each one excelling in something. Clare in everything. Pippa was an accomplished artist, sang beautifully, got above average grades in academic work. Eleanor, the tallest, usually took the lead in the school play, was flamboyant, liked to be noticed, made people laugh. 'A personality' they said about Eleanor, someone you couldn't help noticing.

The gong sounded and conversation stopped immediately. Mother Brendan, who had been *in loco parentis* during their school years, tucked her arms inside her cowl and put on a brave face as she always did at this annual occurrence—when the rooms, dormitories and corridors were cleared of chattering voices and the convent was plunged in silence. A sort of gloom seemed to descend on the community as they went about their tasks, as though they needed the children to complete their vocation. Even an experienced nun like Mother Brendan hated to say goodbye to favourite girls, some of whom she knew she would never see again, despite what they said. After all, sharing them so intimately with their parents, they had become her children too.

'Now girls,' she said briskly. 'Those who have not finished packing their trunks please go to the locker room and do so immediately; and those whose desks are still full see that they're emptied and the lids left open. And

13

those . . .'

The instructions were concluded with a few brief words of farewell, especially to those who were not returning, though she had privately said all her goodbyes.

She, for one, would miss Clare and Pippa, but perhaps not Eleanor so much. She was always too knowing, too quick with her answers, a shade too independent. Mother Brendan felt she led, and the other two followed. She felt quite apprehensive about what would become of Eleanor in later life. Clare, she knew, would do well and succeed, and Pippa too, though perhaps in an unexpected direction. In her heart of hearts she nursed the secret hope that Pippa, in the fullness of time, might achieve her wish to convert and maybe even become a nun. Pippa would always be gentle and loving, put herself out for other people. She would make a wonderful religious.

Naturally there were no classes that morning, and after Pippa, Clare and Eleanor had seen their trunks taken to the hall, they split up and supervised the excited and disorganised juniors in clearing out their desks and gathering up their bits and pieces scattered throughout the school. Pippa especially was adored by the little ones who clung to her until the very last minute.

*     *     *

It was nearly noon. Parents were already arriving, cars drawing up in the driveway.

By arrangement, the trio slipped away and met at the top of the steps leading down to the lake. They said nothing as they swiftly descended but, once on level ground and as they set out along the path, impulsively they flung their arms around one anothers' waists: friends, bosom pals, schoolgirls together, they knew, in this way at least, for the very last time.

*     *     *

*October 1966*

The wind gusted along the narrow street blowing an old tin can along in its path. The noise of the can reverberated throughout the empty office, making it hard to concentrate. When, momentarily, the wind dropped, the can stopped rolling and Eleanor began to read through her copy, checking the sense, the punctuation, the number of words.

The wind started up again, the can began its clatter and, with an exclamation, Eleanor left her chair and was more than half-way across the room when the office door opened and Ted McGuinness came in, pausing on the threshold as she nearly cannoned into him.

'Hey there,' he said, putting a hand on her shoulder. 'Where are you off to?'

Eleanor looked up with an apologetic smile, still rather nervous of Ted, especially if he should touch or brush against her.

'I'm just going out to stop that can making a noise. It's driving me bonkers!'

Ted looked over her head towards the window. He was a large, powerful man, with heavy features: an Irishman with black curly hair and blue eyes that seemed to have a special twinkle for Eleanor.

Though she'd made a lot of mistakes when she started on the *Darlsdon Echo*, Ted, the editor, was always patient with her, helpful and constructive. She was a little in awe of him.

He stood aside and Eleanor sprinted down the narrow stairs and out into the street, but the wind had died down and the can was nowhere to be seen.

A very thin cat came up to her and rubbed itself ingratiatingly against her trousered leg. She reached down to stroke it. She loved animals, and wondered if it was a stray. She'd seen it before. One day she might pick it up and take it back to her bedsit. But her landlady would have a fit. Also, there would be no one to look after it. It wouldn't be fair.

Eleanor returned to her office where she found Ted reading through her copy. She stood for a while watching him. His opinion mattered. He had taught her everything she knew about journalism.

She took a cigarette from the pack on her

desk, offered one to Ted, who shook his head, preoccupied with her copy.

'Good!' he said, rising from her desk. 'You've got talent, young lady. Wasted in a place like this.'

Ted was right. It was a dead-end job in a dead-end town, but Eleanor Hamilton was ambitious. Ted had said she was wasted in this place, but she was learning. All top journalists started on provincial papers. She had her dreams.

\*     \*     \*

Eleanor thought about the cat as she heated her baked beans up on the gas ring in her bedsit. She was very lonely and the cat would be company. But it would also be a tie. She was only going to give the paper a few more months and then she'd be off. She already scanned the trade press for jobs; had written— so far without success—to one or two of the big chains. She knew she would get there in the end. The *Darlsdon Echo* was the local paper in a small run-down Lancashire town where the cotton mills had closed and the mines were fighting for survival. Situated on the Pennine range, it was a grimy, depressing sort of place, where the only thriving trade was that of the licensed victualler. There were ten public houses—one on nearly every corner— an hotel, two fish and chip shops, a curry

17

house; but nowhere decent to eat. For that you had to travel into the surrounding countryside—pretty and not too far away.

The food at the hotel, like the accommodation, was awful. When the town was prosperous it had been a thriving concern, but now it was run-down, just like everything else. The number of unemployed was well above the national average.

There were many other similar towns, with rows of terraced houses in serried ranks astride the valleys, spirals of smoke issuing from so many identical chimneys. The steep streets were mostly cobbled. Children played in them, or rode their bicycles dangerously downhill. There was nothing for young people to do. It was as if they could see into the future, and it was bleak. More and more as the mills closed the future that faced them was unemployment like their fathers who returned on Fridays, with grim faces, clutching their wage packets and wondering how much longer their jobs could last.

After she'd eaten, Eleanor curled up in the chair before the gas fire and opened her book. Downstairs, she could hear the sound of the Bakers' TV. Mrs Baker was her landlady, and she lived with her teenage son, Denis. No one knew what had happened to Mr Baker; no one asked. Mrs Baker was the sort of woman who didn't encourage questions.

She was a mystery but not a very interesting

one and Eleanor thought that she knew as much about her as she wanted to know. She had a job but Eleanor didn't know what she did.

Eleanor usually went to bed at about ten and was always the first person in the office.

Her work was her life.

\*　　　\*　　　\*

Eleanor scarcely thought back to her schooldays in the convent. She only went to Mass when she was at home. Her parents would have been shocked.

Her father worked long hours as a salesman, travelling in fitted kitchens, which were becoming popular. You got rid of your dressers and cupboards and gas stoves and installed a new fitted version. Her father couldn't be described as a handyman, nor had he any skills as a carpenter. He had undoubtedly chosen the wrong occupation. He always did. He didn't earn a salary, but worked on commission. Although a rather sad figure, he was an irreproachable husband and parent. He had very little imagination, whereas her mother's was extremely fertile. Her life was beset with hidden fears and terrors, and at one time she suffered acutely from agoraphobia. She was permanently on medication.

Home was a semi-detached, three-bedroomed house on a busy main road in a

19

suburb of Manchester. It was from here that her father left to go to work, usually for a few days if he was travelling, and to here that he returned to comfort his nervous wife. During his sales trips, she usually whiled away the time staring out of the window from behind net curtains, safe from the world she could only look out on, yet imagining some dreadful accident that might make her a widow and dependent on the State.

In recent years her mother had seemed to improve, maybe because of all the medication she'd been prescribed. Nevertheless, it seemed an awful way to live.

Because of her mother's bad health, Eleanor had been sent away to school. Her mother's brother, George, who was a prosperous farmer, helped out with the fees. Eleanor thrived and did well enough, despite bouts of misbehaviour. But university would still mean being dependent on her uncle George, whereas a job meant freedom. She'd never regretted what she'd done.

\*　　　\*　　　\*

The following day Eleanor went off to work as usual, unaware that her life was about to change dramatically.

It was a normal sort of day. There was the regular morning conference, where events were discussed and jobs handed out. She was

20

to interview the man who was to be the next chairman of the town council. Not much excitement there, except that he was a leading light in the Labour Party, and rumour had it that he was extremely corrupt. Jobs for the boys. Ted warned her that not a whiff of this must appear in the paper or they'd be sued for libel. The chairman-elect was a friend of the managing director of the group which owned the *Darlsdon Echo*, so the interview must be flattering. Nothing about council money getting into the wrong hands.

There were only two reporters, Eleanor and a youth called Charlie. With Ted they had to cover the town. A lot of stuff came in on the wire from agencies. There was a typist, Mavis, who also answered the telephone, but spent a lot of time on it talking to her boyfriend; and a freelance photographer, Ed.

After her interview with the chairman-elect, Eleanor had to try and persuade the owner of a local mill to tell her the truth about whether it was to close or not. Rumour had it that the shutters could go up before Christmas. And what a miserable time that would be for about fifty families.

Eleanor recalled what a tough time her family had had when Dad was between jobs. Some of the mill workers would never get another.

She was through by five, and went back to the office to type up her stories. She had just about finished when Ted appeared at the door of his room, a scowl on his face.

'Have you seen Charlie?'

Eleanor shook her head.

'Well, when he does come in you can tell him he's got the sack!'

Eleanor sat back and looked at Ted. 'That's hardly my job, Ted. I'm afraid you'll have to do it yourself—if you're serious, that is.'

'He isn't here and he didn't ring in. I've had about as much of that young man as I can stand. I'll have to get a replacement. In the meantime, you'll have to help me put the paper to bed.'

They worked hard until about nine. There was no sign of Charlie, so Eleanor wrote some extra copy, making up a few stories, and they dug up a fuzzy picture taken on a rainy day of employees protesting outside a mill that was about to close and captioned it. It would fit in nicely with the current mill story.

'Just time for a bite to eat,' Ted said, glancing at the clock on the wall as he handed the copy to the cyclist who had come to collect for the printers. 'Care for a curry, Eleanor?'

'That would be nice.' Eleanor paused. 'Won't your wife be expecting you?'

'My wife never expects me,' Ted said enigmatically. 'Get your coat.'

\*        \*        \*

It was a raw night and Ted took her arm as they hurried through the deserted rain-swept streets to the curry house. The only occupants, apart from the staff, were a furtive looking couple sitting closely together in a corner.

The manager bustled forwards to greet them.

'Nice to see you, Mr McGuinness. Very cold night.'

'Very cold, Vikram.' Ted blew on his hands, rubbing them together. 'A nice Tokka-E-Bahar for two, I think. Is that alright, Eleanor?'

Eleanor shrugged as she gave her coat to the manager. 'Whatever it is sounds alright to me.'

'It's spiced lamb cooked over charcoal.' The manager directed them to a table and they sat down. 'Together with vegetable curry and fried rice. And some samosas and chapati to start with, Vikram.'

'Certainly, Mr McGuinness. And to drink?'

'Is lager alright?' Ted looked across at Eleanor who nodded agreement.

'Two lagers, Vikram.' Ted smiled at Eleanor and offered her a cigarette from his packet. 'Well, that makes his night. Not much custom.'

The Indian restaurant wasn't very atmospheric, dimly-lit with cheap paper lanterns and faded, plum-coloured flock wallpaper.

'It's a wonder that places like this survive,' Eleanor commented as Ted leaned across the

23

table to light her cigarette.

'Oh, it has a good trade at lunch time, and on Saturday nights you can hardly get a table. Don't go out much, do you, Eleanor?'

'Not really.'

'A girl like you ought to have more of a life.'

'I don't really have the time or the energy.' Eleanor looked pointedly at Ted who sat back in his chair observing her thoughtfully. 'Besides, I go and see my parents most weekends.'

'No boyfriend?'

Eleanor shook her head.

'We must do something about that.' Ted took a deep drag on his cigarette, his eyes still on her. 'There is a possibility that sometime next year I'll be promoted.'

'Well, what has that to do with me getting a boyfriend?'

'Wait. I'm coming to it.'

Ted paused as Vikram came up with the samosas and chapati, and two lagers carefully balanced on a tray.

After a few sips of her lager and some samosa, Eleanor felt better. She had in fact been very hungry. She looked across at Ted. 'You were saying?'

'I'm in for promotion. If I move to the group headquarters in Tambridge I'd like you to come with me. I think I can get you a better job, and there'll be more people for you to meet. It's possible, anyway, the office here will

24

close. They're running it down as it is. More and more news is centralised. I want to replace Charlie, but they've told me to hang on. Ignore what I said today. I was angry. Anyway, if the office closes, Charlie certainly doesn't get the chance of a new job, not with me anyway.'

'And when will this be?' Eleanor finished her samosa and wiped her fingers on a paper napkin.

'Maybe in the summer.'

Vikram returned with another tray and removed their plates.

'The tokka will be a few more minutes, Mr McGuinness. We cook it very fresh.'

'That's alright,' Ted smiled. 'There's no hurry. Another lager please, Vikram.' He looked across at Eleanor who indicated that her glass was still half-full. As Vikram went off, Ted lit another cigarette.

'Interested, Eleanor?'

'I'll have to think about it.'

'What is there to think about? You don't want to stay in a dead-end job like this for the rest of your life, do you, Eleanor?'

'I thought I'd rather like to go to London. I've been looking at jobs in the south. I've learned a lot and I'm grateful.'

'I think you'd be making a mistake.' Ted looked at her gravely. 'I'm sure you'll do well, but you have a lot to learn. A better job here will give you more of a chance in Fleet Street later on. You're still very young. Maybe

25

women's editor of a group newspaper. If you went to London now you'd have to start at the bottom, believe me. Besides,' Ted's hand moved slowly across the table and closed over hers, 'I'd miss you, Eleanor. I've become very fond of you. You know that, don't you?'

\*     \*     \*

In a way it was all so predictable.

Perhaps coffee back at her place hadn't been a good idea, but Ted had grown very emotional as he blurted out his life story: his early marriage, the realisation he was growing away from his wife, Eileen.

Ted was only thirty-two—she'd thought he was older—and he also thought life was passing him by, and that Eileen, who came from a small local village, was holding him back. She never liked to entertain. She didn't socialise. She said the children wore her out. Four children in five years.

By the time Ted finished, it was nearly midnight and even patient Vikram was showing signs of restlessness, of wanting to close the restaurant and go home.

'I'll see you back,' Ted had said, and it seemed so callous and, yes, rather childish to leave him in such an emotional state on her doorstep.

Besides, nothing could happen. He was her boss.

26

Eleanor liked Ted, but she had never thought of him in terms of attraction, of intimacy. She was a convent girl; he was married. She wouldn't dream of looking at another woman's husband.

She had never seen Eileen. No one had. As Ted said, Eileen didn't entertain or socialise, and everyone imagined she was rather shy. There was a photograph of her and the kids on Ted's desk. She looked pretty, but someone who'd met her said she photographed well.

The gas fire spluttered and the clock in the church tower struck midnight.

Eleanor said, 'You ought to go.'

'I can't go now,' Ted said sleepily. 'It's too late.'

'Well where will your wife think you are?'

'She'll think I'm on a job. I'll ring her first thing in the morning.'

'Won't she be worried?'

Ted laughed as if he found the idea amusing. It seemed to sum up their relationship. The picture emerged of the bored husband and the tired wife, both disillusioned with their lives. Eleanor was conscious of contrasting emotions: a feeling of intense nervousness and apprehension coupled with a growing sense of excitement, almost of recklessness.

She knew this was a dangerous situation. Maybe Ted had planned it. She was naïve, inexperienced, trusting. She also knew little or nothing about sex and sexual attraction.

She'd always wondered what it would be like.

People said you weren't complete without it.

*      *      *

*February 1967*

'It's great to see you.'

'And you.'

Mark Pearson seized Eleanor's bag and they walked towards the station exit.

'I hear you got married?' Eleanor looked up at Clare's elder brother who grinned.

'You attached yet?'

'Not likely.' Eleanor settled into the front seat of the car which was parked just outside the station.

'A career girl?'

'I guess so. For the moment anyway.'

Mark turned out of the station precinct and drove up the familiar High Street towards the Pearson home—a large detached house with a drive on the outskirts of Wolversleigh, where she'd attended school. It was only about five miles from the convent, but many local families had sent their children to board because it was considered rather common not to. It also gave the impression that you might not have been able to afford the fees. Pippa's home, too, was only a few miles away. It was

Eleanor who had been the outsider, coming miles away from Manchester, but her Uncle George farmed near Wolversleigh and knew that St Catherine's was the right sort of school for his niece, given her mother's poor state of health.

'Clare's got some news.' Mark turned in through the imposing gates and gave Eleanor a mysterious smile.

'Don't say she's getting married!'

Mark's smile widened.

'I'm not supposed to say.'

'I don't believe . . .' Eleanor began, but at that moment they arrived at the front door which flew open and Clare rushed to greet them, arms extended.

'Oh it's so *good* to see you,' she said, hugging Eleanor. 'It's been ages. Did Mark tell you . . . isn't it *exciting*?'

'Mark didn't say . . .'

'I'm getting engaged. We're announcing it tonight. It's so thrilling.'

Eleanor took her friend's hand and squeezed it. 'But who?'

'Andrew Thornton. I don't think you know him.'

'Is he at university?'

'Oh no. I've known him forever. He's a partner of Mark's.'

'An accountant?'

'Don't say it like that!' Clare tapped her friend sharply on the arm. 'He's not stuffy.'

29

'I'm not stuffy,' Mark protested.

'You are a bit!' Clare said. 'And you'll get stuffier . . .'

'Oh come on you two,' Eleanor said laughing. 'We could be here all day. Happy birthday, anyway.' She kissed Clare.

'I'll take you to your room,' Clare clasped Eleanor's arm, 'and tell you all about Andy.'

*       *       *

Clare's father, Dr Pearson, was a large, rather formidable man—more feared than loved by his patients. He was an old style family doctor whose ego and innate sense of superiority were boosted by the deference and obsequiousness of patients and family alike. Christopher Pearson came from a long line of Pearsons who had been medical practitioners in the town. He had married Edith Wright whose father was a prosperous mill owner, and whose family also lived in a sizeable house on the other side of Wolversleigh. Edith Pearson had also been a pupil at St Catherine's Convent run by the nuns of the Society of St Catherine. They, rather like Dr Pearson, considered themselves superior to the nuns who ran a nearby rival establishment for the care and education of Catholic girls in Wellesley Place.

Eleanor was fond of both of Clare's parents. They'd always been very kind to her and, after she'd changed and had had a good gossip with

30

Clare, they greeted her warmly in the lounge where they were waiting for cars to take them to the hotel. Accompanying them was Andrew, who was slightly shorter than Eleanor had expected, not particularly good looking, a rather solemn-looking young man with glasses, not a bit like she'd imagined.

But love was blind.

He had, however, a pleasant smile and opened up to Eleanor when introduced. He told her he had met her before, and when she confessed she couldn't remember the occasion, he told her he'd attended the school play in their last year at St Catherine's. She nodded agreement but, in reality, she couldn't honestly recall meeting him.

It must have been then, unknown to Eleanor or Pippa, Andrew began to court Clare. He had just completed his Articles and started his first job. He was ten years older than her. She had told Eleanor in the bedroom that he was solid and reliable, with very good prospects; the sort of man she'd be happy with, someone like Daddy.

Eleanor suspected he might also be dour and unimaginative. In a way she saw him as a foil, a counterpart to Clare's vivacity. She would always outshine him, and he would adore her.

And no, she wasn't too young. She knew her own mind. She would graduate in the summer and the wedding would be in the autumn.

31

Eleanor was invited to be a bridesmaid.

\*　　　　\*　　　　\*

Clare's party was held at a local hotel. It took the form of a dinner for sixty guests, with dancing afterwards for a much larger number—mostly young people, Clare's schoolmates and friends from university.

The people at the dinner were family; Clare's parents, her brothers Frank and Mark, Mark's wife Chrissy, uncles, aunts, cousins and older friends of her parents, and colleagues of her father. There was also a sprinkling of ex-St Catherine's girls, many of whom Eleanor had not seen since school. Pippa was not there. Eleanor didn't know why. The men wore black ties, the women evening dresses, mostly short—though those of some of the older women were long. Some looked as though they'd been in mothballs a very long time.

Eleanor had bought a new dress, pale blue taffeta with a square neck and three-quarter length sleeves. She thought it was slightly too dressy. Tall, pale with mouse coloured hair, she wasn't very good with clothes. Having spent most of her life in school uniform, and with a mother as a poor example, Eleanor felt that she lacked dress sense. Despite the impression she knew she made on other people—assertive, self-confident—in reality she felt different. She had always enjoyed acting, and so, in a sense, in real life she felt herself to be playing a part. She was not at all the person she appeared. She considered herself personally unattractive, lacking the physical beauty and vivacity of Clare; the almost alluring femininity of Pippa. Until Ted had shown an interest in her she worried that she lacked sex appeal and maybe for that she was more grateful than wise.

And Clare, on this sparkling occasion of her twenty-first birthday, did indeed look both beautiful and vivacious, happy, bubbling with excitement. She danced dutifully with her brothers and father, but mostly with Andrew. Eleanor noticed how close he held her.

At midnight there was a roll of drums, the lights in the ballroom were extinguished, and a huge cake with twenty-one candles was wheeled in on a trolley while the band played *Happy Birthday To You*, and everyone sang. Then, in a voice brimming with emotion, Dr Pearson announced the engagement of Clare to Andrew, who drew a ring from a box and put it on her finger. The newly-engaged couple embraced. Many of the older ladies present wept.

Eleanor didn't quite know how she felt. Stunned, perhaps a little jealous. After all, the future looked good for Clare; all set out on a nice straight path. No money worries, security, status. One could have predicted that, from now on, her life with Andrew—also from a

Catholic family—would be a smooth, untroubled, one.

Somewhere behind her she heard Clare's mother murmuring to a friend.

'He's such a nice boy. One of us.'

Wolversleigh was a very Catholic town and the old Catholic families like the Wrights, the Pearsons and the Thorntons were really what counted; people one knew, people one had been to school and attended church with; people with the rocks of stability, money and religion in common.

Eleanor realised then what she should have realised before—but she was too young—she didn't really fit in.

At school Eleanor had never been conscious of the social superiority of the Pearsons vis-à-vis her own lower-middle class family: her father, the unsuccessful salesman, and her neurotic mother. She had been accepted into their home as a friend of their daughter, but she realised now that they were probably really patronising her, being kind to her for Clare's sake and because basically they were people who were kind to the poor, the disadvantaged and animals.

But she wasn't one of them, and they'd known it all along. Like the poor, the disadvantaged and animals, she was a breed apart.

\*     \*     \*

On the train home Eleanor thought a lot about Clare, Andrew and the Pearsons and realised what a gulf there was between her life now and theirs. It had existed before, but now it was much wider.

What was more, if they'd known about Ted she'd be beyond the pale completely. No good Catholic girl would have had an affair with a married man. She thought how nice it would be if her life could be simple and uncomplicated, like Clare's. How nice it would be to be able to be open and show off your man to the world.

Her relationship with Ted worried Eleanor. She knew it was wrong. It was also unsatisfactory, because they never went anywhere together except the Indian restaurant, and that wasn't often. But Ted mattered to her. She'd convinced herself that he was a kind, caring man and, although she knew little about love, she thought he was a good lover. She enjoyed sex. She thought it was pleasurable, even addictive. The more you had, the more you wanted.

Sometimes they went back to her room at lunch time. Her landlady worked, and the other inhabitants were out at that time anyway. It was much better than Ted's infrequent, furtive visits at night.

She also tried to convince herself that she was important to Ted, because she thought perhaps that she was in love with him.

She stopped going to Communion altogether.

*       *       *

Ted popped his head round the door of his office.

'How was the birthday?'

'It was great.'

He came into the office and perched on the edge of her desk. He looked around him, and then bent forward to kiss her. Eleanor pushed him away.

'Don't!' she hissed.

'What's the matter? There's no one here!'

'Not yet.' Eleanor looked at the clock. Not quite nine. As usual she had come in early.

'I missed you,' he said. 'We could have spent the weekend together. Eileen took the kids to her mother. She's not very well.'

'Who? Eileen?'

'No, her mother.'

'Oh I'm sorry.' Eleanor scraped her hair back from her head. 'My friend's got engaged. I can't get over it. She's only twenty-one.'

'I was married at twenty. A father at twenty-one.'

'Were you?' Eleanor looked interested. 'I didn't know that.'

'Eileen was only seventeen.'

'Maybe that's why you don't get on. You

36

were too young.'

'I didn't say we don't get on. We just don't have so much in common. We've drifted apart. Look, how about lunch time?'

'Not today.'

'Why?'

'I can't explain. I feel out of sorts.'

'That's just because your friend's got engaged. Nice, Catholic girl is she? Good family? Makes you feel uneasy.'

'Yes it does.'

'I'll make you feel better at lunch time. Go on.' Ted reached out and ruffled her hair. 'You know you'll feel better.'

And she knew she would.

But there was also something more serious that was troubling Eleanor.

\*     \*     \*

Of course they went back and made love, and it was wonderful. It seemed to banish all her inhibitions, and she no longer felt gawky, naïve and awkward, but a woman of the world who had been initiated into the mysteries of sex.

They lit cigarettes and she blew smoke into the air.

'I've missed two months,' she said, finally voicing her apprehension.

Ted sat up in bed, turned and looked at her. 'So?'

'Well . . .' she paused.

'You can't be pregnant.'

'Why not?'

'Because I've been so careful. It's probably your hormones. Anyway, you better get some sort of contraception, just to be sure. You should have thought of that before.'

She had. But contraception was sinful. So, of course, was sex outside marriage.

Ted had been in a good mood, the lovemaking had been joyful, but now he looked cross. She'd spoiled a good afternoon.

But still she was worried. She was usually never late, whatever Ted said about hormones.

'When you go to the doctor you'd better get a test to be sure,' Ted said. He got out of bed and began to dress, his back to her, every movement expressing disapproval. 'And if anything has gone wrong you'll have to get rid of it.'

Eleanor was sorry she'd spoken. It was, after all, quite on the cards that Ted wouldn't understand.

# CHAPTER TWO

# MARCH 1967

Eleanor sat in the middle of the small Lady Chapel of the busy city church. In front of her the altar was lit with a single spotlight and two large candles. The statue of Our Lady, placed above it, looked kindly down. Her hands were outstretched and around her head there was a crown of stars. To one side of the altar stood a large brass candelabrum containing rows of guttering votive candles placed there by the faithful.

It was a cold March day, just after six in the evening, and the home-bound traffic had been awful.

Eleanor hardly knew London, and it rather frightened her, but Pippa had met her at Euston and they had had tea in the station café before going to the church.

Pippa had been very composed, calm, certain she was doing the right thing. She had wanted to be a Catholic since she was fourteen, and this was the day of her reception into the Church. As her closest Catholic friend, Pippa had telephoned Eleanor and invited her to attend the ceremony.

Eleanor didn't really feel part of the Church any more, but she couldn't refuse. Besides, she wanted to see Pippa. Maybe Pippa could return the favour—though it would be an awkward subject to bring up on the day of her reception.

The priest was fairly young. He had dark curly hair, rather like Ted, and was also Irish. Ted was an Irish Protestant, born in Belfast, but he had been brought up in Liverpool where his father came to get work, and he no longer had an Irish accent.

Eleanor was not required to play any part in the brief ceremony, and she sat quietly in her pew watching and thinking about the past, and their schooldays. About the things that had happened since: Clare's engagement and her own affair with Ted.

Pippa's call had been unexpected. They no longer corresponded as they used to, or talked on the telephone. But as soon as she heard Pippa's voice she'd felt she wanted to see her, and be with her on such an important occasion. She'd asked Ted for a few days off and had taken the train to explore the big wide world. She was convinced that Ted thought she was job-hunting.

The priest made the sign of the cross over Pippa, who was now a Catholic. The following day she would make her first Holy Communion, which Eleanor had also promised to attend.

Pippa stood up and the priest shook hands. Eleanor rose from her seat and went forward.

As she embraced Pippa she saw she'd been weeping. She put her arms round her and hugged her.

'Well done,' she said. She felt like weeping too.

It was a strange emotional moment, and after a few more words with the priest the two women went slowly up the main aisle of the church and out of the imposing front portico.

*    *    *

Pippa's bedsit was not unlike Eleanor's three hundred miles away. It was cramped, rather gloomy and in an insalubrious part of north London—that grey area between Camden Town and the Euston Road known as Mornington Crescent. From the window you could see the main railway lines from Euston to the north—the line on which Eleanor had travelled. Trains passed every few minutes, their reverberations shaking the building and making conversation all but impossible.

'I don't know how you can work here,' Eleanor said as the room shook again.

Pippa smiled. 'It's cheap.'

Pippa was preparing for finals and scattered around the room were books, papers and cards needed for revision. After making a cup of coffee for them both, she rather guiltily hurried around tidying up, while Eleanor went to the window and stood watching the trains.

Despite her gift for art Pippa had lacked the confidence to apply to art school. Besides, her mother had thought that the life of an artist was not an option her daughter should seriously consider and that a university degree, possibly leading to a career in teaching, would provide a firmer foundation for her future.

Pippa felt she had to agree. After all, though good at art, no one seemed to think her work was outstanding. But she had always been very good at English, and had read this for her degree, hoping eventually to add art to her course when she did her postgraduate diploma in education.

Pippa was a very self-contained young woman, something of an enigma to her fellow students, as in many ways she had been to her schoolmates. She had neither sought nor inspired intimacy. No one knew much about her, and even after two-and-a-half years she had made acquaintances rather than friends. She didn't socialise, but went to classes each day and returned home each night—rather as though she already had a job. Occasionally she attended functions organised by the Arts Society, but on the whole she had missed out completely on the fun and camaraderie of university life.

Maybe she had felt that nothing could replace the harmony she had once enjoyed with Eleanor and Clare; or maybe she already knew that once she was a member of the

Church she loved so much her destiny lay very closely within its confines. She was already distancing herself from the world.

But it was wonderful to see Eleanor again, to have her with her at such a special time. Eleanor was still an important part of her life. They had known each other since they were small girls, and that bond was irreplaceable, even if, inevitably, you changed as you grew older.

The room was more or less restored to order as Eleanor, busy lighting a cigarette, wandered back from the window and perched on the side of the narrow bed.

'I don't know why you didn't wait until after the exams to be received.'

'Why should I? I want to be a full member of the Church. I've waited long enough. My instruction was finished. I was ready.'

'Well,' Eleanor sounded dubious, 'if you're sure.'

'It's too late now.' Pippa sat on the edge of the bed and looked anxiously at her. 'I thought you might be happy for me?'

'I'm happy, if it's what you want; but to me well . . . I don't go to Mass any more except when I visit my parents.'

'Oh!' Pippa momentarily looked disappointed. 'So you won't be coming to Communion with me tomorrow?'

Eleanor shook her head.

'I can't. I'm also having an affair. I feel it

puts me beyond the pale.'

'I see.'

'Are you shocked?'

'I'm not shocked. Maybe a bit surprised. I didn't think . . .'

Pippa rose and began to wander round the room. 'Well, it's just that you don't seem very happy. I thought how mournful and preoccupied you looked when you got off the train. I thought that maybe there was something wrong.'

'I'm pregnant. He's married. I'm *not* very happy.'

Eleanor drew furiously on her cigarette to stop herself crying. 'I realise I'm spoiling your day.' She got up and, opening the window, crushed her cigarette out on the ledge. Then she shut the window and looked at Pippa. 'Sorry.'

Pippa came over to her and took her arm. 'That's awful. What are you going to do?'

'He wants me to have an abortion.' Eleanor sat down on the bed and, taking out her handkerchief, gave her nose a good blow. 'It's got to be now or never. I'm about four months gone. Ted, the father, knows a doctor . . .'

'Oh but you *couldn't*!' Pippa, her expression horrified, sat beside her friend.

Eleanor reached out and took her hand. 'That's what I feel. I mean it's wrong, ethically wrong.' Eleanor's eyes wandered round the room. 'Do you think if I came to London I

44

could stay somewhere near here?'

'You mean by yourself?'

'By myself, but near you, near someone I know. That would make it anonymous. I can't go home and tell my parents, and I don't want to stay in Darlsdon where everyone will know, including Ted's wife.'

'And Ted . . . if you decided to keep the baby, would he support you?'

'Oh no, I'll have it adopted.' Eleanor glanced at Pippa. 'Don't you think? I mean it's the only thing to do, isn't it? I couldn't possibly keep a baby or look after it. It wouldn't be fair, either to the child or to me.'

\*　　　\*　　　\*

*August 1967*

In later years they were to call it The Summer of Love, the months of hippiedom and flower power. The American guru Timothy Leary's gospel of turning on and tuning in crossed the Atlantic with a vengeance. Being young, being hip, was what it was all about. It was the age of psychedelic drugs, meditation, maharishis and The Beatles—whose manager had just been found dead while they were on retreat in Wales. They hurried back to London proclaiming how shocked they were. John Lennon was reported to have said they didn't know where they would have been without

Brian.

It was the age of self-expression, and the Duke of Bedford, not to be outdone, was hosting a three-day jamboree for the Flower Children at his home in Woburn Abbey.

But for Eleanor Hamilton in her bedsit the reality was very different. It was a warm, dry summer and she baked in her attic room in Camden Town, alone and afraid. Her twenty-first birthday in June was no cause for celebration. It came and went unobserved, except for a trip to a West End cinema and a meal at a steak house.

Eleanor had left the paper and travelled to London in the spring. At that stage, her pregnancy wasn't too obvious, and she'd had no difficulty finding a job as a temporary secretary with an agency. She told her parents that she'd landed a good job on a newspaper. She lied to them all summer about her prospects in order to avoid going home.

But it was a lonely time. Pippa was busy with her finals, and they saw little of each other. Besides, there was that vague air of disapproval or, rather, embarrassment on Pippa's part. She was too nice a person, too charitable, openly to disapprove of her friend. All the same the inference was there: with a married man Eleanor should have been able to say 'no', which she would have done had she taken her Faith more seriously. God would have given her the grace to refuse.

Eleanor registered at a north London hospital and went for regular checkups. Everything was fine. She posed as a married woman separated from her husband and wore a wedding ring, telling the authorities that because of the break-up of her marriage she would not keep the baby. She contacted a Catholic Society that dealt with adoptions, and soon the formalities were completed, the papers signed.

It was a very bleak, soul-destroying process, for which Eleanor had to steel herself. But she had no doubt at all that she was doing the right thing, not only for the baby, but for herself. Unencumbered she could begin life afresh, with a new job—hopefully in newspapers—and she would succeed. This was just a blip, something that one had to learn to put behind one. Unfortunate, but it happened.

Ted had thought she was crazy. An abortion was such a simple affair these days. There was even a new Act of Parliament to make the whole thing easier. But she couldn't do it. She didn't want to. Her Catholicism was deep enough and strong enough to convince her that it was wrong to take a life, and she would make some childless couple happy by giving them a baby.

This childless couple seemed to take shape in her mind as she tossed on her bed, or wandered listlessly in Regent's Park at the top of the road. She would never forget that summer: the number of happy couples who wandered through that park with prams, children, and dogs, as if to emphasise her own loneliness and misery. Fathers and mothers were united in the marital bond, their children lawfully conceived and born without stigma.

Often she'd get back to her room, after she'd toiled up the stairs, and weep.

She would always remember it as the unhappiest period of her life.

*     *     *

After her finals Pippa went home, though she planned to return to London in the autumn to attend the Institute of Education from where she was going to qualify as a teacher. She had promised to return nearer the birth.

Eleanor had given up her job at the last moment, and had to make do on very little money. This deprivation made her realise more than anything how impossible it would be to keep the baby, even if she wanted to.

She laid a hand on her tummy. She was very large. Any day now. She tried not to think about the child within her, but she could think of nothing else. She hoped it would be a boy, because somehow she felt it would be easier for a man to manage on his own. A man would be more practical; perhaps more understanding and less inclined to blame the mother who had abandoned him.

No, not 'abandoned'. That was completely the wrong word. She was not going to bond with a baby who would be taken from her soon after birth and given to a good Catholic couple who were already waiting to welcome it into their home.

The baby lurched and Eleanor felt a stab of pain. She had a horrible feeling that the birth was imminent, and Pippa wasn't here. There was absolutely no one in the whole world to whom she could turn. Being practical, Eleanor had, of course, thought of this eventuality and made arrangements. Her case was packed and she would take a taxi to the hospital, a short ride away. Nevertheless, she clutched her stomach, turned her face to the wall and wept. She would never forget the grey-green wallpaper with a diamond-shaped pattern that made you feel dizzy if you closed your eyes.

That night the contractions started. Eleanor lay in the dark, gulping for air, alone and afraid. She waited and counted. No mistake. At first they were infrequent, and then they came more quickly. She was afraid her waters would break and, feeling groggy, terribly frightened, she heaved herself out of bed, dressed and grabbed the little case that was ready and waiting in the corner.

She switched off the light, opened the door and crept down the stairs. The house was silent.

As she stood outside on the step, she could

hear the faint sound of a clock striking two.

Eleanor closed the front door and stepped on to the pavement, hoping and praying that a taxi would not be long coming. She was just off Camden High Street and taxies plied at all hours back and forth to and from the West End.

God had not been very good to her, so she supposed she would not find a taxi easily, but she was wrong. Within two minutes one turned off the High Street, its bright welcome orange light like a beacon in a harsh, uncaring world.

She hailed it. The taxi stopped and the driver took one look at her in the streetlight.

'Cor blimey, love. Hop in. I ain't got much experience as a midwife!'

*     *     *

Eleanor lay in her hospital bed, the baby in a crib by her side. It was a practice in the hospital, and she didn't want to draw attention to herself by objecting to its presence. Nor could she. He was a beautiful baby—a boy as she'd hoped—and he didn't have Ted's horrible black hair but a little mousey thatch like hers, and a very fetching smile.

She called him Simon because she liked the name and, oh, how she wished that she didn't have to give him away. He was such a dear baby, and although he slept most of the time he seemed so happy with her, content with the

50

world, not with the slightest inkling that they were to part.

She didn't breast-feed him. She couldn't. She knew that if she did they would never part from each other.

Eleanor held out a finger to Simon and he grasped it. Gently she picked him up out of his crib and cuddled him. She could feel his little heart against hers, and a sense of pure maternal love swept through her. She held him very tight, aware of his scent, his baby perfume of talc and oil. She went each day with the other mothers into the nursery to bathe him. She knew she was courting danger, but she had to let Simon know that she loved him, hadn't spurned him, would help to give him a start in life.

Then she looked up and saw Pippa, flowers in her arms, looking down, smiling at her.

'Sorry I didn't make it.'

'It was a few days early. I managed.'

Pippa nodded. Eleanor would manage. Everyone knew that. If she didn't manage so well people would have made more of an effort to be there when she needed them.

In many ways it was her misfortune that she could and would. People would always be able to depend on Eleanor, but it wasn't mutual.

Pippa looked at her cuddling Simon and raised her eyebrows imperceptibly.

'Changed your mind?'

'No.' Eleanor carefully placed Simon back in his crib, tenderly covering him with his soft blanket.

'He's beautiful.' Pippa leaned over the cot and made a cooing noise.

'He's beautiful,' Eleanor said sternly, 'but he's not a doll. He's a human being. I could not be a good mother to him. I could not give him the life he deserves, and there is a couple with money and a nice house who want him very badly. It would be terribly selfish of me to keep him. It's all arranged.'

'It seems such a pity,' Pippa said.

'Oh do shut up!' Eleanor turned her face away to hide the tears that had suddenly come into her eyes.

*       *       *

During the night she was conscious of some movement in the ward by her bedside, but her sleeping pill had done the trick and she didn't wake up.

The next morning she discovered she'd been moved to a side ward where she was alone, and there was no crib by her side. As she lay digesting what had happened, Sister came into the room and gave her a quick sympathetic smile as she placed a cup of tea on the locker by the bed.

'It *is* what you wanted, Mrs Hamilton.'

'He's gone?'

Eleanor found herself fighting with the strange lump that had suddenly come into her throat. She'd asked that when the time came, he should be removed without her being told. If she saw him being taken away she'd howl the place down. Sister sat down on her bed and took her hand.

'It *is* for the best. I think you know that. It is a very hard life for a woman with a baby on her own. Simon now has the very best chance in life, and you can begin all over again. You're only twenty-one. You must put this out of your mind.'

The tears poured down Eleanor's face and Sister gripped her hand.

But when eventually she looked at her, Eleanor fancied that Sister had gone all emotional too.

\*　　　\*　　　\*

*May 1968*

The nuptial High Mass was celebrated by the bishop who was an old friend of the Pearson family. The deacon was Father Michael Pearson, a first cousin, the sub-deacon Father Gerard Thornton SJ, Andrew's uncle. It was a very Catholic wedding.

Clare had no doubt about her love for Andrew, and she really felt that the happiest, the most fulfilled moment of her life was when they exchanged their solemn vows at the altar in the middle of the Mass in front of the

53

bishop, with Michael and Father Gerard looking benignly on. As husband and wife, they received Holy Communion together. It was a moment of great solemnity, great beauty. The sun streamed in through the east window and bathed the sanctuary in glorious light as the choir sang *Ave Verum* according to the old Latin rite.

The interior of the church of St Anthony of Padua, a nineteenth-century gothic pile set on a busy main road, was a mass of white lilies and orange blossom which blended with the white and gold vestments of the clergy, the rich, heavily embroidered altar cloths. After signing the register, the newly-married couple proceeded down the aisle followed by six little bridesmaids and two pages. Dr and Mrs Pearson and Major and Mrs Thornton joined the procession, and then Clare's brothers, Frank and Mark Pearson and Mark's wife Chrissy, Andrew's brother, Peter, sister-in-law, Dorothy and his younger sister, Pam.

The organ blared out Widor's toccata and the doors of the church were flung open upon a scene of a crowd waiting in brilliant sunshine, jockeying for position, the trees in the churchyard bending under the weight of pink and white blossoms waving gently in the breeze.

Clare wore a waisted dress of oyster silk with a long straight skirt and a tight bodice with tiny pearl buttons up to a high, scalloped

54

neckline. The long sleeves were made of lace, ruched at the wrists, and her veil was also of lace, secured by a garland of tiny white, gold and blue flower buds. This she had worn over her face until the moment of marriage when her bridegroom drew it back and kissed her. Her attendants had helped secure it in the vestry so that it now trailed behind, borne above the ground by her little bridesmaids, two of whom were Andrew's nieces.

She stood at the door of the church looking at the crowd of well-wishers who broke into exclamations of delight as the bridal pair emerged from the church door. Suddenly a full peal of bells crashed out, mingling triumphantly with the strains of the organ.

For the next hour photographs were taken in every conceivable combination. She and Andrew alone, with their parents, with the full family, with the bridesmaids and pages and, finally, with as many people who could crowd in.

After that, the bells still pealing, she and Andrew got into a silver Rolls Royce which drove them to the country house hotel outside the town where the reception was to be held, a steady stream of cars following them.

Eleanor had arrived a little late, but managed to be on time for the ceremony. She was, after all, not an attendant, having pleaded pressure of work.

She thought Clare was probably relieved

because they'd hardly seen each other since the twenty-first birthday party. She'd started a new job on a provincial paper in Essex, so the excuse was half-true. Eleanor stood rather shyly in the line waiting to greet the bride and groom. Once more she felt excluded, out of place, and wished she hadn't come. Well she wouldn't come again to any Pearson 'dos'. This was the last. Certainly she wouldn't come to any christenings. Gradually she would detach herself from Clare and her like.

Then she saw Pippa, together with a group of old St Catherine's girls, and she joined them. Kisses, embraces, were exchanged.

'How are you?'

'Where have you been?'

'Long time, no see.'

So many questions. No time for replies. Not yet. Some of them she hadn't seen for several years. Pippa stood a little to one side looking at her. They hadn't seen each other since Pippa visited the hospital. After that she'd gone abroad. Eleanor had finally gone home to make her peace with her family and to try in some way to come to terms with her loss. For it was a loss. Not a day passed but she thought about Simon. She and Pippa greeted each other a bit awkwardly, brushed cheeks.

Pippa's blonde hair was concealed under a straw hat, and she wore a simple cotton dress that she'd probably had a good many years. It had a pattern of flowers and a plain yellow collar.

Pippa wore no make-up, her complexion was so good she didn't need it. Her skin was pale, her lips naturally rose-coloured and her eyes a curious, azure-blue.

She was fey, she was vague, but somehow people noticed her. Men's eyes swivelled in her direction, but she seemed oblivious to them. When she smiled her cheeks dimpled, and she looked really pretty. Slightly dowdy, a bit old fashioned, but pretty. Eleanor, sitting behind, noticed how reverently she'd received Holy Communion at Mass, remaining on her knees, head bent in prayer for ages.

'Doesn't Clare look lovely?'

'Lovely. But then we knew she'd make a lovely bride.'

'The first of us to be married.'

'Not quite. Mary Barlow was married before Christmas.'

'Pippa, what *have* you been up to?'

'Eleanor, tell us about your new job?'

'Margaret, someone said you were going abroad . . .'

'Joan, how's your mother?'

There was a whole group of them, most of whom she'd known since they were very young. Yet already she felt apart, detached, different. What did they know about having a baby and giving it away? Of an affair with a man who did not love her and with whom she had completely lost touch? She even felt a sense of

57

achievement. Of having, somehow, become suddenly grown-up and more worldly-wise than them.

Chat chat chat. Eleanor was quite glad there were so many of them, and when they reached the bride there were girlish cries and whoops—slightly artificial—lots of laughter, while Andrew, a little bemused, looked on, his round glasses giving him a rather detached, owl-like expression.

'She certainly didn't choose him for his looks!' sotto voce, as they moved away, from someone meeting him for the first time.

'He's really awfully nice.'

'Solid, dependable.'

'Also quite rich. The Thorntons own a lot of property and I heard Major Thornton has bought them a house.'

'Lucky Clare.'

They moved on, accepted champagne, canapés, chatted to more old school friends. Pippa and Eleanor stuck together for company. Then a sit-down luncheon. It was a bit hot. Clare looked very animated, Andrew more relaxed. The speeches went on forever. The day seemed to grow even warmer.

Pippa and Eleanor caught up with each other's news.

'How have you been?' Pippa asked.

'Fine.'

'No, really?' Expression rather anxious, concerned.

'Really fine.'

'No regrets?'

A shadow passed over Eleanor's face and she shook her head.

'Please don't talk about it.'

'OK. I won't, but it's terrible that we never see each other.'

'I know; but as a rookie they keep me working all hours.'

'We definitely must meet before I finish at the Institute.'

'Oh definitely.'

There was a sense of strain. The camaraderie, the intimacy was broken. Maybe Pippa felt guilty because she hadn't kept in touch, and there was embarrassment on Eleanor's part because, of all the people there, only Pippa knew her secret. She wished she didn't.

'I'm going to be a nun,' Pippa whispered suddenly, and Eleanor felt herself grow rigid with shock. She looked at her.

'Did you say a *nun*?'

'I'm entering in the autumn. St Catherine's Society.'

'My God!' Eleanor looked across at Clare and the contrast between her two friends couldn't have been greater. Clare, a beautiful bride, vivacious, in her lovely wedding dress, on the brink of a glittering, happy, fulfilled life; a wealthy, obviously devoted husband; a lovely home; surely a family would not be long

59

coming; and dear old Pippa beside her: sweet, pretty, just a little dowdy, a little subdued, a bride of Christ.

And somewhere in between these two extremes was she, Eleanor Hamilton, not yet quite a failure but, certainly, not a success, already knocked about by life. A single mother who had given away her baby, and whose own future was uncertain.

'I hope you'll come to my profession,' Pippa whispered, so that only she could hear. 'Clare too. I'd like you both to be there.'

\*　　　\*　　　\*

But it was Clare's day. She enjoyed it all; the preparations, the ceremony, the speeches, dancing with Andrew, with her father and brothers, being the belle of the ball. It was a bit like her twenty-first birthday all over again, though this time there was a difference; she was a married woman. From being quite small she had always wanted to be married; she knew she would be good at it.

She'd never worked since leaving university with an upper second in maths. She always wanted to be a wife and mother, never a career woman. Andrew's father had bought them a beautiful house, and her parents had furnished it. She'd spent weeks getting it ready: supervising the decorating and hanging curtains. She'd combined it with fittings for

60

her dress, the bridesmaids' dresses, the uniforms for the little pages.

The day had gone perfectly, the nuptial Mass had been wonderful. It was all like some beautiful Hollywood film in glorious Technicolor, with a choir of angels. At times the scene had been all misted over in sweet smelling incense, the thurifers lifted aloft to the high altar, or the bishop incensing her and Andrew, reminding her of the Corpus Christi procession. Days of her youth. Finally, it was time to leave. She would have liked it to go on forever but now came the nuts and bolts of marriage, the reality. She and Andrew alone together.

Time to go up to one of the bedrooms that had been reserved for them and change. She in one room, Andrew in another. They were to drive to the Continent and motor through Europe. The first night would be spent at an hotel a few miles away.

Helped by her mother and one of her many cousins, Clare changed into a pink suit with a white blouse, two strings of pearls, and a white hat and shoes. She stood in front of the tall mirror admiring herself; her ringed fingers with pink polished nails clutching a white leather bag. Several times she twisted her new wedding ring round her finger. How well it set off the large sapphire and diamond engagement ring Andrew had given her.

'You look lovely,' her mother said. 'Really

lovely.' She sounded very emotional and there were tears in her eyes. She kissed her daughter tenderly on the cheek. 'I hope you will be very, *very* happy. All your life, precious.'

\* \* \*

It was rather strange to be alone together in a bedroom. Once the porter had left their luggage and Andrew had tipped him and the door closed Clare was visited by a sudden, unexpected feeling of awkwardness. It would have helped if Andrew had come up and put his arms around her, but he seemed awkward too. He went over to his case and opened it, fiddled around, began taking out his things for the night. She noticed a pair of pyjamas and a dressing gown.

On a table by the side of the bed was an ice bucket with a bottle of champagne and two glasses.

Clare took off her hat and placed it on a tallboy, unfastened her pink jacket and hung it in the wardrobe. Then she sat on the bed and undid her pearls.

They had never slept together, though there had been some very heavy petting. Even that she thought was sinful, and she had mentioned it in confession, numbering the numerous occasions among 'impure thoughts'.

Several of the girls at university had had affairs, but Clare thought they were silly. She had some idea that she had kept Andrew's interest because she wouldn't let him go all the way. So far, but no further. He respected her for it. She was sure of that.

Her Catholic faith had never been really put to the test by sex, and now that she was married she was glad she had kept to her principles. That Andrew had kept to his. They had saved themselves for each other and what would a sacred day like today have been if they hadn't, with the nuptial Mass and them taking Holy Communion together? A mockery. She was a good Catholic girl and she had married a good Catholic man.

Clare felt a hand on her shoulder and turned.

'Penny for them, darling?' Andrew had his tie off, his shirt undone and his braces hung by the side of his trousers. In his hand was a glass of champagne which he handed to her.

'I was thinking,' she said, smiling as she took the glass.

'What, darling?' His voice sounded rather thick.

'I was thinking, well . . .' she looked at him slyly over the rim of the glass . . . 'it's all OK now.' She felt a heightening of desire and, putting her glass to her lips, slurped half the contents.

Andrew sat beside her, his own glass in his hand and drank from it. He seemed quite flushed and breathless, his spectacles misted

63

over. He put an arm round her waist and drew her towards him, at the same time removing his spectacles and putting them carefully on the table by the bed.

He kissed her full on her open lips, expelling into her mouth a jet of champagne that rushed down her throat. The unexpected mouthful of liquid, mixed with warm saliva, produced a sharp, erotic sensation and she felt decidedly randy. Taking her glass and putting it with his to one side, Andrew finished removing her pearls, fumbled with the buttons on her blouse and, not too skilfully, undid her bra, while his own trousers obligingly fell to the floor.

Clare lay back on the bed and he leaned over her gazing with some awe at her naked breasts. Previously he'd only ever felt them through her clothes in the dark. He clamped a nipple firmly in his mouth, his eyes closed in rapture. Clare feverishly wriggled out of her skirt and tights, kicked off her pants until they lay beside her bridegroom's crumpled pinstriped trousers on the floor.

What happened next, and several more times that night, was well worth all the years of frustration involved in keeping the commandments of God and the Church.

In the small hours of the morning Clare turned to her husband and lover and rested her head on his chest.

Now she felt well and truly married.

# CHAPTER THREE

# AUGUST 1972

'What do you seek?'

'The mercy of God and the grace to do His Will.'

'Do you seek it with your whole heart?'

'Yes, Father, I do.'

The priest, sitting in front of the altar, then clasped Pippa's hands between his, covered them with his white stole, and prayed that grace might be granted to Pippa, who had taken the name in religion of Sister Mary Frances, to perform her role in the religious life of the community.

In days gone by, women making their final vows had been dressed as traditional brides in white dresses with long veils. There had been a tiered wedding cake afterwards at the feast to which parents and relations were invited. For many parents, facing the loss of a beloved daughter, this had been an ordeal. For others, an occasion of joy. Whichever view you took, the imitation of the marriage ceremony, the notion that a woman in religion was being married to Christ, a spiritual lord rather than a temporal one, seemed to emphasise the occasion.

But following the Second Vatican Council,

religious orders had been asked to reform themselves, to make the nun more acceptable for the modern day. So, in place of a wedding dress, Pippa wore a dark suit with a calf-length skirt and a white blouse. Instead of being clothed in the black habit that went back to mediaeval times, she wore a short veil which exposed the front of her pretty blonde hair.

Pale-faced, diminutive, Pippa, who had never worn make-up, looked fragile, in many ways prettier than before she had entered the Society. The plainness, the very severity of her garments enhanced her natural physical assets. In the world she was not exceptional; out of it and in the company of many of her fellow nuns who were frankly plain, she could almost pass as a beauty.

With Pippa were two other young women making their vows. In previous years there might have been a dozen or more. But the reforms of the Vatican Council had, paradoxically, led many to question the value of the religious life and scores abandoned it.

For Janice Sidgwick, Pippa's mother, there was neither joy nor sorrow, just a complete lack of comprehension as to why her daughter had become a nun. She sat at the back of the chapel of the mother house where Pippa, after four years in the novitiate, was making her solemn vows.

The Society had been founded early in the nineteenth century by a pious Italian lady of aristocratic birth who named it after St Catherine of Siena, the town in which she was born. The object of the Society then was the education of aristocratic young women who would be taught good manners and versed in the ways of piety, docility and obedience. Under the guidance of the foundress, who was well-connected in Italian society, the Order flourished and spread abroad to other European countries. But, by the mid-twentieth century the ideas of the foundress had expanded to include the education of girls of all classes, in addition to which it embraced higher education and opened colleges for advanced learning.

Janice might have understood it better if Pippa had wanted to be a missionary, or had joined an Order more biased towards good works. She felt there was something anachronistic about the Society of St Catherine in the late-twentieth century and many of its houses were closing.

The service came to an end, the three newly-professed nuns moved down the aisle of the chapel after the priest, accompanied by the Mother General, who had come from Rome, and other dignitaries of the Society.

Janice spied Pippa's two school friends, Eleanor and Clare, standing at the back. They saw her as they turned towards the aisle to watch the procession, and waved.

Thank heaven, Janice thought, for familiar

faces.

Outside the chapel a throng had gathered. Everyone seemed to know everyone else. The other two nuns seemed to have cohorts of relatives and friends. Janice greeted Eleanor and Clare, who stood a little aside from the others, and they decided to move away from the entrance and into the sunshine where there was to be afternoon tea.

The English mother house, in which Pippa made her solemn profession, was a beautiful manor house set in rolling acres near the sea in Sussex. The emerald lawns were in perfect condition, there was an abundance of blooms in the herbaceous borders, and little tables and chairs were set out under the trees. For all the world it seemed to resemble the upper-class English stately home it must once have been, and not a convent of nuns dedicated to poverty and the service of God.

'I'm so glad to see you.' Janice sank into a chair and took a cigarette from a packet. 'I must say I found this an ordeal. Of course, you know we're not Catholics.' She bent her head to light her cigarette, and in her rather faded good looks it was possible to see how Pippa resembled her, and how she too might become. She wore a creased blue frock and a blue felt hat, carried a white plastic handbag, and when she had her cigarette going her pale blue eyes gazed questioningly up at her daughter's former school friends. 'How well you both look,' and, noting Clare's size, 'a baby on the way I see.'

'Number three.' Clare sat next to Janice and kicked off her shoes to ease her aching feet. 'We already have a son and a daughter. We Catholics breed like rabbits you know!' She laughed deprecatingly, managing at the same time to sound rather smug. She wore a pretty light blue two-piece, a skirt and a loose top, obviously maternity wear; but she looked smart and, at the same time, comfortable. She was hatless and so was Eleanor, who wore a white linen suit with a navy blue blouse which made her look professional, competent, smart.

'I'm so glad for you, my dear.' Janice briefly touched her arm. 'So happy for you. But then I always knew you would be happy, and contented.'

She paused and looked meaningfully at Eleanor, as if to imply that was something she had not expected of her. And, indeed, Eleanor's relationship with Janice had always been a little prickly, as if there was something about her she didn't quite understand. 'And you, Eleanor? Are you married yet?'

'Not yet.' Eleanor occupied the third chair.

'A career girl, I expect. Pippa says you're a journalist. I always knew you would do well.'

'I haven't exactly done *well*, Mrs Sidgwick, but I get by. I'm the women's page editor of a group of newspapers here in the south. I live in Essex.'

'Well that sounds very important. I wish Pippa could have done something like that. Made something of her life. She is so artistic. I think she could have done well in the arts, or perhaps been a painter. I never in my wildest dreams thought she'd be a *nun*.' Her tone left no doubt as to how she felt about that.

'In my opinion she *has* made something of her life,' Clare said defensively, but Janice sighed and continued.

'I have always worked hard, you know. My husband deserted me after Pippa was born, leaving me to bring up two young children. My son John is a chemical engineer and lives in America. I hardly ever hear from him. Now I feel Pippa is lost to me too.'

'She's not *lost* to you. She'll be able to come and see you. In the old days of the Society, when we were all young, she wouldn't have been allowed to, but now she can. They have much more freedom . . . Ah . . .' Clare looked with relief across the lawn. 'Here is Pippa. I think she looks very well and very, very happy.'

Pippa was walking slowly across the lawn to where her mother and friends sat in the shade of a tree. She wished her mother hadn't come. She hadn't asked her to. Her years at boarding school had separated her from her mother and elder brother. They had a loving but difficult, strained relationship.

However, she stretched out her arms as her mother rose to greet her, and hugged her.

70

'Mummy. Eleanor . . . Clare.'

Kisses, more hugs were exchanged. Pippa sat down. 'It was so sweet of you *all* to come.' She looked at Clare. 'Clare, another baby. How lovely!'

'The third.'

'I know. Aren't you lucky? You must write when it's born, or tell me all in your Christmas card.'

Christmas cards were now all the women exchanged.

Soon, Eleanor thought, they would probably stop altogether. There was nothing that really they had in common any more. There were affectionate memories, but now they had all gone their very separate ways.

It was difficult to get a proper conversation going. Where, after all, did one begin? Three people, almost strangers, with the added complication of Janice.

Soon after tea, pleading pressure of time, Eleanor and Clare left Pippa, still seated with her mother, to drive back to London.

\*       \*       \*

'My, that was embarrassing. Most.' Eleanor looked both ways as they came to the main gates of the convent, not quite sure whether to turn right or left.

'Right,' Clare pointed. 'That's the way we came in.'

71

She leaned back in her seat and looked at the countryside. 'I didn't feel embarrassed. Just a bit awkward. I didn't think Mrs Sidgwick would be there. I don't think I'd have come if I'd known she was coming. I felt Pippa had to have someone.'

Just like Clare, so thoughtful. And it was an awfully long journey for someone who was about six months pregnant. Eleanor had been shamed into going because Clare was. Otherwise she'd have given it a miss. There'd been something rather detached about Pippa when Simon was born. Something a bit critical and uncaring. Maybe it was simply a lack of understanding, or embarrassment, or both.

Clare took a last look at the convent as they drove past it. 'It really is a lovely place. Those nuns know how to choose the nice spots, don't they?'

'They do indeed. Our convent grounds were heavenly. I often think of them in odd moments. Heaven knows what's going to happen to the Society in future.'

'Why do you say that?'

'So many are leaving, aren't they? So few joining as well.'

'I suppose so.' Clare paused. 'You've left the Church, haven't you, Eleanor?'

'Just about.'

'Any particular reason?'

'I don't think I had faith. I didn't have your background either. My parents were not very

72

religious.'

'I couldn't do without God and the Church. I couldn't exist.'

'And does Andrew feel the same?'

Clare looked at her in surprise. 'Oh yes. Of course.'

'I think something has gone from the Church. I loved the ritual and the Latin Mass, and I so much preferred the old habit the nuns wore. It was so sweeping and graceful, so elegant. I thought they looked hideous today, in those ill-fitting suits and thick lisle stockings, those awful tatty little veils.'

'Then your faith *can't* have been all that strong.' Clare's tone was censorious. 'Details like that are unimportant.'

'They were important to me and to the Church for nearly two thousand years.'

The gulf between them was getting wider. No doubt about that. Pointless to argue about religion. Pointless to argue about guilt, which was why Eleanor felt she had really left the Church.

Clare now spoke hesitantly. 'Eleanor, I wonder if I can ask that other question, the one you avoided on the lawn. Any men in your life?'

The answer was the same: 'Not at the moment.'

'I recommend it.'

'You were always meant to be a wife and mother.'

'And you? What were you meant to be?'
'I don't really know.'
'But you'd like children?'
'Frankly, I'm not sure.'
'We're going to have about six.'
Eleanor swallowed.
Little baby Simon. His face was always there.

\*      \*      \*

As she dropped Clare at the station, embracing her warmly, she felt she wouldn't be surprised if they never met again. She was not even sure, now, that she wanted to.

\*      \*      \*

Eleanor was very weary when she got home. It was nearly midnight and it had been a very long day. She poured herself a large gin and tonic, lit a cigarette and kicked off her shoes. She felt strangely flat, depressed. Maybe it had been a mistake to go to Pippa's solemn profession and, somehow, she had a slight feeling of envy at that great protruding belly of Clare's. It was alright to be a career girl, but it would also be nice to have the comfort and security of Clare's cosy life with Andrew and that huge family about her.

Sometimes, Eleanor felt, she had nothing. No one.

Of course she had promised to visit, and to write and . . . Well, she'd probably continue to send a Christmas card for the time being at least.

The day had been stilted, unsatisfactory. Yes, now, in retrospect, she was sorry she'd gone. The occasion seemed to have emphasised just how far she, Clare and Pippa, had grown apart, the differences between them; one now a consecrated virgin—she supposed Pippa was a virgin—and the other the fecund, fulfilled mother of nearly three, with herself somewhere in between.

*　　*　　*

Eleanor had a small flat overlooking the bay at Southend, where the headquarters of the South East England Newspaper Group was situated. Women's page editor seemed rather important, had a ring about it, but it was quite a mundane job, sounded better than it was.

She knew it was a dead-end, and if she didn't move fast she'd be stuck there for life. She had progressed from reporter to women's page editor, the page that went into all the group newspapers, rather like the *Darlsdon Echo* and, as such, she pretty well chose her subjects and her schedule.

Twice a year she went home to see her parents—her mother still ailing, her father still hard up and complaining. Little changed.

Every summer she joined some group or other and went on a holiday, usually abroad, sometimes to faraway places like Australia and India.

For two years after the birth of Simon she had led a celibate life, but after that she had a couple of brief unsatisfactory affairs. One with a man at the office; one with a bloke she met on holiday. Neither was serious. She thought she wasn't very sexy. She could go for a long time without it. Had done for some time now.

Eleanor guessed she was pretty much like a lot of women of her age and type who had welcomed the liberal ideas of the sixties and now the seventies without wanting to assume masculine roles or burn their bras. They made fairly good money, had a home of their own, by many standards an enviable lifestyle. On the other hand she had just turned twenty-six, she had been in journalism for nearly seven years and time was definitely passing her by.

\*     \*     \*

Despite the lateness of the hour she felt far from relaxed. On the contrary she felt quite churned up. She had left home early, the traffic in London had been awful and it was a long way to go.

She fixed another drink and flicked on her answer machine and played through the messages.

'Eleanor, Lewis Gould has invited you to lunch with him tomorrow. Don't be late.' The address followed.

Eleanor sat on the side of her sofa and put her head in her hands. An interview with this chauvinistic author was the last thing she wanted, but it was too late to cancel. Len, the current equivalent of Ted, except that he wasn't her lover, would have been furious.

She thought a lot about the events of the day as she got ready for bed. The ceremony of Pippa's solemn profession flitted in and out of her mind, along with disordered memories of childhood as she tried to get to sleep.

But sleep eluded her. At two she picked up a novel by Lewis Gould which she really should have read and that, finally, sent her to sleep.

She woke at seven with a headache and the aftertaste of too much gin.

At nine she rang the office to say she was going straight to Gould's place, which was in a village near Chelmsford. She picked up some more messages, made some calls, had coffee and tried to finish his novel. He was considered a 'literary' writer and consequently, the plot, such as it was, was hard to follow. *A Moment of Life* had recently won a prestigious literary prize, so someone obviously thought it was good. He was enjoying a *succès d'estime* and would probably soon move from Essex to the south of France or Cornwall. Essex wasn't really fashionable for an up-and-coming novelist.

Len had wanted him to be interviewed because his attitude towards women was supposed to be reactionary. Might provoke controversy. Good for circulation.

\*     \*     \*

Eleanor found herself in Chelmsford just after noon, and dawdled a bit until she arrived in the village where Gould lived. She identified his cottage on the outskirts, and drove past it. Then she parked nearby and hurriedly finished reading *A Moment of Life*. It was very hard to understand why it had been so successful, except that it had the backing of a reputable publisher and from the photograph on the jacket Lewis Gould looked rather dishy. He also had a wife and two daughters.

Because the lane in which the cottage stood was narrow, Eleanor left her car where it was and walked back. It was a very pretty thatched cottage, double fronted with a tiny garden massed with hollyhocks, dahlias, Zinnias and Antirrhinums. Along the whitewashed walls ran a couple of rambling roses, pink and white. Eleanor opened the gate and walked up the short path to the front door. It was just before one and she could hear a clock chiming the hour inside.

There was a curious air of emptiness about

the house, and she was beginning to wonder if her journey had been in vain when the door opened and Lewis Gould appeared on the threshold, greeting her with a smile.

Yes, he was dishy. Pity about the wife.

'Miss Hamilton?'

'Yes.' Eleanor smiled back.

'I hope you haven't been there for too long. I was out at the back.'

'No, I just arrived.'

'Fine. Do come in.'

They shook hands and Eleanor entered a rather dark and narrow booklined hallway from which ran a staircase leading upstairs. At the other end was a large, pleasant, but very untidy room into which Lewis conducted her. It seemed to be a combination of lounge and study. By the open French windows was a cluttered desk with a typewriter surrounded by books and papers scattered on the floor and furniture. A large cat curled up on one of the easy chairs facing the fireplace. Being August, the fire wasn't lit.

'Sorry about the mess.' Lewis scooped the protesting cat from one of the chairs and, dusting it down with his hand, pointed to it. 'Do sit down. Unfortunately my cleaning lady's away. I hope you're not allergic to cats?' Eleanor shook her head but nevertheless gingerly took a seat.

'Drink?' Lewis walked over to a table on which there was a number of bottles. 'I thought we'd go to the pub for lunch, but have a drink first. Is that OK?'

'Fine.' Eleanor looked round wondering where Mrs Gould was hiding herself.

'What can I get you?' Lewis stood back surveying the array of bottles, and clasped his hands. 'Gin, whisky, sherry, vodka . . .'

'Gin and tonic. Just a splash of gin.'

Lewis turned and began opening bottles and pouring the contents into two glasses.

He was tall with straight black hair, rather long and untidy, strands of which fell over his lean face, a beaked nose and intense, knowing brown eyes. He wore black steel-framed spectacles and his dress was casual: a white and blue check shirt and jeans. There was the suspicion that he hadn't shaved that morning. He seemed engaging and ready to be friendly, not quite what she'd expected.

He was not *quite* as dishy as his picture, in which he'd not been wearing glasses, but she found him attractive in rather an intellectual, Arthur Millerish kind of way, though much younger. Lewis handed her a glass, smiled again, poked his spectacles up his nose, swept back his hair with his free hand and held up his glass.

'Cheers. It is "Miss" Hamilton, is it?'

'It is, but you can call me Eleanor if you like.'

'And why did you decide you wanted to interview me, Eleanor?'

80

'Actually my boss suggested it. Len Turner. I think he's a friend of yours.'

'"Friend" is not exactly the right word.' Lewis screwed up his nose. 'I think we met in a pub. Not that I'm complaining. I'm always glad of publicity.'

'It seems you're doing rather well.' Eleanor reached down and produced her pad from her handbag.

'Oh, is the interview starting now?'

'When you like.' She smiled. 'I didn't want to miss anything.'

'Have you read my books?' He knitted his brows and peered at her closely.

'One, I have to confess.' Suddenly confronted with that rather ferocious stare the title went from her mind. 'It's called . . . It's your latest.'

'*A Moment of Life.*'

'That's it.'

'I suppose you thought it was awful. It's not a woman's book.'

'I found it quite hard to understand in all honesty. Maybe I'll read it again. But I'm really here, Lewis, to talk about your life. That is of more interest to our readers, as well as the way you write. Your family . . .' she looked around.

'Drink up,' Lewis commanded, looking at her half-full glass. 'I booked the table for one, and it's nearly half-past.'

*          *          *

It was the sort of small cosy village pub you expected to find in a remote part of Cornwall, rather than suburban Essex. There had been no need to book a table. The bar was not very full, and the dining room almost deserted. Eleanor declined another drink and they went straight into lunch.

'I agree,' Lewis said as they studied the menu. 'If I drink too much at lunch time I can't write another word.'

She settled for a tuna salad and half a pint of lager. Lewis had ham and eggs and a pint of bitter.

'Now tell me about yourself,' he invited, leaning across the table.

'No, you tell me about *yourself*.' Eleanor, once again, reached for her pad. 'I'm here to interview *you*.'

'Well, I'm thirty-five, born in London. Father a dentist, mother a housewife. One sister, married. Educated Dulwich College and King's College, London. I taught for a time.'

'What did you study?' Eleanor busily scribbling, looked up.

'French.'

'And what made you decide to become a writer?'

'Well, I always wrote. I mean I contributed to the school and college magazines. I was writing while I was teaching. My first novel was

82

published when I was twenty-five.'

'And what was that called?'

'*Innocent Beginnings*. It won the Schneider Award for a first novel.'

'And did you then decide to give up teaching?'

'Oh no. You don't make money from a first novel.'

'But you don't teach now?'

'My father died and left me a bit. Also my wife had money.'

He thoughtfully chewed his lip and there was a pause as the food arrived. Eleanor put her notepad on one side.

'Is your wife . . .'

'Divorced.' Lewis took a sip of his beer.

'Oh, I'm sorry.'

'Nothing to be sorry about, except that I miss the girls.'

'It said on your jacket blurb . . .'

'Well, that was written some time ago.'

She sensed he didn't wish to pursue the matter.

'I feel I'm talking about myself all the time.' Lewis finished his ham and eggs, sat back and again gave her that penetrating, disconcerting stare. 'Incidentally, that was very good.' He indicated his plate.

'The food here is good.'

'I eat here almost every day. I'm not very domesticated.' He looked at his watch. 'Shall we go back to my place and have coffee? I think we can talk more easily there.'

'Well,' looking doubtful, 'I should be getting back.'

'But you hardly know anything about me.'

'That's true.'

'And I know absolutely *nothing* about you.' Big smile.

*       *       *

Eleanor wondered how long the cleaning lady had been away. The place was in a mess. There were dirty crocks in the kitchen sink which looked as though they'd been there a very long time. Lewis didn't seem to know where the coffee was and she had to rescue two cups from the sink, rinse them through and dry them. She wondered how long he'd been divorced.

'I'm pretty hopeless domestically,' he said as he carried the tray with the coffee cups into the sitting room.

'I can see that.' Eleanor sat down again and got out her pad.

'Do you know, I like outspoken women.' He gazed at her admiringly. 'Where do you live, Eleanor?' He put the tray down and passed her a cup.

'Southend.'

'What a horrible place.'

'Actually it's rather nice.' Defensively, she put her pencil aside and looked at him. 'I like

84

the sea.'

'I do too, but not at Southend.'

'Where would you like the sea?' She put her cup to her lips.

'Say, Greece? I love the Mediterranean. Have you ever been to Greece?'

She nodded. 'I've been all over. I like travelling.' She thought of all the dreary 'Singles' trips, but it wouldn't do to let him know about those.

'Where did you go to school?'

'In the north of England. It was a convent.'

'Ah!' There was a speculative light in his eye. 'Are you a Catholic?'

'Sort of. They say once a Catholic always a Catholic.'

'I see.'

There was a pause. Eleanor finished her coffee, took up her pencil and wondered what else she could ask him. She felt rather nervous, curiously disturbed, as though some new dimension had entered their relationship since they returned to the cottage. It was not hard to define what it was: sex.

After all, with the kitchen in such a mess it would have been easier to have had the coffee in the pub.

'I find you very intriguing, Eleanor.' Lewis had been standing by the window drinking his coffee and, coming over to her, casually put his empty cup on a table nearby. Then he stood looking down at her. 'May I ask you

85

something?'

'Ask away,' she said, trying with difficulty to keep a lightness in her voice.

'Are you engaged, in love, having an affair . . . anything like that?'

Eleanor shook her head, keeping her eyes on her pad.

'What about this Len?'

She burst out laughing. 'He's my boss. He has a very possessive wife and five children.'

'All the more reason.'

'Oh no. Nothing like that.'

'Well, I hope we see each other again.'

She gazed at him not quite knowing what to say. Too late. He bent down and swiftly kissed her.

*     *     *

She felt rather dirty, a bit sordid. It was only four in the afternoon and she'd known him three hours. He had become her lover and they'd made love twice. He started again almost as soon as he climaxed the first time. It had been heady, exciting, crazy. She'd never known anything like it. Now all that had passed and she felt disgusted with herself and her performance, as if she'd never had a man in her life before.

He was asleep and she thought she'd creep out of bed and go away. She was quite sure this was one of those brief adventures that led

86

nowhere. She also decided he would be disgusted with her. He was chauvinistic. She was a convent girl and she'd given in so easily. He'd think she was sex-starved, that was it.

She began gently to turn back the bedclothes and felt a hand round her waist.

'Where are you going, Eleanor?'

'I've got to leave,' she said rather frantically.

'Why?' The hand tightened on her waist.

'Because I have to.' She looked at him. He had rather a quizzical expression on his face, hard to fathom, but it wasn't disgust. 'Look, you may not believe this, but I've never done this before.'

'What? Made love? You could have fooled me.' He began to laugh.

'No, hopped into bed with someone I'd known five minutes. I feel rather ashamed.'

'Don't be silly. I like you. I really do.'

'You say that . . .'

'I mean it. I do. I like you lots.'

\*      \*      \*

Len said: 'How did the interview go, Eleanor?'

'It went fine,' she said, poring earnestly over her notes which she was trying to transcribe on to the typewriter.

'Why are you blushing?' Len leaned over her desk and looked at her closely.

'I'm not,' she waved a hand across her face. 'It's just so hot in the office.'

87

'Lewis Gould,' she began, 'one of the most successful younger novelists of this generation, lives in a picture-book thatched cottage where I interviewed him on a bright summer's day. There are rambling roses on the walls, collared doves cooing on the roof and as he opened the door . . .'

I fell in love, she thought. Just like in soppy romantic novels. Can this, really, be happening to me?

# CHAPTER FOUR

# SEPTEMBER 1972

Outside the window of her private room the branches of a tall beech tree waved in the late September sunshine. Clare remembered seeing it before she went under the anaesthetic and it was the first thing she saw when she came to. She lay looking at it; the shining, dancing leaves so like tiny mirrors reflecting the sunlight had a mesmerising quality.

The room was very quiet. Strangely quiet. She looked down at the side of her bed and she knew. Tears filled her eyes and she felt an awful sense of desolation, of loss.

The door opened and Andrew walked into the room, looking tired and, unusually for him, his clothes were crumpled. He was always so neatly turned out, so smart, so very formal. Even when he relaxed at home he looked like someone who found it difficult to unwind completely.

Clare held out her hand and Andrew clasped it.

'The baby died, didn't it?'

Andrew found it hard to contain his tears and nodded.

'It would never have survived.'

'What was it?'

'A boy.'

Now the grief overwhelmed Clare and she put her head against Andrew's chest. He put his arms round her, hugging her tight.

*     *     *

The bleeding had started in the early hours of the morning. It wasn't just a show, it was a fierce flow. The doctor had been called and she was rushed to hospital. Up to then, as with her other two, she'd had a carefree pregnancy.

'Did they explain how it happened? Why?' Clare drew away from Andrew and, reaching for the handkerchief tucked in his top pocket, blew her nose hard.

'One of those things. They can't explain them. It doesn't mean we can't have any more. We must try and forget it, Clare. Put it behind us. We must try and accept it as the Will of God.'

She supposed that this really was the test of faith, to think that God had willed a seven-month foetus to die in the womb. Pippa would have accepted it, might even have explained it; but Pippa had never carried a child in her womb, felt it moving and kicking, communicated with it long before it was born. Pippa had never longed for a large family, felt herself only complete, in a way, when she was pregnant.

90

In the weeks after she returned from the hospital, Clare plumbed depths in herself that she had never known, a feeling of total despair that nothing could relieve or assuage. She felt completely isolated and alone despite being surrounded by love, and she had all the help and support she could ever have wanted. She talked to the parish priest who had known her since she was a child, to the family doctor, Dr Burroughs, who had delivered her. She talked to her mother and father, her brother Mark and to his wife Chrissy—whom she liked and to whom she was close—but still she felt that nothing could reach her, no one could comfort her. Andrew in his own grief tried to help. All to no avail.

The family took her depression badly. No one could have imagined that Clare could be affected like this. Clare who, in many ways, had such a perfect life, wanted for nothing, seemed to have a naturally cheerful disposition, had always enjoyed a serenity that went along with her overall intellectual and physical abilities. No Pearson had ever been in this situation, and it was hard for a Pearson to understand it.

There were days when Clare felt she couldn't communicate at all, couldn't even get out of bed.

Above all she felt she couldn't look after her

two little children, and because of the effect her illness had on them they were taken away to be cared for by their grandmother.

'Mummy is ill,' it was explained to Marcus, who was three and Pauline, two. 'Mummy will soon be better.'

Clare had always been well and happy until this catastrophe, consequently, the children were happy and well-adjusted, and they looked on this as an adventure, a chance to go and stay with Granny and Grandpa, of whom they were very fond.

Dr Pearson understood it least of all. There had never been any mental illness in his family. Pearson women, Catholic women, had borne dozens of children down the generations without a blip. He simply couldn't explain it.

Baffled, he sought the advice of a colleague.

*     *     *

Andrew crept into the bedroom and stood gazing at Clare, a shadow of the bright, alert, lovely woman he had married. Unable to sleep at night, she slept during the day. Andrew had moved into one of the spare rooms.

He drew up a chair and sat by the side of her bed deep in thought. People were so concerned about Clare they didn't seem to realise how much he suffered. Not only had he lost a baby, he felt he had lost a wife; that happy, joyous union was temporarily suspended. As the weeks had passed and Clare seemed no better he wondered if 'temporarily' was the right word, or if he had lost forever the wife he adored.

Clare opened her eyes and blinked rapidly. She saw Andrew and noted the gravity of his expression.

'Andrew, what is it? Something wrong?' She sat up, made as if to get out of bed. Andrew motioned her to stay.

'Darling, there is nothing wrong, nothing to disturb yourself about. The only thing that is wrong is what is the matter with you. We are all terribly worried.'

'Do you think *I* don't worry?' She sank back on the bed. 'I can't get out of my mind what happened to that baby. What had *I* done that God should take him from me?'

Andrew reached out and took her hand.

'You did nothing wrong, Clare. It is something that happened. It happens. Not all babies go to full term. No one can explain why. The thing that worries me, worries us all, is your current state of mind, this deep depression you're in.'

'I can't help it,' she wailed, beginning to cry, rubbing her fingers in her eyes like a child, screwing them up and making them red. 'It's not only the baby but the world seems in such a mess. I can't get over that awful massacre at the Olympics. Those poor people being gunned down . . .'

Clare had got into the habit of brooding on events in the daily news, personalising them as if they had happened to her, like the massacre of nine Israeli athletes by Palestinian terrorists at the Olympic Games in Munich earlier in the month.

'Clare, you're only dwelling on this because you're depressed.'

'You mean you don't care about it, Andrew? I'm surprised at you.'

'Of course I care about it! I think it was awful. But I don't dwell on it. You see, Clare, when you're unhappy, depressed, other things assume a disproportionate significance. They prey on your mind. You're just in a generally depressed and unhappy state, so these things that are awful, no one denies that, take on a special significance because, in your case, of the way you feel about Dominic.'

They had given the baby a name and he had had a proper burial, the tiny white coffin being interred next to countless Thorntons who had pre-deceased him.

'I can't help it,' Clare said again, sobbing wildly.

'I know you can't help it. It's not like you. It's some chemical in your body that's not functioning right.'

'Who told you that?' She sat up again and looked sharply at him. The least hint of something wrong frightened her.

'Well, it's a theory. It's the only one they can

94

find to explain what's happened. It's changes in your hormones following the loss of the baby.'

'It didn't happen before.' Clare's expression remained fixed and stubborn.

'Darling, I've had a long talk with your father and John Burroughs and we think you should go away and have a rest . . .'

'But I *am* resting, Andrew!' A note of exasperation, of defiance, entered her voice. 'That's all I do, *rest*. That's all I seem capable of doing. I am so tired. You have no idea how tired I am.'

'Clare, I have every idea how tired you are. But your father and John and I would like you to go into a clinic for a while. It is a very nice place, very well thought of—very expensive incidentally, but that's no problem—and we think that a few weeks there will . . .'

'No!'

'But, Clare . . .'

'I said "No". No, Andrew. Do you understand? No!'

'Clare, please . . . You do need psychiatric care. You need to talk about what is the cause of this depression. They will also give you suitable medication. Believe me, darling, you will be there no time at all, and once it is sorted we can get on with our lives, have the children back . . .'

'No, Andrew. No. No, no, no.'

Lewis smiled his seductive smile.

'I liked the article very much.'

'Good.'

'You've got talent. You're wasted where you are.'

'Oh no. I don't think so.'

'Yes, you are. If it's any interest to you a great friend of mine is the editor of *The Examiner*. Douglas Jerrold.'

'Oh I think I'm too old for Fleet Street.'

'Of course you're not. How old are you?'

'Twenty-six.'

'Too old? Rubbish! If you like, I'll give Douglas a ring and you can show him some of your work.'

'Well . . .'

'You're not very self-assured, are you, Eleanor? I mean you give the impression that you are, but you're not.'

'It's true I have a lot of doubts.'

They'd met in a pub after work in Southend where Lewis told her on the phone he just 'happened' to be. She felt awkward and uneasy. Still didn't know the man or anything about him, although she'd slept with him. It seemed grotesque and she had this awful sense of shame.

Lewis's hand closed over hers.

'I do like you a lot, you know. You don't believe me, do you?'

'Well . . .' She raised her eyes and smiled doubtfully, 'I'd like to.'

'Then what's stopping you?'

Silence.

'It's that lack of self-assurance, isn't it? I guess you've been badly let down by men in your life.'

'Let's say my love life hasn't been a hundred per cent successful.'

'Well neither has mine. Kay, my wife, left me for another man. It was an awful blow.'

'Oh dear, I'm sorry. Somehow I didn't think . . .'

'I let her keep the children because, as they were girls, I didn't think it fair to insist on custody, though I had every right to.'

'Do you see them?'

'Well, every now and then. They live in Wales. Kay's new husband is a sheep farmer in the Welsh mountains.'

'How on earth did she meet someone like that?'

'She was a friend of his sister's. They were at university together in Cardiff. She knew him before she knew me. She used to talk to him about me, said I was cold and remote.'

'I thought the contrary.' Eleanor looked shyly at him. 'I thought you were very warm and friendly. I expected something different.'

'Look, I meant to ask . . .' Lewis slipped the bar mat in front of him back and forth with his forefinger. 'I mean, I assume you took precautions . . .'

'Oh yes, I'm on the Pill.'

'Oh I see . . .'

'But I don't sleep around. I . . . I once got caught out. I did become pregnant.'

'Oh I'm sorry.' His hand closed over hers again. 'And what happened?'

'I had a baby boy. He was awfully sweet. I called him Simon. I had to have him adopted of course.' Suddenly her eyes filled with tears. 'I was just twenty-one with no help or means of support . . .' She blew hard into her handkerchief. 'My parents would never have understood.'

'And who was the father?'

'He was someone I worked with. It was rather sordid. He didn't want to know. It's something I still feel terrible about. I mean, I often wonder what the people were like who adopted him. I was told they were very nice. But it's always worried me.'

'I'm sure there's no need to worry.' Lewis's tone was gentle, caring. 'Lots of people had to do what you did.'

'I couldn't have an abortion. Being a Catholic . . .'

'I know. I know. Don't distress yourself, Eleanor. Look . . . Aren't you going to show me your flat? Maybe I'll see Southend in a new light.'

\*       \*       \*

Douglas Jerrold was urbane; an editor of the old school. After graduating from King's College, London, he had gone via Reuter's News Agency to *The Times*, *The Sunday Times* and, finally, Fleet Street's top-quality newspaper, influential, privately owned, *The Examiner*.

He offered Eleanor sherry and discussed everything except work for half an hour before taking her to lunch at Simpson's. Lewis was a great friend of his. He had a very high regard for him and his work.

He looked approvingly at Eleanor.

'Do I take it that there's a relationship?'

'I didn't want that to affect . . .'

'Oh I assure you it would never influence me to take you on the staff if you weren't any good; but Lewis is right. I liked the stuff you sent me. Your work is good. Of course you are wasted in that group, churning out stuff for mass circulation. If you stayed there any longer I think it would be very hard for you to get to Fleet Street. It ruins your style. Another coffee?'

Eleanor shook her head and Douglas looked round for the waiter and asked for the bill. Then he stared hard at Eleanor.

'As it happens I have got a vacancy for a feature writer. I'm prepared to take you on a trial basis, say six months. I can't be sure you'll do, but I think you will. Now this is a risk as far as you're concerned because it is possible that if it doesn't go well, we don't suit you or you don't suit us, we shall have to part. You will then be without a job. No security. But . . .' He flashed her his charming smile, 'I think it's worth the risk.'

\*      \*      \*

Eleanor wanted to live with Lewis, but not in the house he'd shared with Kay. She was quite adamant about this. It was the occasion of their first row after she'd given him the news. The evening started off well with dinner in the pub, a bottle of champagne to celebrate.

A formal offer had arrived that morning with terms and conditions of work and she'd told Len, who was not pleased. He said *The Examiner* was a stuffy old newspaper with a tiny circulation that nobody read, not quite *The Times*, not quite *The Guardian*, and she'd soon get tired. But the die was cast.

'I'm terribly, terribly pleased,' Lewis had said.

'I can't thank you enough.'

'You can.' He'd paused. 'I wondered if you'd like to housekeep for me.'

'Housekeep?' She'd stared at him aghast. 'You know I *hate* cleaning . . .

'What I mean is a live-in lover. You don't need to iron my shirts. How about it?'

Well, they'd been together four months. It

100

was now December and she was due to start the new job in January, after she'd served a month's notice.

'You won't need to live in Southend, you can live here.'

He refilled her glass.

'Darling . . . Lewis,' she hesitated, 'can't we begin somewhere . . . fresh?'

'Fresh?' He didn't seem to understand.

'Move, you know. Maybe to London.'

'London! I hate the place.'

'Well Kent, or even Sussex. It doesn't have to be Essex.'

'Eleanor, I think you're missing the point. I don't want to move. I like it where I am. I like the cottage. I love it. It's my home and I want you to share it with me. Surely that's what you want too?' He looked appealingly at her.

'I don't want to share that *particular* cottage. Can't you understand?'

'Not really.' Sulkily he took up his knife and fork. 'Well, let's leave it then, though I think it's silly. I thought you'd be pleased.'

'Oh, Lewis . . .'

'No, let's leave it. We'll meet when we can at each other's places. Except that . . . will you keep on your flat?'

She bit her lip. 'I don't know. I hadn't thought, or if I had, I suppose in my mind I thought London.'

'I'm not living in bloody London,' said Lewis. 'And that's that!'

101

Eleanor had always considered Christmas one of the dreariest, most depressing times of the year. She felt she had a duty to go and see her parents, and this year was no exception. Lewis had wanted them to spend it together, but she had to explain that, for this year at least, she'd have to go north.

She'd go on Christmas Eve and she'd come back on Boxing Day. She'd drive so as not to be dependent on trains.

As usual her parents greeted her with the minimum display of pleasure. There was the bleakest smile of greeting followed by the accusation that they never saw her, they seldom heard from her and, after the barrage of complaints, she wished as usual that she hadn't come.

But this year there was Lewis to think about and the job; a new start in life for the year 1973.

Maybe, at last, things were turning her way.

Her mother was only fifty-five but she looked seventy. In their youth both her parents had been good looking in a thirties kind of way. Her mother was quite tall, strong-featured, fair-haired, steely-eyed. She'd worked as a secretary in a firm where she met Jim Hamilton, then on the first of his many jobs as a rep. He was tall too, a football player, a Brylcreem boy with shiny hair and smiling eyes, suede shoes and a double breasted suit.

One wondered when it had all changed and gone wrong. What had made her mother a hypochondriac and her father such a failure?

Even now he was still talking about schemes, missed opportunities, people who'd let him down. He sat in a corner sucking his pipe grumbling about this and that. Never his fault, always that of someone else. One thing you could say about her father; he never gave up.

Her mother was as usual full of woe about her health. She started almost as soon as Eleanor came into the room. She was having nasty turns and was short of breath. The doctor gave her pills but nothing worked.

'You should see a specialist, Mum.'

'What's the use? They don't know anything.' Always that air of futility.

Her parents lived in the house where she was born and a feeling of flat depression, as great as anything her mother ever knew, descended on her whenever she turned into the street and saw the dreary little semi-detached house looking like all the others, except that the patch of garden in front was less well kept and the curtains not so clean as those of their neighbours.

It was a cheerless place, but it made her feel guilty. Her mother, after all, was an invalid and her father . . . Well what made a person take

103

on so many jobs and succeed at none of them? He sat now in a corner of the sitting room, rheumy eyes misted over with bewilderment and pain, pipe in his mouth, staring gloomily at her.

'What's this about a new job, Eleanor?'

She'd tried to cheer her mother up with the news, but all she got was a bleak stare.

'In Fleet Street, Daddy, on a big daily newspaper, *The Examiner*.'

'Mmm,' her father grunted. 'What did you need a new job for?'

'Well this is better.'

'More pay?'

'More pay and more opportunity.'

'You don't want to get like your father changing jobs all the time.' Reproachful stare from her mother.

'Mother, I have been with Southern Group Newspapers five years.'

'You told us it was a very good job.'

'It was, and so is this. *The Examiner* is a very good paper. Highly thought of.'

'Never read it. Too up-market for me. All print and no pictures.'

'Maybe you'll read it now, Daddy.'

Her father shook his head.

Her mother thoughtfully sucked her teeth. 'It doesn't look as though you're ever going to marry and have a family, does it, Eleanor? You'll soon be twenty-seven. Don't you want children?'

104

'Not really, Mum.'

'Do you have a boyfriend?' Her mother looked at her suspiciously.

'As a matter of fact "yes".'

'Oh! What's his name?'

'Lewis.'

'What does he do?'

'He's a writer.'

'Oh, like you?'

'No, he writes novels.'

'Not much money in novels,' her father shook his head knowingly. 'I hope you don't have to keep him.'

'Are you living together?'

'Not yet.'

'Sleeping together I suppose.'

'Really, Marjorie!' Her father looked disapprovingly at his wife.

'Well they all do it these days, Jim. Don't they, Eleanor? And I don't suppose you go to Church any more. Given it all up?'

'Well, Mum, you're not exactly a regular.'

'That's because I can't kneel or stand and your father hardly ever takes the car out. But at least the Church gave us standards, and sometimes I think you young people would do well to remember that.'

Eleanor didn't reply, and her mother sighed loudly once again, an exaggerated sigh, which was a habit she had, almost like a nervous affliction.

'Well I suppose we'd better do the

decorations. We were waiting for you to come home, Eleanor. You know your father hasn't the patience and I can't reach. Usually you come home a few days before Christmas.'

'Sorry, Mum, I couldn't this time.'

'Sometimes I don't think you have the time for us, Eleanor. Sometimes I feel you'd rather not see us at all. You've got too posh for us. Seems like that to us, doesn't it, Jim?'

Her father nodded morosely.

'You've grown away from us, Eleanor. It's not like having a daughter at all.'

'And now you've got a young man, we'll never see you at all I suppose.'

'Mum, you know that's not true.'

'Well, why didn't you ask him to come with you?'

'Because . . . Well, I felt I should tell you about him first.'

'Are you going to get married?'

'No plans at the moment.'

'I hope he doesn't string you along, Eleanor. It's silly to give into a man, that's what I always say. It bodes no good at all. A man doesn't respect a woman. . .'

'Oh, Mum . . .' Eleanor turned her head away, her stomach already churning.

It was going to be that sort of Christmas after all.

*     *     *

106

'What sort of time did you have?'

'Awful!'

Eleanor sank on to the sofa feeling utterly exhausted and depressed. A great fire roared in the grate and, as she entered the cottage, there was a welcoming feel, a sense of being at home. She'd driven at breakneck speed all down the motorway.

She kicked off her boots and lit a cigarette. Lewis handed her a drink and sat down beside her, one arm casually flung round her shoulder. He kissed her cheek, a tender, intimate gesture that was somehow better than a passionate kiss.

'Tell me about it.'

'I feel so guilty about my parents, Lewis.'

'But, darling, you do everything a daughter should do.'

'No I don't. I see the bare minimum of them.' She gazed at him despairingly. 'But what incentive do I have to go home when they are on at me all the time for my many deficiencies as a daughter? The trouble is they're right, but the constant moaning and nagging gets me down.'

'Poor lamb.' Lewis pecked her cheek again and snuggled up to her. 'I missed you.'

'It was only two days,' she murmured. 'What sort of time did you have?'

'OK,' he shrugged. 'I spent most of it in the pub. I ate there. There were quite a lot of abandoned souls, like me.'

'You'd have hated it at my parents.' She bent forward and threw a log on the fire, then she leaned back against Lewis. 'They are really sad and pathetic. That's what makes me feel guilty. I told them about you.'

'What did they say?'

'Pretty negative. "Supposed" we were sleeping together.' She looked at him slyly.

'Well they were right.'

'They still live in the past.'

'Are they very religious?'

'No, not at all, but they still think a "nice" girl doesn't give herself to a man until they're married.'

There was silence. Lewis said nothing. Marriage was something they never mentioned. Marriage and children. Somehow, because he didn't bring it up, Eleanor couldn't either. She felt it had to come from him, when he was ready for it and, well, maybe she wasn't quite decided on the issue either. There was plenty of time.

'Any post for me?' she asked.

'Oh yes.' Lewis got up and, going over to a side table, produced a stack of cards which he placed on Eleanor's knee. She began to go through them as he resumed his place next to her again after refilling their glasses.

'It's good to have you back,' he said, pressing her shoulder again. 'Look, darling, I've been thinking. It is very selfish of me to want you to live here. I've been thinking about

108

London again. There are some nice parts of London. We needn't be too central. We . . .'

Eleanor paused in her perusal of her mail.

'I was thinking too. It was very selfish of me to expect you to give up your home. After all, it *was* your home before you married Kay, wasn't it?'

'No.'

'Oh I thought it was.'

'No, we bought it together. Fell in love with the place . . .'

'Still I don't feel her "presence" here and I don't suppose it would much matter if I did. I mean it is a very pretty cottage, very comfortable. You like the village and the pub.'

'Let's find somewhere in London as well. I mean you must have a bit put by.'

'Well, yes, I have. I've never been madly well-paid but I never spent much money.'

'And you've got your flat.'

'I rent that.'

'Oh, I see.'

'It's not a decision we have to make tonight, darling.' Eleanor put the cards on the table, threw the envelopes in the wastepaper basket and sat back. 'Nothing from Clare. I wonder why.'

'Who's Clare?'

'An old school friend. Last time I saw her she was pregnant. Maybe that's why.'

'Why what?' Lewis yawned and looked at the clock.

'Why there's no card. Too busy with the new baby, I suppose. I really should have rung and found out how she was.' She turned and tapped his nose with her finger. 'I was too busy with you. After I met you I couldn't think of anything else.'

'Really?'

'Really.'

'That's nice. Let's go to bed,' he suggested.

*      *      *

The first Christmas without Clare since their marriage. It was very hard to bear. He took the children to the clinic to see her but she hardly seemed to notice them. The medical director said she was still in the grips of severe postnatal depression, one of the worst he had seen, but there were signs she was slowly responding to treatment. It would take time. No, he couldn't say how long.

Andrew sat in front of the fire drinking a weak whisky and water. It was Christmas Day, surely the worst he'd ever spent? The children were still with the Pearsons and he was going over for lunch.

Marcus was now three and a half, Pauline two and a bit. Marcus seemed to understand about his mother, but Pauline didn't. They'd both been told that Mummy wasn't well.

It was very hard to think that a woman like Clare, so vivacious and vital, could suffer a

110

mental breakdown of such severity. It just seemed to be so contrary to the sort of person she was. In a million years he never would have predicted this, nor would anyone else.

It crossed his mind that, in many ways, he had assumed a lot about Clare, taken too much for granted. He had left the children, the running of the house, entirely to her. She entertained his clients, cooked delicious meals, played golf—always good at games—graced social functions as only she could.

It was this terrible gap that had made him realise what she'd been to him and how much he had lost.

He had, he decided, been a rather selfish, conventional husband, going out at nine in the morning and coming back at six at night, expecting a drink and a good dinner. The children getting ready for bed would be visited for a play or a story. He and Clare might entertain, might go out for dinner, and as he was also on the town council and in line one day to be mayor, there were quite a lot of social functions to attend. Weekends were busy too.

Like many husbands, he took it for granted that these things would run smoothly. And they did.

It had never occurred to him either that his progress up the ladder of life, the path of success, would in any way be halted.

Andrew finished his whisky, put the guard

in front of the fire, checked that the front and back doors were bolted and locked and went through the door in the kitchen adjoining the garage. He got out his car and drove the few miles to his parents-in-law on the other side of town, almost dreading the large party he knew he would find there.

As soon as he stopped by the front door, the children, who had been looking out for him, ran down the steps and hurtled themselves into his arms. Tears sprang to his eyes as he hugged them. They were so precious that he knew he couldn't be parted from them for much longer. Behind them, smiling on the steps, was Edith, Clare's mother, who had her youngest grandchild, nine-month-old Henry, the son of Mark and Chrissy, in her arms. She looked on benignly as Marcus and Pauline greeted their father and, with his arms round each of them, he ascended the steps.

'Happy Christmas, Mother.'

'And to you, dear Andrew.' Edith kissed him on the cheek and looked questioningly into his eyes.

'Did you go to the clinic?'

Andrew shook his head.

'I may go later. I was there yesterday and there's not much to report.'

A cloud seemed to flutter across Edith's normally cheerful, composed features.

'I simply can't understand it, can you?'

'No.'

'There's never been anything like this in the family on either side.'

'They say it's hormonal. The abrupt ending to the pregnancy: the Caesarean plays hell with a woman's insides.'

'She will recover, Andrew.' With her free hand Edith pressed Andrew's arm. 'I know.'

But would she? He often wondered, but with the family one had to put on a front.

To the Pearsons, and to the Thorntons, appearances mattered so much.

In a way Andrew enjoyed the day, the large family party, the games that followed, the presents under the tree. But all the time he thought of that pale-faced, emaciated form either lying in bed gazing out of the window or sitting inertly in her chair not communicating. Sometimes you felt you wanted to shake her. It seemed so unfair, unreasonable, in a way, self-indulgent. He wanted to scream out: 'I need you, Clare, the children need you. We want you back home. For God's sake, woman, pull yourself together.'

But he knew that wasn't right, it wasn't fair. She literally could not help what was happening to her, or do anything about it.

But even then it was so hard to understand.

By early evening everyone was exhausted. Mark and Chrissy took their baby home to bed. Frank left with his girlfriend Ruth, and Andrew sat in front of the fire with Christopher Pearson while Edith put the

113

children to bed. They were one of the few families left with a live-in maid, but she had Christmas Day and Boxing Day off. Just the time you really needed these people, Edith thought, but that was the way these days, and if you objected they'd leave.

'Well, a satisfactory day I think,' Christopher Pearson observed as he puffed on his pipe.

'Very enjoyable.'

'Missed Clare though.'

'Of course.'

'Last year she was the life and soul of the party.'

'She was the life and soul of everything,' Andrew said, and found himself choking with grief.

His father-in-law looked at him with concern. 'You alright?'

'I feel it's partly my fault, what happened to her.'

'Oh no, it's a medical thing. Nothing to do with you.'

'I should have paid more attention to what was going on at home.'

Momentarily Christopher Pearson looked shocked.

'But you loved your wife and children?'

'That goes without saying.'

'And I suppose there is no doubt you were faithful?'

Now it was Andrew's turn to look shocked.

'I do object to that observation, Father.'

'Sorry.'

'I adore Clare. I would never look at another woman. No, what I mean is I took everything for granted. That it would all go with a swing.'

'And it did. Clare was, is, a very capable woman. So is Edith.'

'You never thought you could do more . . . ?'

'Certainly not. I was a loving husband and father and, I like to think, a good and conscientious doctor. Edith ran the house and saw to the needs of the family.' He looked over at his son-in-law. 'That's how things have always been, Andrew. That's how they *should* be. It's only these new and ridiculous notions about women's liberation that in my opinion threatens the fabric of society. I never heard such rot, and don't you entertain any ideas like that either.'

'Well . . . I still think I could and should do more. I'm going to take the children home, Father, and get a housekeeper and a nursemaid for them. I'm going to try and be a real father to them, not be so patriarchal, see more of them, so that when Clare comes home I can share some of the burden with her.'

Patriarchal, that was it. The age of the patriarch, of which species Christopher Pearson was a typical specimen, was over.

# CHAPTER FIVE

## JUNE 1973

Sheltered by a tree in the clinic garden, Clare was conscious for the first time of her surroundings, the sights and sounds of summer. The rose beds were in full bloom and the herbaceous borders were awash with the variegated shades of lupins; the blues, purples, soft mauves and whites of delphiniums, the reds and pinks of peonies, the bobbing, multicoloured heads of Aquilegia—known as 'granny's bonnet' but, in reality, like little birds in flight—and the burgeoning Antirrhinum, Zinnia and sweet-smelling Nicotiana. Clare looked slowly round savouring it all. If, as it was said, you were closer to God in a garden, she felt He was here.

That morning, for the first time in months, she had become aware of birdsong, very low and gentle at first, barely lilting. She no longer sat immersed in her own troubled thoughts, product of a tormented mind. Just, perceptibly, she could see beyond that low, low cloud to the skies above.

There was no way of describing the state of her mind these past few months, her anger with Andrew who had had her committed— incarcerated she'd called it—into a mental home. No use telling her it was for her own good. It was prison. It was hell. But hell, she slowly came to realise, with a soft side: beautiful surroundings, tranquillity, a pleasant room, kind, helpful staff; everyone there to try and assist her recovery, but she resisted. Her psychiatrist, Dr Ashworth, suggested at first that she didn't want to get better. Clare, when she at last consented to talk to her, felt she could have thrown something at her. There were many stormy sessions.

Slowly the barriers began to break and she, reluctantly at first, then more willingly as her general health improved, started to cooperate, to try and explore the dark recesses of her mind, to understand why she was so unable to forgive herself for losing the baby.

Why she was so resentful and angry with God.

Was it because she had trusted Him and He had let her down? For a time she ceased to believe in God at all, and thought that, maybe, she would never again resume her simple, unquestioning faith. The faith of her fathers for generations past. The counselling, the therapies—relaxation exercises and massage—the rest, above all, perhaps, the medication, had slowly brought her to a stage when she no longer dwelt on herself but tried to look about her, see others, see things, the beauty of nature or hear the sound of birds.

It had all been a long time coming but,

gradually, she was beginning to rise from the abyss, peer above the parapet.

Clare became aware of two figures strolling slowly across the lawn in her direction. They were deep in conversation and, as they came nearer, she saw that one was Dr Ashworth, and the other . . .

'Pippa!' she called softly, getting out of her chair. Pippa looked up and, seeing Clare, ran across the lawn. The two women embraced.

'I'll leave you two to chat,' Dr Ashworth said, smiling that sweet, slow smile that had begun to endear itself so much to Clare. She was about forty, a German Jew who had married an Englishman. She had been smuggled out of Germany as a child, but her parents had been killed in the camps. She answered few questions and would not allow Clare, who wished to, to dwell on this; Clare with her fascination for anything grim and morbid. What had happened to Irma Ashworth was not part of Clare's therapy and she tried gently to detach Clare from her analyst's past and concentrate on her own.

Clare nodded and Irma wandered back across the lawn towards the house, hands deep in the pockets of her long cardigan.

'Oh I'm so *pleased* to see you.' Clare clutched Pippa's hand and drew her down to the chair beside her. 'How did you hear?'

'I telephoned you to say I was coming for the reunion on Association Day . . .'

'Oh Association Day . . .' Every year there was Association Day, the meeting of old students that enabled them to get together, reminisce and exchange news and gossip. Clare had always been one of the main organisers, going at it hammer and tongs to make it a huge success. In fact she had completely forgotten about it.

'Besides, I hadn't heard,' Pippa went on. 'No news from you about the baby, no Christmas card.' She bit her lip. 'I should have got in touch with you before. I do feel guilty.'

'No need to feel guilty. There was nothing you could do. I have been in here since I . . . Well, you heard I lost the baby. That triggered it off. Complete collapse. Whoosh. No one knows why.'

'Yes I heard.' Pippa continued to clasp her hand. 'Andrew told me some, Dr Ashworth the rest. She seems awfully nice.'

'She is. At first I didn't like her. I deeply resented her. I was extraordinarily rude to her but she persevered. I refused to come voluntarily and Andrew had me committed. I felt it was a stigma. The trouble is you don't really think you're ill. You think everyone else is.'

Her face seemed to go blank and Pippa gently shook her hand.

'There's no need to talk about it.'

'I just wanted to explain. I know it's so unlike me. I felt in a way the family were

119

ashamed of me. They felt I'd let them down.'

'I'm *sure* that wasn't the case.'

'You don't know my father.'

It was true Pippa didn't know Dr Pearson well, although to her he'd always seemed a bit frightening. A big man with bushy brows and an authoritative manner. She had never thought of him as someone to whom she could, or would have taken an intimate problem.

'Andrew's been very good,' Clare said quietly. 'He brings the children to see me. He has them living at home, spends all his time with them. He gave up the council to be with them more. That meant a lot to him because he was so ambitious. I couldn't forgive him for a time for having me committed. I thought it was brutal, but now I know he did it for the best. I feel I understand him more. Maybe he understands me too,' she concluded almost sotto voce. 'Do you hear from Eleanor?'

Pippa shook her head. 'Not since my profession. I had a Christmas card. I have a feeling that Eleanor has distanced herself from us, maybe because she's left the Church. I felt that a bit the day you both came to Sussex.'

'I did too. She seemed preoccupied with other things.' Clare's voice trailed off. Studying Clare's face Pippa sensed that she was getting tired. She was very pale, much thinner and certainly a mere shadow of the bonny woman she had been the previous August. The bonny, blooming, pregnant woman. There were dark circles round her eyes which lacked their usual sparkle, such a feature of her as a girl. Above all, the lustre had gone from her beautiful hair which looked lank and uncared for, as if she was no longer concerned about her appearance. Pippa wondered if she'd had electric shock treatment. It seemed an unfathomable mystery to see Clare reduced to such a ghost of her former self.

As if she could read her mind Clare said: 'I often wonder why God did this to me. I mean why does He do these things? Dr Ashworth is German, and her parents and most of her family died in the concentration camps. I try and get her to talk about it but she won't. Why does God do these things?'

'I wish I had an answer.' Pippa looked thoughtful. It was a question one often came up against. 'Nothing really explains the miseries of the world except free will. I mean God doesn't control our lives. He doesn't intervene. He is there if we call on Him to help. And, in His way, He helps us, even if we don't understand how. I'm sure of that.'

'It's a point.' Clare leaned back in her chair and closed her eyes. 'Are you happy as a nun?'

'Very. Very happy. I've been sent to Roseacre ...'

'Ah *Roseacre*!' Clare said in a tone of exaggerated respect.

Roseacre was a house of the Society in

Devon where all the rich or well-connected girls went. It was the Catholic girls' equivalent of Stonyhurst or Downside. 'I bet you have to mind your ps and qs there.'

'It's really a very *nice* place. Most civilised and agreeable. The girls are lovely. I teach history of art which is a joy. I couldn't be happier.' And Pippa did look happy, serene, other-worldly. She'd changed, no longer withdrawn yet not too outgoing. Mature. The expression came into Clare's mind: 'Touched by an Angel'. But she had to introduce something more mundane.

'Don't you miss men? Sex?'

'Not a bit.'

'Did you ever sleep with a man?'

'No.'

'So you don't miss what you don't know?'

'I suppose so. One has a love affair with Christ. It's a different kind of emotion altogether.'

'I don't know how I'll feel about sex now,' Clare said thoughtfully. 'After Dominic, the baby who died.'

Pippa reached for her hand again.

'I think you must try and resume your life when you leave here as though this has never happened. Like an illness, which it is. Once cured you don't have to go back or think about it all the time. If you have your appendix out you don't keep on missing it.'

'Easier said than done,' Clare said.

122

*          *          *

Pippa had not been back to St Catherine's since she'd become a Catholic or entered the novitiate. It was a strange experience to be welcomed back as a nun, and to take her place in the community of which she'd once been a charge. It was a different community from her own schooldays. Then, the nuns had worn the religious habit and bonnet; they had an aura of solemnity and mystery which certainly they hadn't got now—for the most part plain women with shapeless figures which the graceful habit had disguised.

Pippa had been depressed by the abandonment of the habit following the Second Vatican Council, but she realised that it did not detract from the essential point of being a nun, which was giving yourself up to God. You existed for Him and Him alone, service to others was through Him, so what you wore was unimportant. The face, the figure, didn't matter. If most nuns seemed to look plain, then most women without make-up would too. What mattered was the soul of each individual woman in the chapel at Mass on her first morning back at St Catherine's.

Even the Mass was different. No longer in Latin, no longer ritualistic, the priest now faced the congregation and spoke in English. It was all very different from the old days.

123

Many Catholics yearned for them, but what mattered was the unalterable nature of God and the Church. That didn't change.

The community was smaller. Some nuns had left, some had died, some had moved to other houses. There was now a very large lay staff who taught the girls.

The superior was different from when Pippa had been a pupil. When she appeared at recreation after the evening meal, many of the nuns who taught her were present and they greeted her joyfully. Those who didn't know her were introduced. There were a few kind words of welcome from Reverend Mother, and some general chat, before they all went off to bed.

It took Pippa some time to get to sleep because the memories of her schooldays were so vivid they seemed to press down upon her. She saw herself then and now, two different people, almost ten years older than when she left. It seemed like a lifetime ago.

Pippa had been given a small guest room to herself. Some of the nuns still slept in a dormitory and she was thankful that she was spared the tossing and restlessness, the sometimes curious or unpleasant sounds of other people sleeping. At Roseacre the nuns all had their own rooms, but then it was a vast mansion that had once been a ducal home.

Before she fell asleep Pippa's thoughts lingered on Clare who seemed to be recovering from her breakdown; but what had happened to Clare gave one pause for thought, however much one believed in the goodness of God and His mercy.

\*      \*      \*

Sister Teresa of Avila was a nun who stood out for her stature, her authority and her natural, almost striking good looks. She was a polymath, an intellectual like the saint whose name she had taken in religion, the great Spanish mystic of the Carmelite Order. Above all, she was passionate about art which she had taught Pippa or, rather, helped her to develop the talent she already had.

She was waiting for Pippa after breakfast the following morning, having greeted her affectionately but only briefly the night before.

'I knew I had to share you with everyone else,' she said giving her a hug. 'It is so *good* to see you again, Pippa.'

'And you, Sister.'

'I wanted you to have a peek at our art exhibition.' Sister Teresa took hold of Pippa's arm. 'Have you time? This year I think it is particularly good.'

'I'd love that,' Pippa said enthusiastically.

The two women walked, chatting, along the shiny main hall to the school building which contained a modern art room at the top. The windows were open and gave a view over the town.

'I'm so glad it's nice for Association Day,' Sister Teresa said, closing the door. 'Did you see Clare Pearson?'

'Yes. I went there straight from the train. She's much better.'

'To think she always organised Association Day. So sad.' Sister shook her head.

'Maybe she will next year,' Pippa murmured, beginning to walk round the room, inspecting the exhibits while Sister Teresa sat at her desk and watched her.

Pippa hadn't changed, a little graver perhaps, and the two-piece suit and grey blouse didn't exactly flatter her, nor were they meant to; but hadn't they all suffered a bit when they gave up the habit?

Sister Teresa was a rebel when it came to the subject of the reforms. She was a traditionalist and thought they weren't reforms at all but a futile attempt to catch up with the age, to be all things to all men and not succeeding. After all, the Church had remained the same for centuries, and what was wrong with that? The abandonment of the beautiful Latin language was a disaster.

Pippa and Sister Teresa had always been close, drawn together by their bookishness, their intellect, their love of art.

'Do you still paint, Pippa?' she asked, as the young nun finished her inspection, nodding her approval.

126

'Oh yes. I gave up for quite a time while I was in the novitiate, but now at Roseacre Reverend Mother has given me permission to start again. I intend to be very active this summer.'

Sister Teresa looked carefully at Pippa as she spoke, recalling the thoughtful young woman, overtly religious, yet not able to join the Faith, the visionary, the dreamer. She could have gone far, seemed destined to go far. But that, surely, had been halted?

'Do you ever regret entering, Pippa?'

'Oh no!' Pippa looked shocked. 'Why should I?'

'I think you had so much to offer the world, Pippa.'

'But in what way, Sister?'

'As a wife, a mother, an artist.' Sister Teresa rose from her desk and began agitatedly to pace the space in front of it. 'I'm not sure that becoming a nun is the best way to serve God. It is a way, but maybe not the best.'

'You don't regret . . .'

Sister nodded. 'In a way I do, for myself. But I am nearly fifty and it is too late to consider a change. Had the Vatican Council happened ten years earlier I might; but what could I do in the world? Where would I go?'

'You could teach.'

'At my age? Do you think I'd get a job? Where would I live? No, I have been a member of the Society since I was twenty and I expect to die a member of the Society. But you, Pippa, you are young and strong and capable, very gifted, very blessed, and I should think very carefully about spending the rest of your life as a nun.'

Sister Teresa leaned forward and put both hands tightly around Pippa's cheeks looking intently into her eyes.

'Forgive me for approaching you like this, but I had to say it. I don't want you to get to my age and feel you've made a mistake. But please, please don't pass on to anyone, especially any member of the community, what I've said to you.' She glanced at the clock on the wall as it struck nine. 'Now I must prepare for my lesson. Because of Association Day, the girls break up at twelve. This afternoon you'll be able to see all your friends again.'

\*          \*          \*

But two were missing: Eleanor and Clare. They were the important ones, but there were others. Almost ten years on some had married, some had children, some were career women, a lot were teachers. Two were doctors, two civil servants, one an economist. Several were secretaries. Others were missing because they'd gone abroad. Most of them still lived in and around Wolversleigh. Some were well-heeled, the social equals of the Thorntons and the Pearsons, most were not. Their fathers had

had mundane jobs in offices or factories, their mothers stayed at home and they had lived in houses that were terraced or semi-detached. There had been a hierarchy at St Catherine's, a distinction between day girls and those who boarded, whose parents were deemed to be better off. It all seemed rather silly but maybe the freedom enjoyed by the day girls was envied by the boarders who made up for it by an air of exclusivity, a snobbishness that was certainly generations old, since the Italian nuns had set up a house in Wolversleigh in the nineteenth century. The truth was that both sides rarely mixed except in classrooms. Fraternisation was not encouraged. Recreational times were quite separate and when the day girls went home the boarders went off to their own quarters.

Mary Barlow, married before Clare, had five children. Five! Everyone gasped—she was not yet thirty. But then she was a good Catholic, contraception wasn't allowed and she could have twenty by the time she was forty, theoretically more. However she seemed happy with her lot, proud of it in fact, and breezed along like a ship in full sail with a glass of wine in one hand and a sausage roll in the other. She had also, perhaps not unnaturally, put on a lot of weight.

Margaret Potter was unmarried and a teacher in Morecambe, Joan Dixon married to a doctor in Liverpool, Georgina Fox had come

129

back from teaching in Nigeria, and Kathleen Lonsdale was a nurse at Manchester Royal Infirmary.

What a lot could happen in nearly ten years.

They were all over Pippa. Someone had actually joined the community at a time when vocations were down. What was more, Pippa had blossomed. She was not so withdrawn. The Society had brought her out, matured her, made a woman of her. It showed that it didn't necessarily need a man to do that, which was the prejudice that most people had. She was a very good advertisement indeed for the religious life. Mind you, she taught in the poshest convent in the Society. Its flagship. Life was very cushy at Roseacre, rather as it had been in the great abbeys of the past, presided over by the daughters of kings and peopled by noblewomen.

And Clare? Voices were lowered.

'Poor Clare.'

'So unexpected.'

'Such a tragedy.'

'Everything to live for.'

'Didn't seem fair.'

'The last thing anyone thought . . .'

'Andrew was marvellous. He'd resigned from the council, the Rotary Club. Of course being a Catholic he wasn't a Mason.'

'Those poor children . . .'

And so on and so forth.

Eleanor? No one knew what had happened

to her. Pippa had seen her last at her solemn profession. She was a journalist in the south of England. Well, she *had* left the Church, apparently, and she never had attended Association Day, not even once since she left. She seemed to want to break away, lose contact. But she had never been very religious, had she? Got out of Mass whenever she could, and was always first away from evening prayers. She had been liked, admired, envied a little, but never as popular as Clare.

Pippa enjoyed the day, the gossip. The afternoon ended with tea and Benediction in the chapel and the old girls—day girls and boarders together, all barriers down—dispersed, promising to see one another again next year, to write, to keep in touch.

'And Pippa . . . good luck!'

\*     \*     \*

After she'd seen the last one out of the main gate, Pippa escaped along the path that led round the lake. In the height of summer the grounds were always beautiful, the rhododendrons and azaleas in full bloom, the walls festooned with Dog roses. She often used to bring a sketch pad and draw, or sit on the smooth lawn at the top with her paints.

The high grass of the meadow reminded her of how she, Clare and Eleanor used to lie on their tummies planning the future. Even then

131

she knew she was going to become a nun, only she was too shy to say. She wasn't even a Catholic. And now here she was, a professed member of the Society, a consecrated virgin, and Eleanor was a woman who had had a baby out of wedlock and Clare had sustained a serious breakdown in health.

It was almost dark, the lights from the convent were glowing like welcoming beacons guiding her, as Pippa climbed the path to what now was her home.

Maybe, despite Sister Teresa's forebodings, she, Pippa Sidgwick, Sister Mary Frances in the religious life, had chosen the better part, after all.

\*     \*     \*

Dr David Marsden was the director of the clinic. He had trained at the same hospital as Christopher Pearson, but a few years after him, and had gone on to specialise in psychiatry. He was a pleasant, red-haired man with freckles and horn-rimmed glasses that gave him a solemn, rather humourless expression. Not a lot of laughter there.

Dr Ashworth was his deputy, and she sat across from him in an informal semi-circle, Andrew in the middle.

Dr Marsden consulted a pad on his knee, then he addressed Andrew.

'Your wife is very much better, Mr

Thornton. We feel we have the medication right, and her moods are under control. The depression has definitely lifted.' He looked across at Dr Ashworth who nodded.

'She no longer dwells on mournful events. She takes much more notice of things. She is able to be positive. She doesn't sleep all day.

'We feel she's nearly right for release,' Dr Marsden concluded. 'If you would like to sign the papers she can go home any time.'

'That's marvellous news.' Andrew jumped to his feet. 'Today?'

'Well, we want to get her ready for it. We wanted to talk to you first, see how you felt. If you think you can cope. She's been here nearly eight months. We thought maybe start with a brief home visit, get her used to being back. She might regard this as home for the time being, feel safe here. She might even be reluctant to leave.'

'But of course I want my wife at home. The housekeeper and nanny will stay. There will be no pressure on her.'

'I think I'd like to continue to see her every week,' Dr Ashworth said. 'More, if she thinks it's necessary.'

'And the medication?' Andrew looked at the director.

'That should continue for the time being. We can modify it and discontinue it altogether in time, if all goes well.'

'Will she,' Andrew paused, 'will she *ever* be

completely better?'

'Oh there is no question of that. She will make a complete recovery, but . . .' Dr Marsden lifted a finger and waved it gently in the air, 'in view of the severity of your wife's breakdown I would strongly advise against any more children, Mr Thornton. Another pregnancy might result in the same thing, and this time recovery would be more difficult.'

'She so wanted a large family.'

'I think,' Dr Marsden again exchanged glances with his deputy, 'that must be out of the question. We know now that Clare has a weakness and any undue stress or strain could seek it out and precipitate a recurrence. It is clearly hormonal, and the hormones must be carefully controlled. They must not control her.'

'No sex then?'

The director looked surprised.

'Oh I didn't say no sex. You must use an effective form of birth control. I would advise against the Pill on medical grounds. We don't really know its effects yet; but the diaphragm or sheath.' He shrugged. 'There are many effective methods. The best is the Pill, ninety-eight per cent, but we can't use that. The sheath with additional spermicide should be as effective.'

'But we're Catholics. I don't think we could consider methods that break the Church's laws.'

134

'I see. Of course.' Dr Marsden folded his hands and studied the ceiling. 'Well I wouldn't recommend the rhythm method, which is very unreliable. I believe that is the only one acceptable to your Church.'

'Clare's periods are very irregular,' Dr Ashworth said. 'You could never rely on that in any case.'

There was a profound silence for a few moments during which it was possible for each person there to imagine they heard the heartbeats of the others.

'Well then,' Dr Marsden concluded, 'if that is the way you feel, and of course one must respect sincere religious practices, it will have to be abstinence . . . at least for the time being, until after the menopause. I would never answer for the consequences if Clare were to have more children.'

# PART II

*Good at Games*

# CHAPTER SIX

# MAY 1978

Eleanor dabbled a hand in the waters of the narrow *rio*, one of the hundreds of tiny waterways that ran through Venice like capillaries in the body, and felt she'd never been happier. On either side rose solid blocks of stone—houses, palazzi and churches, some of which were as old, or almost as old, as the city itself.

Next to her, Lewis, head flung back, eyes closed, looked asleep. The gondolas were ridiculously expensive and very touristy. They'd sworn they wouldn't be seen dead in one but, what the hell, just for once. This was the last day of the trip.

Lewis had come for a conference of writers, an Anglo-Italian organization whose aim was to promote cultural exchanges worldwide. It was a very nice way of having a good time while professing to be there for something worthwhile and, of course, it was tax deductible. Every day Lewis went religiously to the meetings held on the Island of San Giorgio Maggiore while Eleanor wore out her shoes sightseeing: the Carpaccio in the Scuola di San Giorgio degli Schiavoni, the Tintoretto in the Scuola San Rocco, the Collezione Peggy

Guggenheim in an extraordinary modern building which was also her home, the Gallerie dell' Accademia, the basilica of San Marco and the Doge's Palace, the Giudecca, the amazing Rialto Bridge and, of course, the obligatory day trip to the island of Murano where Venetian glass was made.

At night she dressed up and joined Lewis and the other delegates to attend sumptuous receptions in various private palazzi overlooking the Grand Canal or its tributaries; or delicious dinners in charming trattoria where the conversation and booze flowed, and cigarette smoke rose to the ceiling well into the small hours. And then back to their hotel and, wearily, into bed.

The conference was over. Lewis was exhausted because he'd had to give a paper on the Italian influence on English literature the day before. This had entailed weeks of work, and he'd almost become ill with nerves. He was worn out anyway with talking and walking and arguing and not having enough sleep because, among other things, the hotel room was close, and even in May it was hot. They'd had lunch at Harry's Bar as a treat, the gondola was another, and after that it was back to the hotel for a siesta, then pack, a final meal and home the next day.

'It *has* been glorious,' Eleanor murmured, taking Lewis's hand which lay limply beside her.

'It's been bloody hard work,' he grunted, not opening his eyes.

'But you enjoyed it.'

'You enjoyed it.'

'I thought it was great. I'd like to come again for much longer, wouldn't you? Five days is too short. Have you got a conference here again next year?'

'The year after.'

'Lewis . . .'

'Mmm . . .'

'Maybe it's not the time to say it, but . . .'

Pause. Now that it had come up she felt afraid, but it had been on her mind, on the tip of her tongue for so long now. Venice being such a romantic place made it seem like a good idea to bring it up. They'd had a good lunch, plenty of wine, Lewis was somnolent.

'What?' He opened his eyes and stared at her.

'Nothing.'

'Go on. You were going to say something.'

'No, it's nothing.'

Once again she'd lost her nerve. She lay back and let her hand drift in the water feeling bemused with the wine, half-asleep herself.

*     *     *

Back in the hotel they fell on the bed, made love and went to sleep. When she awoke it was to a perfect sunset. It was a glorious evening.

141

They'd splashed out and were staying at an hotel which had strong literary associations, among them Dickens, Ruskin and Proust. As a delegate, and someone who was presenting a paper, Lewis had his expenses paid, but they'd had to subsidise the stay at one of the smartest hotels in Venice.

Eleanor got out of bed, flung on her light robe and stood by the window looking across to the Island of San Giorgio in whose basilica Lewis's conference had taken place, delegates attending from all round the world. Small boats of every kind were bobbing about, plying their way across the lagoon which looked, as usual, hauntingly beautiful and crepuscular. Numerous clocks were striking the hour.

Eleanor stood there for a long time, and when she turned round she saw that Lewis was awake and watching her. He stretched out a hand and she went over and sat beside him on the bed.

'Where shall we eat?' he asked. 'Would you like to eat here? One last treat?'

'How about that little trat where we were the first night, by the Ponte dell' Accademia?'

'Oh but we have to walk.'

'Don't be lazy.' She leaned forward and kissed him lightly, then went swiftly to the shower.

\* \* \*

142

Like lovers, familiar, relaxed and easy with each other, they walked hand in hand through the narrow lanes, crossing small bridges, as far as the Ponte dell' Accademia. It was a warm, balmy evening and the golden moon shone through the trees in the squares they passed through, throwing into relief the dark shadows cast by the tall palazzi, the many marble palaces of noble Venetians, some as old as the twelfth century, though many had been converted into apartment buildings or municipal offices.

They searched for the restaurant—there had been something romantic about that too—and the proprietor seemed to remember them and gave them a welcoming smile as he showed them to a table in the corner covered with a pink cloth, and brought them enormous menus. They ordered seafood salad and little medallions of veal in lemon, a bottle of Verdicchio and one of Barolo.

'It's been just about a perfect day,' Lewis said, breaking his breadstick into little pieces. 'Home tomorrow. When are you due back at work?'

'Thursday. I'm going to do a piece on the conference.'

'That will help with expenses.' Lewis grinned.

'Oh yes, I think I'll get expenses.'

Lewis looked thoughtful. 'What was it you were going to say in the gondola?'

'It was nothing.'

'It must have been something because of the way you looked. I thought it was important.' His expression was one of impatience.

Eleanor took a deep breath.

'Lewis, should we get married?'

'Married?' Lewis sounded startled.

'We've been together five years.'

'Well that's fine. Why spoil it by getting married?'

'But why should that spoil it?' Her heart sank.

'I think it might.'

'I see.' She looked at the table, aware of that dull, leaden feeling round her heart.

'You know that I don't want to be trapped, Eleanor. That was what was wrong last time.'

'I thought Kay left you for another man?'

'She did. But I still felt trapped.'

'Well I don't want to "trap" you, Lewis.' She knew he must have recognised the sarcasm in her voice.

'I thought you were happy as we were. We are married in a way.'

'I am happy.'

'You've never wanted children.'

'I want children.'

'Well you never said. Really, Eleanor!' Lewis began to sound irritable and they were both relieved when the grinning proprietor waltzed up with huge platefuls of *antipasto de mare* swimming in oil.

'You never *said* you wanted children,' Lewis hissed when the proprietor had turned his back on them. The restaurant was beginning to fill up.

'I felt we should wait, see how things went. Well I think they've gone well. We're happy together. Aren't we?'

'Very. Don't spoil it.'

'I'd like to have your children, Lewis.' She was afraid of sounding soppy, but it had to be said.

'How many, for God's sake?'

'Two.' She tried to smile, but it was forced.

'Children would spoil our relationship.'

'How do you know?'

'Because they spoiled mine and Kay's. They do. They're destructive. Anyway,' he looked at her rather meanly, 'you don't strike me as a very maternal person. You're crazy about your career, you're good at it and, anyway, you had a kid and you gave it away. That's not a very maternal thing to do, is it?'

'That's a horrible thing to say.'

'Nevertheless it's true, darling.'

'I was *twenty-one*.'

'You still gave it away. Other young single women have children and manage to keep them. If you'd wanted to, you could have kept it. My bet is that you didn't want your Catholic parents to know you'd committed a mortal sin.'

'Cheap jibe, Lewis.'

145

They hardly ever rowed. Her stomach was churning and she wished she'd never spoken, certainly not tonight to spoil the idyll of what had been nearly a perfect holiday. She went on: 'You think I haven't regretted it?'

'I've never heard you mention it again from the day you told me not to.'

'I think about him every day.'

'I find that very hard to believe.'

Coldly: 'Nevertheless it's true. Think what you like.'

'Is everything alright, signora?' The proprietor looked with concern at Eleanor's plate, the food scarcely touched.

'Yes, it's beautiful, but I'm not very hungry.'

The proprietor's dejected expression made it look as though he too had experienced a personal tragedy as he regretfully swept the plates away.

'This is all very silly, Eleanor.' Lewis filled their glasses with wine.

'I know. I'm sorry I brought it up.'

'Well you obviously felt you had to.' Lewis sipped from his glass. 'You must have had it on your mind. Now you've cleared the air we can forget it. OK?'

'Yes.'

'Besides, I have no desire to have any more children. I have two and I hardly ever see them. I was not a good, or especially fond father. I find babies tedious. The state of matrimony seems to me archaic, and I'm surprised that you, as an independent woman, don't feel that way too. You've got a wonderful job, one, incidentally, that I helped you to get. Without me you'd probably still be on the *Southend Argus* or whatever it was.'

'Don't think I'm not grateful, Lewis.'

An awkward silence fell between them until their second course arrived which Lewis, as if dismissing the matter, attacked with relish.

But Eleanor hesitated, fighting a sense of shock, almost apprehension, that Lewis's words had inspired in her. There was a deliberate brutality about them, a desire to wound and hurt. 'You had a kid and you gave it away.' Was that what he really thought about her, unthinking, uncaring, not for a moment understanding the trauma she'd been through?

Now she began to wonder how well she knew the man with whom she so trustingly shared her life.

Had she been deceiving herself as to the nature of the real Lewis?

\*　　　\*　　　\*

*June 1978*

They always seemed lucky with the weather on Association Day. It hardly ever rained and this year was no exception. The grounds were in their usual pristine condition, the top lawn newly mown, set with small tables, chairs and summer umbrellas. Below on the lake two swans glided majestically alongside the boat rowed by some of the old girls clowning around, while there was a lot of laughter on the path as others jostled for a place.

The ages of the women present ranged from about seventy plus to fairly recent pupils in their early twenties, yet to make their mark on the world. Most of the nuns and lay staff mingled with the guests.

Jennifer Cuthbert and Ruth Brown stood together on the lawn, teacups precariously poised, viewing the scene.

'I think there are more than usual this year,' Ruth said. 'Must be well over a hundred.'

'I'd say two.'

'Would you really? Maybe you're right.' Ruth's eyes alighted on a figure running energetically between tables, pausing every now and then to chat.

'Doesn't Clare Thornton look well?'Ruth murmured. 'You'd never think she once tried to kill herself.'

Jennifer gazed at her in surprise. 'Oh I never heard that. I thought she just had a breakdown?'

'I thought I'd heard she tried to kill herself and that's why she was committed.'

'Oh no, she was just depressed. I'm sure of that. Anyway, it happened a long time ago. She's well over it now.'

Indeed she was. If Clare ever thought about

148

her breakdown, and sometimes the thoughts did intrude on a busy life, she immediately tried to rid them from her mind. Dwelling on the past, as Pippa had said, was pointless. It was years since she'd taken medication, and Irma Ashworth had moved to another position.

'What are you two whispering about?' Clare smiled mischievously as she caught up with Jennifer and Ruth, contemporaries, a bit younger than herself she thought.

'We were admiring your energy, Clare. You never stop.'

'I'm glad you mentioned it.' Clare reached for a sandwich on a plate on a nearby table. 'I would like to give it up. I've organised Association Day for years and years. Could I persuade you . . .'

'Oh no thanks.'

'No thank *you*!'

Clare sighed. It was always the same. So difficult to get anyone to do anything.

'I thought you'd say that.' She pulled a face.

'You're so capable, Clare. So good at it. You know everyone. Besides you like it.'

'I do like it, but I've so many things on my plate. Apart from my voluntary work, I play badminton and squash twice a week.'

'You were always good at games,' Ruth murmured.

Clare smiled modestly. 'It helps keep me fit. I need to be. I'm chairman of the parents'

149

association, secretary of the old girls' association. I'm on the parish council, a member of the Catholic Mothers' Guild. Besides that I work a day every fortnight at the OXFAM shop and collect for Amnesty International . . .'

'Sounds sickening,' Jennifer muttered. 'All that activity can't be healthy . . .'

'*And* I have recently taken on the Catholic Women's Refuge. Believe me, that *is* a handful.'

'Refuge from what?' Jennifer looked politely curious. She was a rather languid woman, married to an architect who had built a superb house for his family in a village five miles out of town. One of her daughters was at Roseacre, and the boys either attending or down for Stonyhurst.

'You haven't heard of the Catholic Women's Refuge? Shame on you, Jennifer.'

'Battered wives, silly.' Ruth put her cup and saucer on the table. 'What made you get involved with battered wives, Clare?'

'Oh someone asked me, as usual. I was one of those who started the whole thing.' Clare swept back a lock of hair from her brow. Her face was hot and sticky but this enhanced her looks rather than detracted from them. Her pink cheeks and flashing eyes made her look alive, youthful. She wore a pretty white dress with a nipped-in waistline that emphasised her slim, trim figure.

150

'You mean *Catholic* men batter their wives?'

'Some do, I'm afraid. Seriously, if you'd like to know more, Jennifer, give me a ring.'

'I'll think about it. Why don't you ask Mary Barlow?' Jennifer sniggered, nodding her head in the direction of a very large lady in a spotted dress and a wide hat decorated with flowers and, possibly, a bird of paradise.

'Mary Barlow,' Ruth burst out laughing. 'She's got *ten* children.'

'Then she'd be a good one to ask.'

'She'd never find the time.'

'Ten children,' Jennifer murmured to herself, shaking her head.

Clare's eyes seemed momentarily to dull. 'I always wanted a large family. Maybe that's why I like to help women who can't cope. Anyway . . .' She dispelled the cloud and flashed them her brilliant smile, 'Lovely to see you.'

'Oh, do you ever hear from Eleanor Hamilton?'

Clare shook her head.

'I hear she's doing rather well.'

'That's good. Look I really must dash. 'Bye.'

Always on the go. No time to stop. No time to stop and think why was she doing all this?

Because she was happy being busy, that's why. She always had been except for that awful time of inactivity in the mental home, but she never allowed herself to dwell on that now. Never. Or if she did, she'd quickly find something else to occupy her mind, take up

151

even more time.

As usual, the day was a great success. Tea was followed by Benediction, and the chapel was crowded. Kneeling at the back, Clare's eyes wandered to the open window, to the tips of the trees waving in the park and, chillingly, she recalled the view from the hospital window the day she lost Dominic. She bowed her head and, for a moment, was visited by a feeling of intense loneliness and depression. But by the time Benediction was over and the old girls streamed out of the chapel and down the stairs to stand in the shiny parquet hall talking in groups she was her old self, all smiles again, darting backwards and forwards, saying goodbyes, making promises to keep in touch with those who lived some distance from the town that she knew she would never keep.

Which reminded her that she hadn't seen Eleanor or Pippa for years. She must ask one of the nuns for Pippa's address, if she was still at Roseacre, and write.

As for Eleanor, she rather thought that friendship was over and done with. Pity. Above all she recalled vividly the summer days, like today, lying in the long grass, Pippa sketching, she and Eleanor planning a brilliant future . . . She remembered tennis on the court by the lake, rounders on the pitch under the chestnut tree, and the Corpus Christi procession in June.

But then, she had never really gone away.

She remained in touch with the school. Pauline was at St Catherine's and Marcus had been a junior before going to a prep for his father's old school. She was intimately associated with St Catherine's and St Catherine's was with her.

Eleanor had drifted into another far off world and probably had a family of her own by now.

*　　*　　*

Later, after seeing that all the chairs and tables were safely stacked away, and the left-over food either sent down for the boarders' supper or put in plastic bags for disposal, talking over the day's events with Reverend Mother ('another success, Clare, thanks to you') and hurrying home to get the family evening meal, Clare lay reading in bed. She called 'come in' as there was a tap at the door, and Andrew put his head round. She looked up at him and smiled, put down her book.

'How was the day?'

'Splendid.' She patted the side of her bed.

'Well organised I guess.'

She removed her reading spectacles. 'As usual.'

'Clare, I often feel you do too much.'

'Nonsense. I like doing too much. It's good for me.'

Andrew nodded. 'Darling, would you mind if I joined the town council again? I had a

153

meeting with the mayor tonight. He asked me to stand for the Tories.'

'Not at all. Of course I don't mind.'

'By the time I'm fifty I might be mayor.'

'Fifty! What a long way off.'

'It will soon come. Don't forget, I am much older than you. You'll be surprised.'

'Well, I don't want to talk about being fifty. I don't *want* to be fifty.' She paused for a moment. 'By the way, do you know that Mary Barlow has *ten* children?'

Andrew shook his head. 'I don't think I knew Mary Barlow.'

'Anyway she's very fat. That's a consolation, I suppose.'

'You look about twenty-five. I thought how incredibly young and pretty you looked, Clare, in that white dress.' His hand moved towards her and, startled, she gazed into his eyes.

'Andrew . . .'

'Clare, I do wish . . . I do want . . .'

'You know we mustn't.' She put out a hand and firmly removed his from her breast.

'Darling, I feel absolutely *desperate* at times . . .'

'Andrew, we talked about all this five years ago.'

'Yes I know. But I can't help it. I wish I could, but I can't. I have fantasies of sleeping with you. I miss you so much . . .'

Clare looked at her husband of ten years thoughtfully, compassionately, yet she also felt

154

a curious sense of detachment. It was true, perhaps inevitable, that when you didn't sleep with someone a dimension was lacking.

'Really, you'll have to pray about it, Andrew.'

'I do. I pray fervently.' He looked up at her and she was unnerved by the pain she clearly saw in his eyes. 'Do you pray about it, Clare?'

Clare leaned back against her pillow and closed her eyes. This was a subject she hoped would never raise its ugly head again. She had thought separate bedrooms would settle the whole thing. They seemed to live perfectly happily and contentedly together, both with busy lives. It was, after all, what the Church intended if you obeyed its laws.

'Andrew, I have no need to *pray* about it. I went off sex after we lost Dominic. I never wanted anything like that to happen again. I don't even *think* about it, so it has made it easy for me.' She took his hand. It felt very hot, and his eyes looked feverish. 'I *do* love you, Andrew, but we have agreed that things must be as they are. I think you ought to offer up your sexuality to God.'

*     *     *

Clare thought that if Andrew were to talk to some of these battered wives he'd go off the idea of sex too. The house had been bought with private funds in a village near Wolversleigh where there'd been the usual protests from well-heeled citizens who didn't want it in their back yard.

It was a fairly substantial house in pretty grounds, but a lot had needed doing, and much remained outstanding. Funds were always a problem. They had bought it fairly cheaply. Clare had been pivotal in raising money and had donated a substantial sum herself. Somehow, the poor women with their children, their shocking stories of violence and abuse mattered very much to her. As a deeply religious woman, she felt it was the nearest she came to acting out the part of Christ in the community. 'I was a stranger, and ye took me in: Naked, and ye clothed me.' The refuge was named after St Martin, a rich young man who had given his cloak to a beggar.

Clare loved going to the house, doing what was needed, and playing with the children. Some of the women had quite large families and had been subject to years of abuse, in some cases the children too.

Her sister-in-law, Chrissy, who now had four children, also came along to help. Clare and Chrissy were close. They were the same age, though Chrissy was a beautiful blonde with the figure of a model and deep violet eyes. She carried her years well. She had been a beautician before her marriage and had met Mark at a dance at the cricket club to which her brother had also belonged. Chrissy was not a Wolversleigh girl, her family not Catholic, not part of the Wolversleigh set, the Thorntons and Pearsons and Wrights who all knew one another, whose families lived in big houses and went to St Catherine's or the boys' equivalents, St Anthony's for day boys or St Thomas's if they boarded.

But Chrissy had fitted in, she'd conformed, converted. Mark was a good catch, solid, dependable and wealthy. He indulged his wife and she responded so that to all intents they were a happy couple.

Chrissy was the ideal sister-in-law for someone like Clare because they were very alike: vigorous, outward-thinking women with busy, busy lives. Chrissy, though, was even more sporty, swam and played golf with a handicap of seven.

Clare loved both her brothers, but she was closer to Mark than Frank who was now a mining engineer and lived mostly abroad, not yet married and doubtful that he ever would. He was a confirmed bachelor and enjoyed the lifestyle, as well as the money this afforded him. No ties, no responsibilities. He was a very kind and generous uncle to the children.

Chrissy spent a day at the centre every week. Clare spent two, as she was one of its founders and chairman of the trust which ran it. The two women had little time for private conversation; they were far too busy, but they tried to have a gossip over a snack lunch or one of the brief tea or coffee breaks.

Most of Clare's time was taken up with interviewing the women with a view to finding a long-term solution to their problems, but it wasn't a simple or easy matter. Sometimes the problems were intractable and lasted for years. Sometimes the women went back to their husbands and were battered all over again. When they returned, it was usually with a new baby.

This particular day, a few weeks after the June reunion, Clare hadn't even had time to pause for lunch, and was munching a sandwich one of the workers had made for her, and drinking a cup of cold tea when there was a knock on the door and Chrissy came in, a mug in her hand.

'Hello!'

'Hi there!' Clare gave her a welcoming smile.

'Is it OK if I come in?' Chrissy held up her mug.

'Of course. Take a pew.' Clare pointed to a chair near her desk.

'I haven't seen you all day.'

'Well we had a new case last night, as you know, an emergency, and I've spent most of the day on the phone trying to sort it out with the police and our solicitor. I'm trying to get her to press charges.'

'The one with the huge black eye?'

'Yes.' Clare looked savage. 'She's been here

158

before. I think if she pressed charges he'd get a long spell inside, but she's terrified of him. I'm trying to reassure her that she will be protected, but you see,' she looked sadly at Chrissy, 'I'm not sure that I can.'

'Can what?'

'Keep that promise.'

Clare looked out of the window where a group of children were playing happily on the lawn which, for safety's sake, was now enclosed by a high fence. Sometimes the fathers tried to kidnap the children, in order to force the mothers to return home.

'Don't they look happy?' she said wistfully. 'You'd never think the tragedy they had in their lives. Do you know,' she turned back to Chrissy who was watching her closely, 'they're all members of the same family? Imagine *five* children without a home. How are your brood by the way?'

'Oh fine.' Chrissy had an au pair, two dailies and no money worries. Her three sons were all at St Catherine's Junior School which admitted little boys. Her daughter was only two. 'I'm very lucky, very fortunate.'

'We both are. Being here makes you realise just how lucky.'

'I always thought you wanted a large family, Clare?' Chrissy sounded hesitant. 'Perhaps I shouldn't ask?'

'Oh I do. I did . . . but after Dominic,' Clare looked across at her sister-in-law, 'I couldn't

159

stand the thought of another baby. Couldn't bear being pregnant again.'

'I thought you got over that business awfully well,' Chrissy said gently.

'Oh I did, no question. But sex was a problem. I went right off it . . .'

'Oh dear. I didn't realise that.' Chrissy averted her eyes, biting her lip. 'I shouldn't have brought it up. It's none of my business.'

'Really, I don't mind. It's quite helpful to discuss it. In fact, Andrew and I talked about it only recently. From time to time he feels upset . . .'

'Well you can't blame him.'

'Oh I don't blame him. It's a natural urge.' Her bright, clear, intelligent eyes looked frankly at Chrissy's. 'But we're strong Catholics Chrissy. We go to Confession and Mass, we receive the sacraments. There is no question of us, either of us, breaking the laws of the Church.'

'Well . . .' Chrissy put her mug on the table and fumbled in her pocket for a cigarette, 'I don't know what Mark would say if we took that attitude.'

'Well you don't need to. You're young and healthy. Nothing to stop you having more children. You see, I *daren't* for my health's sake. We were both told quite firmly while I was still in the clinic that there were to be no more babies. The rest followed.'

'I'm not going to have any more children,'

160

Chrissy said firmly. 'There is no question of that either. Mark agrees. I've been on the Pill since Helen was born. I think the Church is absolutely nonsensical about contraception, and so does Mark.'

Clare drew herself up in her chair. She had a stern, forthright manner when she chose, and many of the refuge women were wary of it. Few people crossed her. 'Well I don't agree, I'm sorry. The Pope made it quite clear. We couldn't go to Communion with a clear conscience if we'd practised artificial contraception.'

'But isn't that much better than risking your marriage?' Chrissy enquired gently.

'There is no question of our marriage being at risk. We're at one on this.'

'But I thought you were enlightened Catholics?'

'We are. Most enlightened,' Clare's tone was getting prissier and prissier, 'but on certain matters there is no compromise, and this is one of them.'

'But,' Chrissy paused and looked out at the children playing on the 'lawn', 'don't you think that if these women, the mothers of all these unwanted children, practised contraception, the world would be a happier place?'

'Not necessarily. Each child is valuable for his or her own sake. A large family brings much joy. A lot of the women who come here are fervent Catholics. That's why we have a refuge for them, to help them.'

'I think it's absurd,' Chrissy's tone hardened. 'I'm really surprised at you, Clare. It seems that women's liberation has passed you by . . .

'Women's liberation has *not* passed me by, thank you,' Clare said with an edge to her voice. 'Besides, Chrissy, what we do in our own marriage is our business, not yours.'

'Sorry I spoke.' Chrissy took her mug from the table and turned towards the door. 'I shan't mention it again.'

Clare looked thoughtfully out of the window as Chrissy shut the door. The sisters-in-law seldom argued. She didn't think this was a serious matter, and they'd soon be OK with each other. They'd forget about it or, at least, put it out of their minds. No question of that. She'd say something and Chrissy would say something and it would be alright; the matter would be smoothed over. They were both too well-balanced to let it fester or spoil the close relationship between their families.

Besides, she knew that Chrissy wasn't a Catholic in the same way that she was. She had converted to marry Mark. She wasn't forced. She'd said she wanted to. She hadn't become a Catholic in the sense that Pippa had, out of faith and conviction. She'd become a Catholic out of convenience. But Clare had suspected at the time that she wanted a splendid wedding, such as she and Andrew had had,

162

with a nuptial High Mass, a heavenly choir and the church full of flowers and glittering candles. The Church made it clear that mixed marriages didn't get that sort of treatment; a few bleak words at the altar and that was that. No pomp at all.

Chrissy had looked stunning in a wedding dress of Brussels lace with a massive train, six bridesmaids and four pages. It *had* been a lovely wedding, and there were now four children and no doubt that Chrissy and Mark were happy. She supposed that as Chrissy took precautions Mark managed to deceive himself that it wasn't him. It was the sort of tautological way of reasoning that Catholics were so good at. She knew that they both went to Communion, the three boys traipsing after them to the altar like little angels. But, of course, Chrissy hadn't been brought up in the same tradition as Clare and her brothers, going back for generations when Catholics were a persecuted minority creating martyrs for the faith.

It was a very great tradition and Clare was proud of it. Women's liberation was all very well, and she felt liberated, had never felt anything else.

But it had no place at all in matters of faith. Chrissy would never have understood about that.

# CHAPTER SEVEN

# OCTOBER 1981

The barge passed slowly and majestically along the river while the seagulls whirled disconsolately about its bows, scavenging for food. The muddy river and the grey overcast sky somehow reminded Eleanor of that day, many years before, when she had sat in a dingy office in Darlsdon putting together her copy for the *Echo*. A tin can had been blown along by the wind and life at twenty had seemed curiously bleak and lacking in interest.

Fifteen years later, exactly to the month, she had the same dead, almost irrational feeling of emptiness, though in fact her life had changed dramatically and was very full. She now inhabited a comfortable, rather than opulent, office in a building between Fleet Street and the Thames, which she did not have to share with lots of other people—as was the trend these days—composing her weekly column for the paper. 'As I See It' by Eleanor Hamilton always seemed to produce a reaction, at least one or two talking points which were debated on the radio or TV. Occasionally it caused an uproar. She did not deal solely with 'women's issues' but was eclectic, ranging far and wide. Current affairs were very much her line and pungent and acerbic she was—Mrs Thatcher and members of her government being particular victims.

In the years she'd been on *The Examiner* Eleanor had progressed from the anonymous writer of reports and third leaders to by-lines on articles and features that attracted attention. Finally, three years ago, her own column had been launched to immediate acclaim. Sometimes it caused an uproar. A recent report had said that one child in eight lived in a one-parent family, a factor which Eleanor put fairly and squarely on the shoulders of Mrs T and her social policy, or lack of it. She was always banging on about the selfishness of the Tories.

But somehow, today, the column failed to fire and Eleanor was reaching for a cigarette when the telephone rang and a voice at the other end said: 'You don't know me but I know you.'

'Oh?' Eleanor, intrigued, put the phone closer to her ear.

'This is John Rudd of Globe TV. I wondered if we could have lunch one day?'

'Well I don't know you,' she said, 'but I certainly know *of* you. Any particular reason . . .'

'I'm afraid I can't give you any gossip or scandal about the government, but I have got an idea for a new TV programme I thought you might be interested in presenting. Just a chat, you know. Nothing concrete yet.'

Somehow the idea of her own programme on TV, started by no less a person than John Rudd, transformed the day, even though it was inevitable that it wouldn't come off. These things never did. Pilots were made and they didn't work. Anyway she'd broadcast frequently on the radio but she had never appeared on TV. Wasn't she too old? She had crow's feet, and lines on her forehead. Weren't they all young these days?

Eleanor decided for the time being to say nothing to Lewis. Anyway she didn't think he'd be very pleased. For some time things had not been going well for Lewis. He'd had writer's block which engendered depression; or did the depression engender writer's block? She wasn't quite sure which way round it was; but anyway Lewis suffered from it. He spent a good deal of time in the pub, not exactly getting drunk but sitting morosely with a cigarette and a pint of beer in front of him staring at the bar.

Finally, after a lot of effort and encouragement and sympathy on her part, he had completed his new novel and had just delivered it. It was a very slim volume, scarcely novel length, and she thought not one of Lewis's best. But then she had always found him hard to read, a fact she carefully concealed from him. She thought it showed how hard it had been to write. It didn't flow,

166

but she enthused over it nevertheless. Perhaps it was wrong of her to be so spineless, but there it was.

In fact, a lot had to be hidden from Lewis, who had become jealous of her success. He never read her column, or at least admitted to it. He never asked about her work, yet expected her to be constantly interested in his. Goodness knows what he'd say about the invitation to lunch by John Rudd, one of the best known TV producers in London, possibly in England.

\*     \*     \*

Eleanor and Lewis lived in a large house in Belsize Park and most weekends they went back to Lewis's beloved cottage in the village near Chelmsford. Sometimes he stayed there all week, ostensibly to work, but Eleanor knew it was a pretence. The fact was that, apart from his novel writing, Lewis didn't have enough to do, though he would never have admitted it. He didn't garden or take exercise and he never lifted a finger in the house. They had a daily in London and someone who came to clean weekly in the country; but Eleanor did all the shopping and most of the cooking, most of the cheering up and all of the listening. Sometimes she felt that Lewis was not very interested in her at all.

She and Lewis had been together for nearly

ten years and she knew the longer they left it, the harder it would be to part. She felt that she was no longer in love with him and that maybe he had never loved her, and the sensible thing would have been to split. But that time should have happened after Venice three years before when she realised what sort of person Lewis really was. There had been suspicions; but she'd clung on. Maybe she had begun to fall out of love with him then.

The sensible thing to have done would have been to come back home and pack her bags. But love wasn't rational, and relationships were complex, not simple. They were used to each other; they had no one else. Moreover, Lewis needed her; without her he'd fall apart. It was a big responsibility to desert someone to whom you'd given ten years of your life.

Three years ago she was thirty-two, and another start in life might have been possible. On the other hand thirty-five was no great age, at least the television company didn't seem to think so. People said she looked good. And she felt good.

Also she got a lot out of life. She had an interesting job, she met interesting people; she had lunch with someone new or influential nearly every day. Her opinion was sought, canvassed. Eleanor had progressed a very long way from the rather gauche, gawky young woman she had once been; a character, a personality at school but with little self-esteem or self-confidence in the real world. When she met Ted she was grateful to be noticed. However doomed and unsatisfactory that relationship, it had launched her as a woman. It had also introduced her to those twin educators of tragedy and sadness. When she met Lewis it was not with a feeling of inadequacy or gratitude that she perceived his attentions; it was as an equal, eager and ready to fall in love.

Eleanor was now well-groomed, elegant. She wore expensive, sometimes couture clothes and had her hair styled in Mayfair. This had transformed her appearance. It was no longer mousey, but ash blonde with highlights, well-cut, short with soft waves. Her make-up was subtle and assured; she exercised at a gym whenever she could find the time. She smoked and drank in moderation. She was a fit, healthy, good-looking woman.

Time had done all that, time and experience and, of course, success. Success and achievement were great incentives to make the best of yourself, to get the most out of life.

The phone rang.

What did she think about Cabinet Minister Norman Tebbitt, one of Mrs T's hot favourites, and his infamous 'get on your bike' speech referring to the unemployed? Eleanor immediately launched into a heated response and forgot about Lewis, for the time being anyway.

169

*     *     *

## January 1982

Lewis hardly ever got taken to lunch by his agent, or anyone much, these days. He felt he was a has-been and he knew he was deeply jealous of Eleanor. He envied her her vivacity, her talent and her youth. He was very sorry indeed that he'd got her the job in London. That had changed their lives. But for him she'd still be on a suburban paper, not a leading opinion-former. He did secretly read her column and he fumed because he knew she was so good. Why had he got her a job that made her so much more important than him?

She also earned good money, but they had a huge mortgage, two cars, all kinds of expenses. These days he hardly seemed to earn anything at all. His advances were pittances, but he was not motivated to do anything else. He couldn't write poetry and despised journalism. That was for hacks. He'd once tried to write a play but somehow it didn't gel.

Maybe Cedric Williams had good news for him?

Cedric was one of the most successful agents in London. He was fifty-five and the head of his partnership, an old established agency that he had joined from a publishing firm twenty years before.

He was an outgoing, cheerful man and his expression that day he and Lewis met for lunch in Soho gave nothing away. He greeted him with his customary courtesy and offered him a drink.

Lewis liked the restaurant and looked appreciatively around, sat back comfortably in the bar as their drinks were brought and the maître d' appeared with the menu.

'Order what you like,' Cedric said expansively.

'Are we celebrating something?' Lewis looked at him but Cedric didn't reply, seemingly intent on the bill of fare.

'How's Eleanor?' Cedric enquired as, having finished their drinks, they were led to a table where their chosen hors d'oeuvres were waiting for them.

'Oh she's fine. Doing well.'

'I read her column.'

'Do you?' Lewis shook his head.

'Don't you?' Cedric looked surprised.

'I never get the time.'

'I see. I wonder if she'd be interested in doing a book?'

'What sort of book?' Lewis stared at him suspiciously.

Cedric shrugged. 'A biography, a novel. She writes very well.'

'Oh I shouldn't think she has the time. Have you heard from Geoffrey? They're taking an age. I suppose Christmas got in the way. These

171

days all the offices close for weeks.'

Geoffrey was his editor.

Cedric moved the cutlery by his plate.

'Lewis, I have bad news I'm afraid.' He paused and stared at the table. 'There's no easy or simple way of doing this, but Geoffrey doesn't want your new novel.'

'But . . .'

'I'm sorry. I've talked to him. Reasoned with him. I even said you would take a smaller advance, but they simply can't sell you. *Break of Serve* sold six hundred copies. Unless you are very famous, literary fiction does not sell.'

'I didn't see it in any bookshop . . .' Lewis responded heatedly.

'Well, they wouldn't take it. The libraries didn't want it. They can't paperback it. I'm afraid, Lewis, you're too esoteric. Geoffrey said they'd taken five of yours and had done everything to build you up. They have, you know that.'

'Only in the early days,' Lewis grumbled.

'They had book launches, signing sessions, spent a mint on publicity. Put the boat out. No effect on sales. You'll have to change your style or your subject. They feel they just can't go on supporting you.'

'Support!' Lewis squeaked, his tone overloud and hysterical.

Cedric leaned across the table. 'Have you ever thought of doing something different? Changing your subject matter, above all your style?'

'No I have not thought.' Lewis thumped the table. 'I am not going to change my subject or my damned style. What do you think Virginia Woolf would have said to such a suggestion?'

'I don't really think you're in Virginia Woolf's league, Lewis,' Cedric said dryly, 'though perhaps to some people as obscure. I must say I found the new book very obscure. It didn't hold my interest. I hoped Geoffrey would feel differently, but he said he couldn't get to the end. If he couldn't, he was sure no one else would. I don't mean to be insulting but times are hard, the marketplace is tough. If you were to sit down and rough out an outline for a different kind of novel I might be able to sell it for you. You know, a big adventure . . .'

'Oh balls!' Lewis said.

Cedric's manner changed. 'If that really is your attitude, Lewis, I really can't go on representing you. I can't sell you and it's a waste of time trying.'

'You can try other publishers, for God's sake.'

'I have made some enquiries. But no one is interested.'

'You mean at the age of forty-five I'm on the scrapheap?'

'Something like that, Lewis, unless you take my advice. I'm awfully sorry but there it is. Fact of life, old boy.'

'And you've got the flipping nerve to suggest

that *Eleanor . . .*'

'Yes, maybe it was tactless; but you see, Eleanor is popular. I think her stuff could sell. Incidentally, given your attitude today, it's a good thing she earns enough to support you.'

*    *    *

Eleanor could tell as soon as she got into the house that something was wrong. There was an air of menace about the place, worse than usual when Lewis was in a mood. Not that he was ever violent but sometimes she felt a slight frisson of nerves, a definite sense of unease.

To begin with, it was very cold, so the central heating mustn't be switched on. Although it was nearly eight o'clock, the place was in darkness. She'd spent the day in the recording studio doing a pilot and it had gone supremely well. She was the anchorwoman interviewing three witty and talented journalists, representing each of the political parties. There had been much wisdom but also a lot of laughter. She felt she'd got them all going together nicely. Then there had been a very clever cartoon sketch with Thatcher and Tebbitt having a cycle race in which her handbag kept getting caught in the spokes of Tebbitt's wheels sending him wobbling all over the place while Thatcher sallied forth.

John Rudd had been delighted and said he'd call her in a day or so, undoubtedly with a

174

formal offer.

Eleanor Hamilton. TV star. *Newsnight, Panorama, Question Time* . . . who knows where this could lead?

On the way home she'd felt good, but there was also that awful feeling of guilt. No shopping had been done so, maybe, she'd take Lewis, who didn't know a thing about this, out for a good meal and break it to him gently.

She stood for a minute or so in the hall listening. She knew Lewis was in. His car was outside, but he wasn't in the pub. The house had the feeling of a presence. You knew when a house was empty and when it wasn't.

'Lewis?' she called and opened the door of the living room. In the light from the hall she saw Lewis stretched out on the sofa, an empty glass by his side. He appeared to be asleep. The curtains were not drawn and the room was bitterly cold as well.

Her first thought was that he was ill, and she went quickly over to him and stood looking down, unable to see whether his eyes were open or closed.

'Lewis!' she cried sharply. 'Are you alright?'

No reply.

'Lewis!' She took his arm and he brusquely shrugged her off.

'Go away,' he said. 'Get lost!'

'Lewis . . .'

'Oh don't keep on saying "Lewis", I'm not a bloody dog.' Lewis got off the sofa and,

175

stamping out of the room, banged the door behind him.

Eleanor felt shattered, unnerved, angry. She drew the curtains, switching on a couple of table lamps on the way.

She went over to the drinks table and poured herself a large gin and tonic. Then she went into the kitchen for some ice. She reckoned Lewis had gone upstairs. He would be lying on the bed, sulking. She looked in the fridge and, except for some eggs, there was nothing to eat. Omelette, or out. But now she wasn't even hungry.

Eleanor stood for a few moments mentally bracing herself and then walked along the passage to the hall and slowly climbed the stairs. Really, the house was much too big for them. They had bought it in the flush of new love and her job on *The Examiner*, thinking maybe they'd entertain a lot and Lewis's two girls would come and visit. But they hardly ever saw their father, and when they did they didn't stay. They had made no attempt to get to know Eleanor or try to like her.

Maybe in those days—days that seemed so far off now—Eleanor had hoped for a family of her own. She assumed that once they had bought the house that they would progress to matrimony and children. She had given it time, but after Venice it was quite clear that that was not to be.

There was also not much entertaining. She

often worked late and Lewis wasn't particularly sociable. Nor did he have many friends, which seemed curious for a man with literary pretensions. He had cronies in the pub in Chelmsford and had made some new ones in the north London pubs, but they never came home.

When she occasionally did invite people back, men or women, Lewis was almost always churlish and inhospitable, as though defying her to ask anyone again. They had a party near Christmas and that was about that. Eleanor continued to go north to see her parents while Lewis stayed away. He had never tried to endear himself to them and they, in turn, didn't like him.

All in all it wasn't much of a life. Thank heaven for her work.

The bedroom door was closed. Eleanor thought it would be locked, but it swung open as she turned the handle. She saw Lewis lying on the bed, one hand on his brow. She bent down to put the bedside light on, and he cried: 'For God's sake turn it *off*!' His hand crashed down on her arm and she winced with pain. She didn't dare say his name again.

Eleanor stood by the bed feeling completely inadequate, not knowing what to do or say.

Finally.

'Are you not well, Lewis? Is there anything I can do to help?'

No reply.

She went over to the dressing table and fiddled with some of the objects there; the silver-backed brush and comb, the mirror, a bottle of perfume.

'Sodding Geoffrey has turned down my book,' Lewis said in a voice scarcely above a whisper. 'Sodding bastard.'

'Oh dear.' Eleanor spun round, went over to the bed. 'Oh darling, I'm so sorry.'

'I had lunch with Cedric.'

Guilt. She had completely forgotten about that because it coincided with her big day, that was it. She really was very selfish.

'Is there nothing he can do?'

'He doesn't want to go on representing me unless I can come up with an idea, some massive potboiler, sex and violence and all that rubbish. Of course I won't.'

'Of course not.' She sat on the bed and groped for his hand.

'I'm not going to prostitute myself.'

'No you mustn't.'

Another pause, a long one.

'What will you do, Lewis?'

'I shall go on writing like I always write; intelligent, well-crafted literary fiction. I don't intend to change at all.'

And if no one published it, what then? But she didn't like to mention it.

'I wondered if you'd like to go out for dinner?' she said. 'Cheer us up.'

'*Us?* Why should you need cheering up?'

178

'Oh it's been a tough day.' She lied, but she thought it might help Lewis. In fact it had been one of the most exciting days of her life, a step on the road to advancement in a creative and interesting way. The thought did a bit to make up for the drabness of her personal existence which now she could only see getting worse.

\*　　　\*　　　\*

Andrew's father Gerald had started his accountancy practice in 1932, four years before Andrew was born. He was then twenty-five and already a father, his son Peter having been born in 1934. Pam Thornton, the only girl and the last of the brood, was born in 1940, just before he left for the war. She had never married and lived in Italy where she worked for an Anglo-Italian bank. Peter had at first joined the firm but left to take up banking, and was now a senior official with one of the main clearing banks and lived in London.

Both Andrew's parents were alive, his father now seventy-five, his mother, Moira, two years younger. On the fiftieth anniversary of the foundation of the firm it was decided to hold a grand party in the Town Hall. Every notable was on the guest list: the Mayor, the County Sheriff, the Chief Constable, the Lieutenant Governor, the chairmen and managing directors of all the main local firms, many of whom employed Thorntons as their auditors.

The Church was represented by the bishop and many local clergy because of the Thorntons' strong Catholic connections. There were also the leaders of all the Catholic organisations present.

Thorntons was a company with enormous prestige, a reputation for integrity that no one could question.

The senior partner since his father's retirement was Andrew, now also chairman of the town council's Finance and General Purposes committee. In addition he had a finger in almost every pie, and was within a few years of being mayor.

It was a glittering occasion. Andrew, his father and mother, Clare, Mark and Chrissy Pearson, as well as Dr and Mrs Pearson, stood in the receiving line welcoming guests. The men wore dinner jackets, the women had spared no expense on evening gowns and elaborate hairdos. The Lieutenant Governor's wife even sported a diamond tiara. But then she was always considered a bit showy.

Marcus and Pauline Thornton were allowed to watch the proceedings from the gallery together with their cousins, Chrissy and Mark's children, but they were hustled away when the dinner began—a sumptuous meal of five courses served with the finest wines and eaten to the accompaniment of a string orchestra playing in the gallery.

The speeches seemed to go on for hours,

180

everyone praising everyone else. The Mayor congratulated the firm on fifty years of success in the town, the Lieutenant Governor spoke. There was the loyal toast, the town was toasted, the firm was toasted, distinguished guests were toasted, Gerald Thornton was toasted and congratulated on his recent award of an OBE for services to the town. (He had been hoping for a knighthood.)

Gerald Thornton thanked the distinguished guests. Then Andrew, in a heartfelt speech, thanked his father for his enterprise in starting the firm and both of his parents for giving him and his siblings life. Above all, he paid lavish tribute to his lovely wife Clare who was such a rock, who enabled him to do what he did, her patience and forbearance, but for her etc etc. It was a very emotional evening. Sentiment ran high and even at midnight people couldn't stop talking and seemed reluctant to depart.

The only discordant note was struck later by Chrissy who, everyone agreed, had consumed too much alcohol together with the pâté de foie gras, suprême de turbot au sauce Mantua, Carré d'agneau and Delice Thornton, a concoction made of ice cream and a medley of fruits created by the chef in honour of the firm.

Clare thought all night that Chrissy looked out of sorts and Mark seemed dour.

*     *     *

It was perhaps unwise to invite the family home for a last drink except that Peter and his wife Dorothy were staying with Gerald and Moira, Pam was staying with Andrew and Clare and Mark and Chrissy lived nearby. Dr and Mrs Pearson decided to call it a day and went home.

A fleet of chauffeur-driven cars had been hired for the night so drinking wasn't a problem and the following day was a Sunday.

Clare was dead tired and was dying to get to bed but it was rare that all the family were together, and Pam very seldom visited this country.

'Couldn't have been more successful,' Gerald said, when the family were assembled in the drawing room, Andrew and Peter dispensing drinks from the sideboard and handing them round.

'I thought the Lieutenant Governor's remarks most gracious and you made a marvellous speech, Andrew. Very generous. Thank you.'

'It wouldn't have been possible without you, Dad.' Andrew handed him his glass and raised his. 'Or you, Mum,' he bent down to kiss his mother's cheek.

'I thought that an announcement was going to be made tonight?' Chrissy said, sitting down and kicking off her very high-heeled shoes. She had been the belle of the ball, ravishing in

182

a simple black gown while most of the women were overdressed. Wolversleigh society always tended to overdo it when they put the boat out.

'I beg your pardon?' Andrew, startled, looked at her.

'I thought the name of the firm was going to be changed and that it would be announced tonight.'

There was a pregnant silence.

'Really, darling . . .' Mark began.

'Seriously, Mark. Didn't you say? Thornton and Pearson? I thought that was the agreement and it would be announced in front of the Lieutenant Governor, the Mayor and corporation and all the big-wigs. After all we *all* know who does *all* the work in that organization. You do.' She looked at her husband, who was clearly deeply embarrassed.

'Chrissy, please don't spoil . . .' Mark hurriedly finished his drink and put out his hand. 'You're tired, darling. You obviously want to go to bed.'

'I am not tired and I am not drunk.' Chrissy looked about her defiantly. 'I know what you all think. I'm only saying what should be said. You're very lucky I didn't jump up in the middle of Andrew's fulsome speech, as I was nearly tempted to do. I was furious; ratting on a promise. Mark says Andrew is so busy with all his council work he hardly ever sets foot in the place. Mark does all the work, or oversees

183

the minions who do it. Mark . . .'

'Chrissy, *please.*' Mark seized hold of her hand and tried to pull her out of her chair, but she sat firm, refusing to budge.

'Thornton & Pearson, Chartered Accountants. I thought it was all agreed.'

'Well it was not,' Andrew said testily. 'Mark is a senior partner and no one doubts his worth, but a name change was never agreed.'

'It *was* suggested,' Mark said petulantly. 'I did actually think there might be some announcement.'

'But not *agreed*,' Andrew insisted, raising his voice.

'It has always been "Thornton and Co",' Gerald said gruffly. 'I didn't know a decision had been made.'

'We would have consulted you, Dad, in due course.'

'I think this is all terribly petty,' Clare butted in. 'It really *is* spoiling a lovely evening, Chrissy. Couldn't all this be sorted out some other time?'

'No time like the present I say,' Chrissy said firmly. 'If it is not agreed here, now, tonight, with all the family present, I think Mark should leave and start his own firm and then we'll all see what happens to Thorntons. If you ask me, it will collapse like a pack of cards. And then you'll realise who really does the work.'

'I'm terribly sorry, Gerald,' Mark turned to

the titular head of the firm. 'I didn't mean all this to come out this way, or on this night.'

'It would all have been swept under the carpet if I hadn't brought it up,' Chrissy said. 'I thought with the family all here it was a very good opportunity.' She looked at Andrew's sister. 'What do *you* think, Pam? You know about finance.'

'Oh please don't involve *me*.' Pam reached for her silver evening bag beside her on the sofa. 'I do think we should all go home and this can be sorted out another day.'

'Trust you,' Chrissy said loudly. 'The whole damned Thornton family sticking together.'

A shocked silence seemed to reverberate like an echo round the room, and even Chrissy decided it was time to go.

\* \* \*

Clare sat in the back of the car, her head against the headrest.

'I can't believe it happened,' she said. 'It ruined the whole evening.'

'What got into her?' Pam asked.

'She was drunk,' Andrew said shortly. 'She'd had too much. Anyway, she's a bitch.'

'She's not a bitch,' Clare looked at him indignantly. 'I'm very fond of Chrissy, normally. I've never *seen* her like this.'

'But did you all decide to rename the firm? I can't believe something wasn't said.' Pam tried her best to sound reasonable.

'Mark does a lot of work. He has been pressing. I am very taken up with council work. I am due to be mayor in a few years. It's important to me. I suppose he thinks I don't do anything at all. But we have so many good staff the business virtually runs itself. No one can accuse *me* of neglecting my duties. I think Chrissy decided to bring things to a head, in this silly way. Well it won't. Dad is dead against it.'

'Oh he does know?' The car turned into their road and Clare looked at him.

'Well it came up but he wouldn't hear of it.'

'Did you tell Mark that?'

'Look I don't want to fall out with Mark.'

'Then you are being a bit deceitful?'

'Not at all. I didn't honestly think it was a very important matter, or that it mattered so much to them. If I had I would have done all I could to avoid this fiasco.' Andrew angrily gnawed at a nail.

'I'm afraid this will create an awful crisis in the family,' Clare said thoughtfully. 'I wish you'd all been more frank. Even so, I can't imagine what got into Chrissy, or what motivation she had to ruin such a happy evening. To make it so public.'

Andrew's hand closed over hers.

'Put it out of your mind, darling. Don't get upset. We can't have you getting ill again. I'll sort it all out soon and we'll forget it ever

186

happened . . .'

'Besides, what's in a name?' Pam said and lit a cigarette.

# CHAPTER EIGHT

## MAY 1986

It had not been a life of hardship, but one of joy. Eighteen years a nun and Pippa had never regretted a moment of it. At times she thought it had been too good, she had enjoyed it too much. There was no struggle, no deprivation, no self-sacrifice apart from the petty annoyances of living in a community of women.

But Pippa somehow managed to overcome even these. She remained detached, otherworldly. Opinion was divided on Pippa. Some people thought she was wrapped up in herself, others thought she was a mystic. But Pippa knew she was not a saint. She was as she was by nature and not because of any closer union with God than the rest of the community. It was just that she found religion beautiful as she found art, or nature, beautiful. She communed with nature in the same way that she communed with God. Sometimes she thought that the two were indivisible and she suspected herself of a kind of pantheism into which it did not do to delve too deeply, certainly not to mention to her confessor.

Except for one break when she had gone to South Africa, Pippa had remained at Roseacre since her profession. For five years she had stayed at a house of the Order that taught pupils even more privileged than those who attended Roseacre: the children of wealthy English-speaking South Africans who lived in the smart areas of Cape Town and Bloemfontein.

The building was well-appointed with Table Mountain rising behind it and the broad sweep of the Atlantic to the front. Here, too, Pippa taught art and art appreciation. She lived in an elegant house nearby with a room of her own. She saw very little of the black people who contributed the bulk of South Africa's population and were still kept in oppression by the Nationalist Government which had ruled for so many years.

From her bedroom window she could see Robben Island where Nelson Mandela and other revolutionaries were imprisoned. But all this passed her by. She had no interest in politics and knew little about race relations. Some of the nuns cared, but most of them weren't interested either. They had black servants in plenty, and boys who kept the garden and fetched and carried. They were good to them and treated them well but every night they went back to their homes, segregated by the Group Areas Act.

Pippa liked South Africa, apart from the climate which didn't suit her. She was frequently unwell and it was decided she should return to England.

So back she came to Roseacre where she resumed her work. Her health improved and, in time, it was as though she had never been away.

Pippa returned with a clutch of paintings and, not long after she got back she exhibited her work with local artists in Plymouth, and several regional newspapers singled her out for special mention. After that she exhibited regularly with the local art group and occasionally, if her students were up to standard, she would encourage them to exhibit too. Most of them were not, with one recent exception.

Maria Tardini was very English despite her Italian surname. She had an Italian father and an English mother with whom she had lived since she was very young when her parents divorced. But she looked Italian, with shiny black hair and a pale olive skin, melting deep, velvety brown eyes and a firm sculpted mouth. By any standards she was beautiful.

She had been a boarder at the school since she was small but Pippa only got to know her well when she began to develop as an artist, showing exceptional talent.

Nun and girl were drawn together by that love of art combined with love of nature which were the pivots of Pippa's emotional and spiritual life. Maria was not very pious. Her mother was not a Catholic and she was only brought up as one because of the promise made to her father who lived in Rome and whom she visited each summer at his house in the hills above Lake Como.

To the other pupils Maria was simply teacher's pet, but some of the older nuns frowned on the relationship, considering it too close.

Pippa disregarded this as she disregarded everything tawdry or sordid. She was above tittle-tattle.

The Sister Superior even talked to her about it, but she rose above it, disdaining criticism and smutty innuendo, confident in her own probity, her view of the world. Besides, she knew what was the truth, if others did not.

\*       \*       \*

Pippa sat in the art room waiting for Maria. She was finishing a painting she had done of the bay at twilight. It was a lovely day and the window was wide open, a breeze blowing in from the sea. Maria and Pippa were to go sketching, something they often did in the surrounding countryside after school or at weekends. They usually set off with pads and soft pencils, occasionally easels and paints, and spent the day out of doors doing what they liked doing best: practising their art. Maria had just turned seventeen and Pippa was hoping that she would be the first of her pupils to go to the Slade School of Art in London and become a professional.

Over the years rules regarding dress in convents had become even more relaxed and Pippa had long ago abandoned the drab two-piece suit and unbecoming short veil. Today she had on a blue denim dress open at the neck. Her legs were bare and she wore white sandals. The only clue to her calling was a crucifix on a chain around her neck. Her head was bare.

She felt a presence and, looking round, saw Maria gazing over her shoulder.

'Oh you gave me a fright,' she said. 'You tiptoed in.'

'No I didn't. It's just that you were so absorbed.'

'Everything ready?' Pippa asked, eyes shining. 'It's going to be a lovely day.' To be alone with Maria was always a special source of joy.

It was a Saturday morning and they were to spend the whole day out of doors. A picnic had already been provided by the kitchen staff, and the convent car was waiting for them in the drive.

Pippa gave a final dab to her canvas, stood back looking at it critically and then she gathered up her things and followed Maria, who was dressed in jeans and a T-shirt, out of the house.

Pippa had been one of the first nuns to learn to drive after the convent acquired a car. It was used for shopping and excursions such as this. There was also a minibus for larger parties.

The two women stuffed their pads and sketching things, the picnic basket and cardigans in case it got chilly, into the boot. Pippa got into the driving seat and they started off, heading for the southernmost tip of Devon where there were craggy rocks and coves and plenty of wild flowers and interesting scenes to sketch and paint.

'Did you always want to be a nun?' Maria asked suddenly while Pippa had her eyes fixed on the winding road ahead of them.

'Yes. I think so.'

'Things were very different then weren't they?'

'Very.'

'I mean you had to wear long habits and you weren't allowed out.'

'Well not after *I* became a nun. By then the habit was on the way out, but when I was at school it was quite strict. Of course I wasn't a Catholic. I became one after I left.'

'And you never wanted to marry and have children?'

'No.' Pippa glanced at the girl by her side. 'You are all my children.'

Maria gazed thoughtfully ahead. 'I don't know why you're a nun at all. I never think of

193

you as one.'

'I really do have a vocation,' Pippa said quietly. 'If you didn't you couldn't. It isn't a hard life but it is circumscribed. You have, within reason, to be obedient. You have no personal possessions, no money. On the other hand, it enables me to lead a life I like, dedicated to work and prayer and the company of delightful young people like yourself.'

She gazed fondly at Maria who brushed her arm. Maria was devoted to Pippa. She had a very vague butterfly-like mother who had a string of men friends and was often abroad. Her father had married again and was more interested in his second family. Maria often felt lonely and unloved, but the convent had given her stability. And her relationship with Pippa, whom she called by her Christian name, had given her security.

'I shall miss you terribly when I go,' she said.

'But we'll keep in touch. If you go to the Slade I'll come and see you and we'll go to exhibitions at the Tate and the Royal Academy. Look,' Pippa pointed ahead of them, 'there's the coastal path and the rocks. It's a lovely spot for our picnic.'

She had driven past Hope Cove and along the narrow winding coastal roads to a tiny bay which they both knew. It was set in a wild landscape with rocks jutting out of the sea. Around them were fields of waist-high grass nearly ready for cutting. It reminded Pippa of St Catherine's and the summers with Eleanor and Clare, and swans on the lake and the huge chestnut tree heavy with pink blooms by the tennis courts.

'I was very happy at school,' she said, parking the car carefully in the car park above the cove which was approached by a very steep path. 'It was a very beautiful place. Like Roseacre.'

'Did you ever want to go back there as a nun?' Maria was busy getting everything out of the boot, the pads and picnic basket and collapsible stools, one easel with paints, sunhats, cardigans and an umbrella.

'Dear me,' Pippa laughed, 'we have brought a lot of things. We shan't be able to carry them all to the beach.' She looked regretfully at the steep winding path ahead of them.

'Oh we'll manage,' Maria said cheerfully. 'You know we like it here.'

'True,' Pippa acknowledged, and she left Maria to carry the easel and the folding stools while she followed more slowly with the rest of the items. The cove was deserted. It was not yet holiday time and there were few people about. Such fine weather in May was unusual. In a month's time it would be packed with tourists and day-trippers.

They put the rug down on the sand, Pippa set up her easel and stool and put on a broad-brimmed sunhat. Maria didn't seem to share

Pippa's eagerness to begin work. She lay on the rug staring ahead of her and then she removed her trainers.

'I must go and have a paddle. The sea looks gorgeous.'

Pippa looked fondly at her companion.

'Of course, dear. We have the whole day ahead of us to work.'

Pippa looked at the expanse of empty sand ahead of her, framed by the huge rocks with the steep cliffs on either side. The sea was as smooth as glass and in the centre of the imaginary frame was Maria, head bent, toes digging into the sand as she wandered towards the water.

Pippa, charcoal in hand, paused. She was suddenly visited by a wave of nostalgia for her youth, a desire to be young again like Maria, to be so talented, so, in Pippa's opinion, very beautiful, like a Florentine Madonna by Fra Lippo Lippi or Fra Angelico. She was never that, never beautiful. She knew her fey, fragile looks had appealed to men and she'd had a few chase after her at university. But the relationships had been platonic. She was never in the least tempted that they be otherwise, never curious about sex, and the men soon lost interest and went away.

She was sure Maria would have many admirers, many lovers. These days everyone had affairs. Maria wouldn't hold back as she, Pippa, had, and not only out of the desire to give herself to God, but also through fear. Sex had frightened her, and it was very convenient to think one was saving oneself for a bridegroom who was sexless. Therein lay no difficult choices, no act of surrender.

Maria was now walking along by the margin of the sea and Pippa shook herself and resumed her broad, light charcoal strokes which she would later fill in with thick colour. Maybe one day she and Maria would go to Florence together and what a feast of sensual delight they'd have, visiting the galleries, the churches containing the great works of art of the past; Brunelleschi's Campanile, the Duomo, the Ponte Vecchio, the Pitti Palace, Michelangelo's David.

When Maria returned she stood for a moment watching Pippa and then threw herself on the rug and dug her toes into the sand.

'It's lovely there. I wish I'd brought my bathing costume.'

Pippa peered at her from under her hat.

'Maria, it's *much* too cold to swim.'

'No it isn't. The water's lovely.'

Pippa glanced around. 'Why don't you have a dip in the altogether? There's no one about.'

'Oh!' Maria looked up, eyes shining. 'Do you think I dare?'

'I don't see why not. Anyway there is nothing shameful about the human body, clothed or unclothed. If only people weren't so

197

prurient. Take the towel, go behind that rock and cover yourself until you're in the water. I'll keep watch.'

'That's a wonderful idea.' Maria jumped up and, seizing the towel, disappeared behind the rock to emerge in a few seconds with it wrapped round her.

'Lucky we brought one,' Pippa said grinning, and her eyes returned to her canvas as Maria sped off. 'And when you come back you can do some work,' she called, but she didn't think the girl running towards the sea heard a word.

She watched her as she stood by the water's edge clasping the towel tightly round her, seized, Pippa didn't doubt, by those few moments of awful indecision as to whether or not to take the plunge. Should one run forward, or back? She looked round, saw Pippa, hunched her shoulders and, casting aside the towel, raced into the water. A couple of seconds later she flung herself into the waves.

It had been a beautiful sight, a breathtaking moment as that slim brown, naked body rushed into the water. Pippa couldn't take her eyes off her.

Maria didn't stay in long. After a few splashes she re-emerged and, gathering up her towel, ran across the sand and threw herself down on the rug shivering.

'Oh it *was* cold,' she said, her teeth chattering. 'But it was lovely. Why don't you

198

go in, Pippa?'

'I haven't a nice young body like yours,' Pippa murmured without raising her eyes. 'Mine is old and wrinkly.'

'I shan't look.'

'No I don't want to.' She gazed at Maria who, without a trace of self-consciousness, spread herself out on her back, eyes closed, soaking in the warm sun. She had small pointed breasts with dark-red nipples which remained erect, even when she was lying down. Her pubic hair was thick and black, her stomach taut and shiny. Her whole body glistened. She could just have been showing off, flaunting herself. Pippa thought she looked magnificent. She swallowed hard.

'Would you mind if I sketched you in the nude, Maria?'

'Of course not.' Maria sat up and shaded her eyes against the sun. 'You said there's nothing sinful about the human body.'

'Nothing at all.' Pippa began to erase what she'd done and started all over again. 'It is made in the image and likeness of God. Most of the great masters have painted the nude.' She looked across at the young woman who had lain back on the rug again, and thought of Gauguin and his voluptuous Polynesian women with sensuous faces and small, pointy, red-tipped breasts. She did a few lightning strokes. 'After I've finished we'll have something to eat and then you'll have to get down to work yourself this afternoon, young lady.'

'I could lie here like this all day,' Maria murmured. 'I feel so lazy.'

'If you don't cover yourself you'll get sunstroke!'

*     *     *

In the democracy that was now a feature of convent life Sister Bernadette, superior at Roseacre, was something of an anomaly. She yearned for the old days, the old habit, the old routine and ritual, the old discipline. She was now fifty-five and had entered the Society at eighteen, straight from school. She had taken final vows five years later after graduating from Cambridge University with a first in chemistry, a subject which she taught throughout the school, and many of her students went on to university.

She was Dublin-born, her family also Catholics of the old school. Two of her brothers were priests and another sister a missionary in Ecuador.

Sister Bernadette had longed to serve God, but not in the missions. She was persuaded that her fine intellect could serve Him in other ways, and it had.

Sister Bernadette was going through the names of new girls due to start in September, and making sure that the parents had all paid the fees, when her telephone rang and, glad of the break, she answered it.

'Sister Bernadette?'

'Yes, Father Casey.' The lilting tones of a fellow Dubliner were familiar to her.

'Can you spare me a moment?'

'Of course, Father.' She settled back in her chair.

'Well, I have just returned from the summer art exhibition in the village hall . . .'

'Oh how was it?' Her rather cheerless face broke into a smile.

'I have something very disturbing to report, Sister.'

'Oh?' She sat forward in her chair.

'There are several portraits of a naked girl who, I'm sorry to say, I recognise to be a pupil at your school.'

'Oh my God!' Sister Bernadette said, clasping her chest. 'Sister Mary Frances!'

\*    \*    \*

Father Casey was waiting at the door of the village hall of Mapperwick. Like many towns in England, August was carnival month; time to elect the carnival queen and princesses and elevate some local girls to dizzy heights they had never dreamed of; to decorate floats and parade them through the streets and, of course, to have the annual art exhibition of local talent at the village hall. The artists were all amateur, and there was the usual mixture of gifted and not so gifted. Country scenes and bowls of flowers predominated. No one could remember a nude ever having been exhibited before, and the news had spread quickly. Within a few hours of the opening a small crowd had gathered in front of the group of paintings showing a young girl in the nude on a beach surrounded by rocks and the sea.

'There's a large crowd there already.'

Sister Bernadette purposefully made her way towards the door.

'Have you spoken to Sister Mary Frances?' Father Casey hurried after her.

'Not yet.' The superior pursed her mouth grimly.

'Well then, can you take them down?'

'Most certainly I can,' and Sister Bernadette made her way through the gawping onlookers, now three-deep and, with a polite 'excuse me' and 'do you mind?' began to remove the paintings from the wall. Happily for her they were all hung at an accessible height.

The crowd stood back, visibly disappointed, and there were one or two protests. Then a stern-faced gentleman with a large yellow badge of office on his lapel approached Sister Bernadette and demanded to know what she was doing.

'I am removing these portraits,' she replied, looking at him in surprise. 'They have been exhibited by mistake.'

202

The man fingered his badge authoritatively. 'Do you have the artist's permission?'

'Yes.' Sister Bernadette had little regard for truth where the honour of the school was at stake.

'Well . . .' the man momentarily looked confused, 'it is not *normal* until the exhibition is over.'

'It is over as far as these paintings are concerned.' Sister Bernadette handed one of the larger ones to Father Casey and asked him to take it to his car.

'They are very, very good,' someone else called out. 'Somebody said the artist was a nun.'

Sister said nothing and, having removed all four pictures from the wall, gave another two to Father Casey who, perspiring, had hastened back and, tucking the remaining one under her arm, nodded to the confused assembly and followed the priest out of the gallery.

A trained cat burglar could hardly have acted more swiftly or efficiently.

'Thank goodness you saw those in time!' she gasped, sinking into the passenger seat. 'I think we have avoided an enormous scandal.'

'We hope!' Father Casey slipped the car into gear. 'What a good thing I was at the opening.'

'What a good thing it is the summer holidays.' Sister Bernadette let out a loud sigh. 'The ways of the Lord are indeed wondrous.

I'm quite sure He is on our side.'

*       *       *

The pictures certainly had merit. But then Sister Bernadette knew that Sister Mary Frances was a very good artist. Personally she was not one of her favourite members of the community, but she knew she had talent.

She had never felt really comfortable with Sister Mary Frances, seldom at ease. There was no doubt she was extremely pious, sincerely so, and some claimed to have seen an aura about her as she returned from Holy Communion, eyes downcast, hands tightly clasped in prayer.

However she was clearly a non-conformist, had a will of her own and was over-familiar with the girls. She had favourites and favourites were not permitted. Although the Second Vatican Council had done its best to strip nuns of their mystery and dignity, she felt Sister Mary Frances had gone too far, so much so that she was scarcely a nun at all and even allowed those favourites to call her by her Christian name.

As far as Sister Bernadette was concerned, it was difficult to see why she had become a nun. She could have been a pious lay woman, and then she could have had all sorts of questionable friendships and hung what nudes she liked on exhibition walls.

Sister boiled over at the thought of what might have happened had the press got wind of this, if Maria's parents, or the parents of other children, got to hear about it. She decided that Sister Mary Frances was out of her senses.

There was a tap on the door and Sister Bernadette called 'Come in'. The pictures were arranged in a row against the wall, so that they were the first thing you saw when you entered the room.

Pippa, on opening the door, appeared dumbstruck by what was in front of her. She stood for several seconds while Sister Bernadette observed her carefully, curious to see her reaction.

Finally Pippa looked at her superior and gestured helplessly towards the paintings.

'I have removed them from the exhibition,' Sister Bernadette said. 'And I am waiting for an explanation.'

'I think they are my best work.' Pippa gazed fearlessly at her superior.

'Are you not ashamed?'

'Not a bit. It came naturally one day when we were sketching at Kittle Cove. Maria went in to swim and I asked permission to paint her in the nude. It was done on the spur of the moment. A beautiful girl in a beautiful setting.'

'Did you never realise what harm you could have done? Thought what people would say?'

'No. I never did.'

'A pupil of the school . . .'

'No.'

'What deductions they would make?'

'What do you mean by "deductions"?'

'That there is some sort of unnatural relationship between you and this girl.'

'That is ludicrous, monstrous, and you know it,' Pippa cried angrily.

'Nevertheless people make them, and I have had occasion in the past to speak to you about your familiarity with your pupils, especially, latterly, Maria Tardini.'

'What *are* you suggesting, Sister?'

'I am suggesting that you might have feelings for her that some people would consider unnatural. Those pictures have a suggestion of intimacy that, I confess, quite shocked me.'

'I do have feelings for Maria,' Pippa spoke thoughtfully, 'and I am not ashamed of them. It is a kind of love, but it certainly is not physical. I imagine it is similar to the emotion a mother feels for a child. We are also drawn together by our love of art, *and* her talent.'

Sister Bernadette invited Pippa to sit down and she sat opposite her. Her expression altered and when she spoke again her tone was softer, her manner less censorious.

'Sister Mary Frances, the world has changed very much, certainly since I was young. Relations between people of the same sex are quite common now, whereas before they were frowned upon. But, as nuns, we have forsworn these strong emotions for either sex. I am not suggesting anything of a carnal nature occurred, but I do think you have behaved very foolishly.'

'You think the great artists who painted nudes were in love with their subjects?' Pippa demanded aggressively.

'Sometimes I believe they were.'

'Well I am not and I deeply resent this inference.'

'Nonetheless many people will assume it. It will look bad for the Society. I am therefore suggesting, Sister, in your own interest, that you leave this school and go to another house. I think you should stay out of the classroom for some time, maybe work with disadvantaged people. We have a house in Stepney, East London where they deal with drug addicts and other unfortunates in society. I have spoken to Mother General who has given permission for you to transfer.'

She leaned towards Pippa and gave her a smile of encouragement. 'Maybe for a while you should give up your art. Offer it up to God, Sister, as your penance.'

\*　　　\*　　　\*

Pippa sat on the train, her small suitcase on the luggage rack above her head. Other than that, and her art, she had no worldly goods. But the pictures did not belong to her because a nun had no possessions and Sister Bernadette had refused to allow her to take any of her paintings, however harmless, with her. One of the nuns with whom she was friendly told her that, as far as she knew, they had already been disposed of.

They had lost no time in arranging for Pippa's transfer to the London house. In a day or two everything was settled. She was asked not to make elaborate farewells to the community, but to keep, where possible, to her room. She spent a lot of time in the art room tidying up for her successor. There she shed many tears, especially when she looked at Maria's folio of paintings and drawings. Maria, of course, was on holiday in Italy.

That morning a taxi had arrived and with her single suitcase in her hand she entered and drove off. No one came to say goodbye.

As the car went along the drive Pippa turned to take a final look at the house where she had been so happy for so many years. It was her home. Standing well back at one or two of the windows she fancied she saw the faces of women to whom she had once been close.

Apparently not one of them had come forward to defend her, or plead for her.

Pippa had never been to the house in Stepney, but she imagined that the nuns would

208

have been briefed about the reason for her transfer. At least their superior would know. She felt a deep sense of anger and humiliation at the insinuation that she had even contemplated a sexual relationship with a pupil in her care.

She hadn't slept for nights, and there was this deep sense that God had deserted her. In her hour of need He had abandoned her.

The train drew into Waterloo and Pippa, unable to move, her heart thumping, sat gazing out of the window.

London. She hated it. Memories of dingy lodgings in Mornington Crescent, too much traffic and noise. The turbulence and uncertainty of adolescence. A guard came along the platform and tapped sharply on her window.

'Everyone out of the train please, madam.'

Gingerly Pippa got down her case and walked towards the door. As she alighted on to the platform to join the crowd hastening to the exit she saw two females dressed in sombre suits, sensible shoes and half veils gazing expectantly at the train. A sudden feeling of overwhelming terror possessed her. She saw them with their grim, tight, unsmiling faces, representatives of a place full of strangers, perhaps hostile to a sinner who had been put in their midst, suspicious about her motives. No doubt there would be a reprimand from Mother General, a priest would remonstrate with her. No one would see or understand her point of view.

Panic took over. The two silent nuns on the platform seemed to Pippa like gaolers waiting to escort her to prison.

So, like a prisoner in transit, she decided to give them the slip and make a break for freedom.

# CHAPTER NINE

## APRIL 1987

Clare thought this was one of the worst moments of her life, perhaps *the* worst moment. She would always remember sitting in the Head's study, quiet and composed, or ostensibly so, with Marcus, white-faced, sitting between her and Andrew. The long thin figure of the Head was silhouetted against the dormer window, and beyond him strapping youths in white were practising for the cricket season.

Marcus, who was an excellent sportsman, should surely be among them?

Andrew was saying 'I can't believe my son is a thief.' His voice seemed to echo round and round in Clare's head.

'Of course he is not a *thief*.' She looked to Marcus to deny it, but he remained sitting with his head bowed.

'I'm afraid Marcus has admitted it,' the Head said, rising from his chair. He wore a black clerical suit with a white collar and a black academic gown, the sides of which he clutched authoritatively. 'There have been a number of thefts throughout the year . . .' he turned and looked at them gravely, 'years in fact, that have mystified us. Finally a trap was laid for the culprit and Marcus was caught red-handed. The thefts were mainly from studies when the boys were out and we kept a round-the-clock watch on the senior boys' study. Imagine our amazement when a member of the study, Marcus, a senior prefect and highly regarded member of the school was soon going through his friends' belongings, people who trusted him. So you can see how despicable the deed was. You can imagine their shock.

'Marcus has admitted to this and previous thefts. He says he does not know why he does it. There is no need. He is not short of money and we do not have a drug problem in this school. I'm afraid Marcus is a compulsive thief and I am expelling him immediately. I would like you to take him home with you. In this case, and solely in the interests of the school, not of Marcus, we will not prefer charges, but please never write here for a character reference.' The Head paused ominously. 'Have you anything to say, Marcus?'

Marcus shook his head.

'At least you could say "sorry".' His father turned on him. 'I am absolutely appalled by what I have just heard.'

'I am sorry,' Marcus mumbled. 'I have said I am very, very sorry.' As if still in a state of shock he relapsed into silence. Clare's heart bled for him.

'The evidence is irrefutable,' the Head emphasised, 'and it will remain so. Marcus's cases are packed and ready for collection round the back of the building.'

The Head looked meaningfully towards the door, but Andrew and Clare remained as if glued to their seats.

'I really am rather busy.' The Head glanced pointedly at his watch.

'What about A levels?' Andrew asked suddenly. 'Don't they start in a few weeks' time?'

'We shall have to sort out something about that.' The Head made a note on a pad on his desk. 'I can't say just at the moment, but his form master will be in touch with you. Now . . .' he looked again at the door.

'But you must understand we are terribly upset,' Clare burst out, tears in her eyes. She was resentful at his apparent lack of pastoral concern. Marcus had been at the school since he was thirteen. Weren't the clergy supposed to care about their charges? 'If Marcus is sorry and promises not to do it again . . .'

'Not a chance, Mrs Thornton. His fellow pupils have already put him in Coventry. He has brought shame on himself and the school. I do understand your anguish and, believe me, you have my heartfelt sympathy. But Marcus has put this school to a considerable amount of trouble, all to catch one miserable thief.' His lip curled contemptuously. 'I do not feel sorry for Marcus but I am, believe me, very sorry for *you*.'

Clare lay on her bed, aware of a terrible pressure on her temples. She had simply felt she couldn't cope and burst into tears as soon as they arrived back in the house. Not what she'd meant to do at all, but she hurried to her bedroom, and took four Paracetamol tablets. The journey home had been awful. She and Andrew in the front, Marcus slumped in the back. Scarcely a word had been said. No one knew what to say. As a mother, her moods wobbled uneasily between compassion and anger.

What a terrible end to a school career, one of such promise. It made you fear for the future.

Marcus was now with Andrew, who had insisted on seeing him alone. At last she managed to nod off, and when she awoke Andrew was sitting by her side.

'Are you alright?'

Clare gingerly felt her head. 'I thought it would burst.'

'I'm terribly sorry.' He reached out and took her hand.

'It's not your fault . . . but, Andrew, how *could* he? What made him do it? Did he say?'

Andrew shook his head. 'He claims he doesn't know. He says he's done it for years, petty pilfering, little things. If he'd been caught

214

before something might have been done to help him.'

'But what *can* one do?'

'I suppose he'll have to see a psychiatrist.'

Thoughts of the clinic, Irma Ashworth . . . But it was such a long time ago. Fifteen years.

'Do you think there's a weakness, Andrew? Something genetic?'

'What do you mean?' He looked puzzled.

'You know, when I had that breakdown . . .'

'That was hormonal. I'm sure this is nothing to do with hormones.'

'It might be. Teenagers, adolescents. Big changes going on. You'd think the school would have *tried* to understand.'

But Andrew was more preoccupied with appearances, of what the family would say.

'The thing that worries me is if this gets around. How can we explain him coming home, for instance?'

'We'll have to say he had a breakdown,' she faltered. 'Just like me. People will say it was in the family. Brought on by stress, pressure of exams. It is a *kind* of breakdown, isn't it? Oh, Andrew . . .' She pressed her fingers to her head and started to cry again. 'What a terrible, terrible thing to happen.'

He put his arm round her and tried to comfort her.

\*     \*     \*

They had been so proud of Marcus. He was bright, attractive, good-looking. Good at games, a chip off the old block. He was a school prefect, an icon to the younger boys, and expected to do well.

Whatever possessed him? Marcus didn't know. At first it had begun as a dare when he was younger, and then he found it hard to resist just taking little things, anything, that didn't belong to him. It was a sort of challenge, a rush of blood to the brain. A blemish in a life thought by everyone, his parents, friends, teachers, to be perfect. It was the secret that only he knew and often when he stole things he returned them after a while or discarded them. He didn't need anything he took. He just wanted to see how good he was and how long he could go on doing it before he was found out.

But he was terribly sorry to upset his parents, particularly his mother. He would have done anything to be able to make it up to her.

*       *       *

Pauline Thornton was bewildered by her brother's behaviour, but she took it less seriously than her parents. She thought it was silly rather than a crime. She thought he was an ass. It was something he would grow out of, she was sure of that.

216

Pauline had always been less perfect than Marcus. She was a day girl at St Catherine's and not particularly bright. She was certainly not stupid, but she didn't shine as her mother had. She was especially bad at games. Neither did she boast the good looks of her mother and brother. She had the rather gaunt Thornton features, sallow skin and lacklustre hair. She had bad eyesight, like her father, and wore glasses; but she was a natural leader, a wonderful mimic and very popular at school. She seemed to have no hang-ups or resentments and was content to plod on, not very ambitious, not very clever, but nice. Everyone loved Pauline.

In the days after Marcus's disgrace she was the mainstay of the family, comforting her mother, cheering her father up, consoling her brother.

Things could change. It wasn't the end of the world.

Pauline went along with the idea that Marcus had had a breakdown brought on by overwork, and was to take his A levels under supervision at a local school. She managed to persuade her mother that Marcus needed a lot of love, not chastisement, and her father that he needed help.

For the next few weeks Marcus stayed mainly in his room revising, determined to do well in his exams and take up the place he'd been offered at university, to try and expunge

217

the memory of the shameful deeds of his past.

*    *    *

*June 1987*

All the talk was about Pippa Sidgwick and the fact that she'd left her convent the year before and vanished. No one knew what had become of her. She had disappeared without trace. Clare had known about Pippa, as the nuns at St Catherine's had asked her at the time if she'd heard from her.

The facts of the matter were very hard to come by. Pippa had had to leave after some misdemeanour, the nature of which had not been disclosed. But she was being sent to a house of the Society in London where she would be given work and looked after. There had been no suggestion that she was being suspended or expelled.

She had got on the train for London but, apparently, had never arrived at the other end. Two nuns had been there to meet her. The police had been informed, and had made extensive enquiries, but so far she had not been traced. She was just another statistic.

It was very hard to think of a woman of forty, a nun who had been used to a certain standard in life, simply disappearing. It had worried Clare a good deal and continued to worry her throughout the year. She thought of

Pippa being abducted and murdered, her body lying in some hole. But nobody else seemed to share her fears. Pippa was officially a missing person, not a missing body.

It happened all the time, but never to someone one knew. After Marcus was expelled she found herself dwelling on Pippa's fate and she knew that, to some extent, the darkness of that year long past was returning.

But as usual, for Association Day, Clare tried to dispel her cares and threw herself, heart and soul, into the preparations. This year there seemed more old girls than ever. They crowded along the path leading to the lake, and huddled in little groups on the lawn or in the field, clinging on to their hats, if worn, because of the wind. Several pairs had changed into tennis gear as soon as they arrived and were playing vigorous doubles on the courts. The usual horseplay was going on with the boat, normally indulged in by the younger members of the Association who had left the school in recent years. Gales of laughter drifted up towards the more sedate members sitting at tables on the lawn who, in turn, looked on with amusement at what the young things were up to. If someone fell in, it wouldn't be the first time.

The weather in the morning had been a bit worrying with dark clouds scudding across the sky, and one had to face the prospect that plans could be ruined and tea might have to be taken indoors.

However by two o'clock the sun seemed determined to shine, the caterers prepared to lay food out on the table and the first guests had started to arrive. This year there must have been upwards of two hundred of various ages and sizes, all dressed in bright frocks except the nuns, who wore grey or blue suits, but had now discarded their headdresses to reveal hair that seemed to be uniformly shades of white or grey. Nuns were getting older because vocations were fewer. Not many women these days were tempted to join religious orders unless they were the far-out Tibetan variety involving saffron robes and shaven heads. This was the trend in nuns these days: religious societies of various kinds with more glamour attached, as well as the opportunity to travel to exotic parts.

Clare still, reluctantly, Secretary of the Association, was soon surrounded by her contemporaries, who were anxious to hear the latest news, or the lack of it, about Pippa.

'But of course I haven't seen her for fourteen years,' Clare said, 'not since she last visited St Catherine's.'

Others knew snatches, tried to fill in.

'She went to South Africa. She loved it there. Maybe she went back?'

Heads were shaken. 'Apparently the climate didn't suit her which was why they sent her home.'

'But she loved Roseacre. She told me she was very happy there.'

'I always had a card from her at Christmas.'

'What *happened* exactly?'

That was it. No one knew.

Another little group stood on the lawn drinking tea.

'I think Clare looks less well this year. Of course I haven't seen her for some time.'

Jennifer Hughes-Johnson, previously Cuthbert, gazed across at her critically. She'd missed the last few class reunions because her husband had run off with another woman and it took her some time to clear up after the mess and to find a new one. Women like Jennifer never liked being husbandless. They depended on men for their self-esteem, their *raison d'être*, and, very important, comfort. But now things were alright again and she had emerged from her chrysalis to grace Association Day with a brand new wedding ring and even larger diamonds on the new engagement ring than on the previous one.

Margaret Potter followed her gaze. She had not found even one husband but had borne it in good part, was a deputy headmistress at a comprehensive school and generally enjoyed life though, if she had a secret sorrow, it was that she had not had children of her own and now it was too late.

'She had a lot of stress with her son,' Margaret said.

'Oh?' Jennifer looked interested. 'What happened?'

'He had a breakdown and had to leave school.'

Joan Dixon grimaced. 'Just like his mother. It must be in the family.'

'He was very bright, a clever boy like Clare.'

'Over-stretched himself.'

'Someone said there was more to it than that.' Ruth Brown's expression was knowing.

'Oh do tell . . .'

'I don't really know.'

'Go on.'

'Well it's just gossip . . .' Ruth lowered her voice and the little coterie pressed in on her.

'They *say* he was expelled, but I don't know why.'

'Wasn't he a Stonyhurst boy?' Jennifer looked shocked.

'No. He went to his father's old school, St Thomas's, in the Lake District. Apparently he did very well.'

'Such a handsome attractive boy. Very like Clare.'

'And the girl so plain. What a pity.'

'But very nice.'

'Oh very.'

'She's here today somewhere,' Joan Dixon looked around, 'helping out.'

Clare could see them all, chatting away, but gossip had lost some of its appeal since one had become the subject of it. She was aware that a lot of people knew Marcus had been expelled because they had sons at the school. It was hard to bear, especially when you had led a bit of a charmed life, things had gone so well, apart from the odd blip: nice children, successful husband, shortly due to be mayor.

She felt terribly tired. Marcus was in the middle of A levels and never went to bed before two or three am. This made his mother fret a great deal. She told him that As didn't matter, but they did. He had a place at university and he wanted to start a new life, expunge the last one and make his parents proud of him again. It would be an uphill task. A psychiatrist was digging into his past at great expense to Andrew, who kept on telephoning him and asking if he'd yet discovered what had made his son into a thief? Clare wished he wouldn't, but she knew he was ashamed of Marcus and was afraid that he might spoil his mayoral year.

Clare looked about her and thought back on past reunions and what one discovered about people who had been one's contemporaries, or who had come before or after. She knew Jennifer had a new husband who evidently had a lot of money. There were now many women she didn't know at all because it was twenty-three years since she'd left the school, and she thought of Pippa who had disappeared, and Eleanor who had become a personality and was frequently on TV. She had been tempted once or twice to contact her but then thought better of it. What was the point?

Much water had flowed under the bridge since they had last seen each other. Besides, Eleanor was a success whereas she, Clare, was conscious of a feeling of failure, of things not having gone as well as one might have hoped, especially since Marcus let the family down so badly by being expelled from school. It made you fear what might come next.

'Are you still Secretary of the Association, Clare?' She turned and saw Mary Barlow, at least she *thought* it was Mary Barlow, though this woman was slim and quite elegant.

'You don't recognise me, do you, Clare?'

Clare beamed: 'It *is* Mary . . .'

'It is,' Mary laughed jovially. 'I lost five stone. The doctor said I'd kill myself if I had another baby.'

'So what did you do?'

Mary bent her head conspiratorially towards Clare. 'Don't tell the Pope, but what does everyone do? I mean, how come you only have two children?'

'Well . . .' Clare looked at her feet.

'Exactly. Where would we be without the Pill?'

\*　　\*　　\*

Clare was rather shocked that someone as religious as Mary Barlow, a good Catholic mother who had had ten children, had disobeyed the laws of the Church. She had never known Mary Barlow really well, so she didn't feel it was the time or the occasion to discuss with her the subtleties of the Church's teaching on contraception. She wondered what Mary Barlow and many others would say if they knew that she and her husband hadn't made love for fifteen years in their scrupulousness, their eagerness to carry out the Church's commands, to lead good Catholic lives? Maybe if all those years ago she, Clare, had not been so frightened after her breakdown, so adamant, they would have found a priest sympathetic to their predicament and practised some sort of mechanical contraception. Even then she doubted whether she could have lived with her conscience. She had always had an acute sense of sin.

It made you wonder, actually, what most of those women who came to the Association meetings did in their own private lives because the Church's attitude to sex went against all current secular thinking and behaviour on the matter. Not only was contraception widely practised but so was abortion—no one thought twice about that. People lived openly together, no longer considering it sinful if they weren't married, and homosexual relationships were commonplace.

Jennifer Cuthbert had been divorced and

remarried, though not, of course, in church. Yet she seemed happy to attend Association meetings—no sense of sin apparent there—and, perhaps, maybe had her own form of worship which made her at ease with her conscience.

It was really quite difficult to be a good, conventional Catholic in the modern world.

On the other hand, one had to assume that hundreds of thousands of happily married couples had a normal sex life, didn't have too many children *and* enjoyed the comforts of religion. If one were not so inhibited it would be quite interesting to know how.

Clare got back at about seven, knowing that Andrew would be out at a council meeting and Pauline had left with some fellow helpers to go to a movie and get a McDonald's in the town. She deserved it. She was a very hard-working eager sort of girl. One good thing about her not going to university was that she would probably do a secretarial course and get a job in Wolversleigh, so that she could continue to be mother's little helper at home. Hopefully, too, like mother, she would marry a local boy and live nearby and send her children to St Catherine's, thus continuing the family tradition.

Clare garaged her car, took some shopping out of the boot and went through into the kitchen where she found Marcus sitting at the table eating baked beans on toast and reading

226

the evening paper.

'How was today?' Clare bent down to kiss his cheek.

'OK. I think I passed.'

Marcus was doing Physics, Chemistry and Maths and today had been his last exam. Clare had had him at the back of her mind all afternoon.

'Oh good.' She started going through the carrier bags and putting the goods she'd bought at the supermarket away.

'How was your old girls' day?'

'As usual.' She turned and smiled at him. 'I am a *very* old girl now.'

'I'll never be an old boy,' Marcus said sombrely. 'Maybe it's just as well because they sound awful.'

'Marcus . . . darling . . .' Clare sat next to him and took his hand. When she looked at him she saw a mirror reflection of herself: dark curly hair, alert intelligent brown eyes, broad nose, firm mouth, very tall. She ached when she thought of what had happened to him, the apparent destruction of a young life, young hopes. She squeezed his hand tightly. 'I don't want you to brood on this. It's all in the past.'

Marcus fixed her with a stare.

'Thing is, Mum, it is *not* all in the past. It is very much in the present. Dad won't let me forget it for a minute. Last night he was still banging on about it. How *could* I let the family down? What would my grandparents say, and

227

how hard it was to keep it from them. Well tell them, I said, let it all hang out. I don't give a fuck.'

'Darling, please don't use that kind of language.'

'Sorry, Mum.'

Clare felt upset, not so much about the F-word as that she knew that Marcus was right. Andrew would not let go. It seemed to obsess him. Why? Why? Why? It rather obsessed her too, only she tried not to let it show, but she thought about it constantly.

Marcus reached into the pocket of his jeans and produced a crumpled pack of cigarettes. He smoked a lot which also annoyed Andrew, who had given up. Pauline had never started. Marcus leaned back, lit his cigarette and exhaled. 'Mum, now that the exams are finished, I want to go away. I feel I can't stay on here any longer.' He paused uncertainly. 'Frankly, Mum, I don't know how you've put up with Dad all these years. He's a puffed-up prick.'

'Marcus, *please* . . .' Clare felt her cheeks redden.

'He is. I know you don't sleep together . . .'

'That's nothing to do with how I feel about Dad. I do not think he is . . . what you called him.'

'Then why do you sleep apart? I don't know any other couples, parents of my friends, or former friends as I don't have any left now, who have separate bedrooms.'

'Years ago after my breakdown I was told not to have any more children in case it brought about a recurrence.'

'I see.' Marcus gazed at the tip of his cigarette. 'But aren't there ways and means . . .'

'Please, Marcus, I'd really rather not talk about it.'

Clare got up and went over to the sink where she began to wash vegetables for the evening meal, though she didn't know when Andrew would be in and Marcus appeared to have eaten.

'OK, if that's what you want.'

'It is what I want. I'm much more concerned about you. I don't mean about what happened but about you going away.'

'People have years off. I would like to postpone going to university and travel a bit. I want to get right away from all this business, away from Dad. Away from Doctor Christie.'

'Isn't he doing you any good?' Clare gazed at him anxiously.

'Yes he's a nice enough chap.' Marcus flicked ash into an ashtray. 'I don't object to him. But I know why I pinched things. I knew it was stupid and I'd get caught.'

'Then *why*?'

Angered by his insouciance Clare leaned over him, wiping her hands on a towel. '*Why*, Marcus?'

'I thought life was too boring, too perfect. I

229

can't explain it, but I had to do something daring, make a blemish. I don't know if you can understand this, but I think I've got it out of my system. I didn't think of the consequences on you, particularly you, or on the family. It wasn't as though I was safe-breaking. I didn't realise I'd be quite such a pariah, all my friends would be disgusted and desert me. They thought I was a creep. I haven't got one left from school. They thought what I did was awful. It was awful. It was silly and contemptible and I want to go away and forget it. If I can I want to come back to a clean slate in a year or two.'

*     *     *

Clare waited up for Andrew to come home. He was late and it was after eleven when she heard the car and, after a while, the garage door shutting. Moments later he appeared in the drawing room where she sat, feet up, watching a late-night movie on the TV.

As soon as she saw Andrew she switched it off and, looking at her with concern, he came across.

'Are you alright?'

'I'm fine . . . I wanted to talk to you.'

'Is something wrong?' Andrew immediately looked anxious. But there was also something else. He looked rather afraid, as though he'd committed some misdemeanour. He turned his back on her and went to pour himself a drink, looking at her as he held up the bottle.

Clare shook her head.

'Marcus wants to go away,' she said when Andrew took the chair opposite her. 'Right away, far away. India or Australia, travel round the world.'

'Bloody cheek.' Andrew took a gulp of his drink.

'No it's not a cheek. Why is it a cheek?'

'Well where is he going to get the money for all this?'

'From us. I think he deserves it.'

'*I* bloody well don't.'

'I am aware of how you feel, Andrew, and so is he. Your attitude is driving our son away.'

'Well what do you expect me to do? Sing his praises?'

'I want you to try and understand him more. He is very sorry. He knows he did wrong and he thinks the reason was that everything was too perfect.'

'Balls.'

'No it is not "balls", Andrew. He was sick of being good. It was something to do with a good Catholic home, I think.'

'Then why didn't Pauline go round stealing things?'

'I don't really understand why Marcus did it; but he has always been highly strung and Pauline isn't. She's sensible and she also has none of Marcus's gifts . . . and advantages. I

231

mean Marcus is very good-looking.'

'So is Pauline.'

'Well we think so, but she's not conventionally pretty in the way that Marcus is handsome. He is also clever and gifted at games . . .'

'Oh don't give me this claptrap, Clare.' Andrew ran his free hand over his face. He did look tired and very drawn.

'Well I think you should make an effort to understand . . . and not be so very busy, Andrew. You have no time at all for the children and very little for me. You are too involved in too many things. You hardly have a night at home, and yet we know from what Chrissy told us on that awful occasion that it's not work that keeps you away.'

'I simply don't know what you mean. It *is* work.'

'Yes, work for the council.'

'I'll be mayor in a couple of years. It's very important to me, and it should be important for you. It's an honour. As for giving you and the children more time. They are both grown up. And you . . .' he looked across at her. 'What about your own good works? What about your OXFAM and your Amnesty and your Catholic Women's League and your Catholic Women's Refuge and your Old Girls' Association? You spin around like a top. You've hardly been a wife.'

'What do you mean I've hardly been a *wife*?'

232

she spat indignantly.

'You know what I mean. We haven't slept together for fifteen years. At times I've felt tempted. You can hardly blame me for burying myself in my work.'

'But, Andrew, I thought we . . . understood the reasons. They haven't changed.'

'Why didn't you have a hysterectomy? Why didn't you get rid of your bloody womb and be a wife to me? I'm not a saint. Why didn't anyone think of that years ago, or have your tubes tied or something . . .

'Because there's nothing wrong with my tubes or my womb,' Clare said icily. 'It's mutilation you're suggesting. You can't remove healthy organs. No respectable doctor would do it. Anyway it's against the law of the Church, and I thought that all our lives we have lived by its rules, or tried to.'

For a moment husband and wife stared at each other as if conscious at last of long-suppressed resentment on one side, of incomprehension on the other, of a dreadful chasm slowly opening between them.

'And look where it's got us,' Andrew said with a weary sigh. '*And* our son.'

# PART III

*The Bride of Christ*

# CHAPTER TEN

# SEPTEMBER 1989

'The body of Christ,' the priest intoned and Pippa, raising her head to receive the Host, looked straight into the eyes of Father Casey, and then quickly looked away again. But he gave no sign of recognition and as he moved on she returned to her pew at the rear of the church and sank on to her knees in prayer.

Mass over, Pippa remained where she was, still on her knees, head bowed, her mind and heart consecrated on her union with God— that precious time each day when she could forget her earthly woes and think only of Him whom she had elected to serve.

Finally, as the congregation dispersed, the lights were put out in the church and she sat back on the pew, still preoccupied with thoughts of God.

She was aware then of a presence beside her and she stiffened. A hand briefly touched her shoulder and a voice said: 'Sister Mary Frances.'

After a moment she looked up.

'So you did recognise me, Father?'

'Of course I did.' The priest removed his hand and looked at her intently. 'Of course I did.'

Pippa wore a threadbare grey coat wrapped tightly around her. On her feet—incongruous in autumn—were white sandals, and a scarf was tied round her head. She wore no stockings and her legs were purple and swollen. Beside her was a bundle of some description. Her face was worn, wisps of faded fair hair struggled out from under her scarf, and Father Casey could see that her hands were grimy, her nails dirty. From her there also emanated a vaguely unpleasant, unwashed smell.

Father Casey was momentarily bereft of words but, as Pippa ventured no explanation for her condition, he finally spoke.

'Sister, we have been very worried about you.'

She nodded but said nothing.

'Could you not have let us have a word?'

Again she didn't reply.

'Sister, you must be hungry. Would you take breakfast with me?'

Pippa was about to refuse and then changed her mind. She was, indeed, very hungry. It was days, perhaps weeks since she'd had a square meal.

'We'll have it in the presbytery,' Father Casey said. 'We will be quite alone.'

The priest got up and she rose to follow him. Her limbs were very stiff and she dragged one of her feet. He stopped to pick up her bundle but she wouldn't let him and took it

238

herself. She shuffled up the aisle after him, through the sacristy door into the presbytery. It was very familiar to her. Twenty-two years before she had been instructed here before being received into the Church.

Now she attended Mass daily, never missing.

One of the curates they passed in the corridor recognised her. Occasionally she was given food if she came round to the back door, or a package was brought to the church and left beside her. Otherwise they had no contact with the bag lady who attended Mass so assiduously. It was as she wanted. Vagrants were often mysterious, silent people and the clergy of this busy London parish offered them what help they could without interference. The curate looked with surprise first at her, then at Father Casey, but no words were exchanged as she was shown into a warm room with a table set for breakfast.

'Do sit down,' Father Casey pointed to a chair beside the fire, 'and I'll ask the housekeeper to lay another place.'

Pippa did as she was told and sat as close as she could to the fire warming her hands. Bliss. It was a long time since she'd seen a gas fire and the heat penetrated her bones which sometimes seemed to crackle with cold.

While the priest was gone she took off her scarf and shook out her hair. She didn't dare look in the mirror hanging over the fireplace.

It was indeed years since she'd taken a good look at herself, but to her appearances never had been important. Still she was a little ashamed that Father Casey should see her like this.

Father Casey returned, followed by a jovial-looking woman whom Pippa also recognised. She often gave her food, and the woman acknowledged her but said nothing. She laid another place, the priest invited Pippa to join him at table and she sat down facing him, but did not attempt to smile.

There was grapefruit to start. Then the housekeeper brought in two plates of bacon and egg, fried tomato and sausage. There was a rack full of toast and a dish of golden butter. Finally she returned with a coffee pot and poured a cup which she put before Pippa, who spooned lots of sugar in it and drank thirstily.

Father Casey watched the colour return to her frozen cheeks and remembered what a pretty woman she had been—pretty and fey, very feminine, and youthful-looking for her age. Now she looked about seventy, and an old seventy at that. He still felt shocked by his discovery and he saw that Pippa was looking at him cautiously, as might a stray dog which, on being rescued from a home doesn't yet know whether it is for good or ill.

Father Casey indicated that she should eat, but he himself seemed to have lost his appetite. He was usually ravenous after early

240

Mass. Pippa, however, had no such inhibitions and quickly disposed of the food on her plate, scarcely pausing for breath. Then she looked up and saw the food on his plate had hardly been touched.

Father Casey shook his head. 'I'm not very hungry. I must say, Sister, I am very distressed at finding you in this condition.'

Pippa shrugged and kept her eye fixed on his plate. As if on cue he passed it towards her and she scooped the untouched bacon and sausage and fried tomatoes on to her own, and tucked in. As she ate the priest began to wonder if he was doing the right thing, if she was as ravenous, as undernourished, as she appeared to be. One heard that starving people shouldn't be given too much food initially, but introduced to it gradually. He saw that the dress she had on under her coat was meant for summer, pathetically thin, almost skimpy—a faded silk reach-me-down. He simply could not believe that this specimen of rag and bones was the happy, healthy woman he had known only three years before.

And who, perhaps, he had helped to bring to this stage.

Finally Pippa decided she couldn't eat any more and put down her knife and fork. When she looked at him she was, at last, smiling.

'That is the best food I have eaten in my entire life.'

'I'm glad then.' The priest lit a cigarette and

leaned towards her. 'I am taking a winter vacation helping out in the parish.'

'Not much of a vacation, Father.'

'I have a sister in a convent nearby and it enables me to see her and to go to some of the London shows.'

'I see.' Pippa didn't seem to be particularly curious.

'Sister Mary Frances, how have you come to this pass?'

Pippa gazed at him thoughtfully.

'I decided I couldn't face the nuns at the new convent they were sending me to. I saw two of them waiting for me on the platform at Waterloo and I simply took off. I didn't give any thought as to where I was going or what. That night I slept in the station. I never meant to make a life for myself on the streets. It just happened. The weather then was good. It was August and I stayed on the Embankment. At night, sometimes, I sheltered near the Savoy! I found that street people are very good-natured and supportive. They taught me how to survive. In return,' she looked serenely at the priest, 'I brought some of them to God. I believe that I have a vocation to be a beggar for God. Living as I do among these, as one of them, I can be more effective than someone dispensing help from a church or a van. Jesus said we should become like children, and I have.'

'Sister,' Father Casey spoke earnestly, 'I am

242

sure God did not mean you to lead the life of a street beggar.'

'But how do you *know*, Father? Who does know the ways of God?'

'Because you are a well-brought up, well-educated woman, a professed nun, an artist . . .' he trailed off remembering his part in her downfall. It was possible that Pippa didn't know this. Hopefully she didn't. Sooner or later someone would have told Sister Bernadette about Pippa's paintings. He was sorry he should have been the first. It had weighed on his conscience for three years. Sharing Pippa's simple faith he felt that, somehow, God had intended this chance meeting in an inner city church.

'I would never return to the Society of St Catherine, Father. I will never forget how they treated me, accusing me of carnal relations with one of my pupils. It was *monstrous*!'

The priest bit his lip. 'Oh I didn't know that.'

'Not in so many words. It was the implication. It was so untrue, so unjust. I couldn't face the community in Stepney. I'd nowhere else to go. My mother is dead, my brother lives abroad and I have no close relations. I think God meant me to discover Him through the street people and that this was His way of bringing it about. He does, indeed, move in mysterious ways.'

'But it is a very *dangerous* way of living.'

243

Father Casey extinguished his cigarette.

'No it is not. You'd be surprised how kind people are, how gentle.'

'Do they know you are a nun?'

'No,' she smiled, 'they think I am an eccentric bag lady; but they listen to me when I talk about Christ, not all of them, but some. Are we not told that God knows when a sparrow falls? I tell you it is true.'

'Sister Mary Frances, you do not look a well woman to me. I see that you walk with a limp, your legs are swollen and you are painfully thin. If you continue like this you may not be able to continue with your mission but will become a burden on society.

'Now listen. I have a suggestion to make. Please hear me out. I do not want you to return to the Society if you don't want to, but my sister who is a nun and lives nearby will find you a bed I'm sure. It is an enclosed order and you will be left alone to do as you wish. But you will have warmth, and the winter is already upon us, nourishing food and medical help which you need. When you are well again you can decide what you want to do. No pressure will be put on you. I will tell Sister Bernadette that you are safe, but not where.' He paused. 'It would have been kind of you to let her know what happened to you. I can't tell you how worried she's been.'

Pippa's expression was mulish. 'If I did not behave well, neither did Sister Bernadette.

244

Why should I think that she cared about me after what she said?'

'I'm sure she regrets saying it. You gave them all a very bad fright. Not a day passes but she and the rest of the community have wondered what happened to you. There will be much joy in heaven on the return of . . .' but he did not say it. Instead Pippa finished it for him.

'A sinner.'

'You are not a sinner, Sister. I think you are heroic. But I do think you need some time to recuperate and get back your strength. The nuns in my sister's convent will be good to you. I promise. Now what do you say to my suggestion?'

Pippa's expression remained mulish.

'I'll have to think about it,' she said. 'Think, and pray.'

\*       \*       \*

'Ladies and gentlemen, pray silence for his worship the mayor and the mayoress of Wolversleigh, Councillor and Mrs Thornton.'

There was a burst of applause as Andrew, in his red robes, the mayoral chain round his neck, walked into the room together with Clare. She wore a long gown and also had a mayoral chain, though not quite as splendid as Andrew's. The full regalia of his office suited him. Over the years he had filled out a little,

245

but not too much; he was almost completely bald, except for a tonsure, and with his sombre countenance and earnest expression, together with his mayoral dignity, he looked the capable and thoroughly respectable member of the community of which he was the chief citizen.

Like royalty, Andrew and Clare bowed to right and left as they slowly proceeded through the chamber of the town hall, gracefully acknowledging the crowd who parted for them, particularly people they knew, before they arranged themselves on the dais to receive guests. The occasion was a reception and dinner in aid of local charities among which was Clare's Catholic Women's Refuge, Amnesty International, OXFAM, UNICEF and a host of other good causes they both supported.

For the umpteenth time in Andrew's mayoral year they stood shaking hands as a stream of people from all walks of life—but mainly well-heeled—were presented.

'How do you do?'

'So glad you could come.'

'How *nice* to see you again.'

And so on and so forth. They oozed charm to the guests in order to milk them for money.

Clare's feet ached and, surreptitiously under her long evening gown, she eased off one of her shoes and rubbed her foot against her ankle. It was nearly the end of Andrew's mayoral year and very relieved she would be when it was over. It had been exhausting but, in its frenetic way, interesting, with trips abroad and an attendance at one of the Queen's garden parties at Buckingham Palace.

Lucy Wallace put her cheek up to be kissed. She was an old girl of St Catherine's, as were about half the women present. Clare could not help feeling proud that Andrew had made it as mayor and that his year had been such a success.

'What a lovely party,' Lucy said. 'Andrew has had *such* a good year.'

Clare smiled mechanically and eased her shoe back on her foot again as they were about to walk in to dinner.

'I can't say I'll be sorry when it's over. We never have a night at home.'

'I wish Jim would take up some local activity.' Lucy looked askance at her husband. 'Get him away from the golf club.'

'If it's not golf it's politics,' Clare laughed ruefully. 'I don't know which is worse.'

'But you, Clare, you're always *so* busy.'

'There's plenty to do. The thing is that, once you take something on, you're saddled with it for life. You wouldn't like to be secretary of the Old Girls' Association would you, Lucy? You'd do it awfully well.'

'Not a chance. Sorry. I've just taken on the treasureship of the golf club so that I can get to see Jim at least at week-ends.'

Lucy waved and slipped away and Clare

stared after her. Not a chance of anyone doing anything really helpful. Sometimes she just longed to get away from it all, simply disappear . . .

'Darling,' she cried as Pauline edged towards her, shyly clutching the hand of her new fiancé, James Morris. Mother and daughter embraced. James, having shaken hands with Andrew, kissed her on the cheek. A professional soldier, he looked very smart in his dress uniform. He was an engaging man, not particularly good-looking but solid and robust, a younger version of Andrew. But there was a snag; he wasn't a Catholic, and didn't wish to convert. Also, Pauline was only nineteen and her parents thought her rather young to consider such an important step. Apart from that, they liked everything about James as a prospective son-in-law. He was six years older than Pauline but already a captain. His future in the army looked good. But despite his undoubted attributes, he wasn't quite the husband Clare would have wished for her only daughter. Apart from not being a Catholic, there was the prospect that James would be sent abroad, and then she would have none of her brood at home.

In the line behind Pauline and James, Mark was chatting to a fellow accountant. Mark usually came alone to these dos. Even though Chrissy was still active with the refuge, she seldom attended mayoral functions.

Mark shook Andrew's hand and kissed Clare's cheek.

'Chrissy has a headache. She sends love.'

As Clare nodded her understanding, there was a roll of drums and the toast-master announced that dinner was being served. Andrew held out his arm and, together, they proceeded into the dining room where a string orchestra struck up airs from Schubert, and waiters and waitresses stood poised at the ready to dart among the tables as soon as the command was given.

Clare and Andrew took their places at the top table next to various dignitaries, and after the bishop said grace a babble of noise erupted among the guests.

Another mayoral function had begun.

\*     \*     \*

'I shan't say I'll be sorry when you're no longer mayor.' Clare kicked off her shoes and collapsed into a chair. It was nearly midnight. She looked across at Andrew who was pouring himself a whisky. 'We have no home life at all. Maybe we could go on a cruise, say for six months?'

Andrew turned and looked at her in surprise.

'Would you give up all your charities?'

'I must say I wouldn't mind. They could all function without me.'

'The question is, would they?' Andrew sat opposite her.

'They'd have to. I have been secretary of the Old Girls' Association for twenty years . . . I hoped Pauline would take over but . . . You never know, James might be sent abroad. Then there'll be no one.'

Clare gazed disconsolately at the carpet as the prospect of all those empty years opened up before her. At one time when she was newly-married she hoped the house would be full of children. Soon now there would be none. To her great sorrow it seemed pretty certain that Marcus would not return from Australia where he had found a job on a sheep farm. There he had no history and it suited him. Even if he had children they would grow up far away from Wolversleigh. And if Pauline went abroad . . . Much as she liked James she wished she had found a nice young man who was a Catholic and had a sensible nine-to-five job like Andrew. Whatever happened in later years it was a good start to married life.

The first five years of their marriage *had* been very happy, and indeed, on the whole, all things considered, given her breakdown and the need for abstinence . . . well, one made the best of life and now, perhaps, they could start enjoying more leisure time together.

Her reverie was broken by Andrew.

'Clare, darling . . .' He paused and downed some more whisky. 'We can still go away, have

250

a good holiday—perhaps not a cruise but . . . well, I have been asked to stand as leader of the council.'

'You wouldn't *dream* . . .' Clare began indignantly.

'It's a great honour and I'd like to. Of course I said I'd discuss it with you,' he finished lamely.

'But, Andrew, I don't know how you *could*. You have had years and years on the council. The mayoral year has been killing, even you complained of not enough time to yourself.'

'It won't be until next year when I've finished my term of office. But the Party needs me. They don't have any good, obvious candidates. Besides, I should enjoy it. I might even, who knows, eventually get a knighthood. Wouldn't you like to be Lady Thornton?'

'No.'

'Oh come, Clare.'

'No, I wouldn't. I wouldn't give a fig about being Lady Thornton if it meant nights on end going to boring social gatherings, chatting to tedious people. And let's face it, half the people in this town are tedious. I tell you, Andrew, I'm *sick* of public life and that's that.'

They had very little else to say after that. They were both tired and went to their rooms without even saying 'goodnight'.

Once in her room Clare took off her dress, removed her make-up, cleansed her face, popped her earrings in a tray on her dressing

251

table, all the time making a superhuman effort to try and calm down.

She went into the bathroom, cleaned her teeth, brushed her hair and, returning to her room lay on her bed.

She was forty-three, not old, but sometimes she felt old. Andrew was fifty-three, again not old. A good age, in fact, to take on more public duties.

The fact was that she was a tired and, sometimes she felt, a disappointed woman. In a way she had achieved a lot in life, and so had Andrew. She knew many people envied them. They lived in a nice house and there had never been any money worries. But there had been two real misfortunes in her life: her breakdown and Marcus's expulsion from school.

They had had such hopes for Marcus. He was a lovely, brilliant boy with a brain and now there seemed no chance of him going to university, of achieving the potential that could have been his. Andrew had hoped he would be a partner in the firm. Instead he was a hired hand on an Australian sheep farm, a dead end if ever there was one.

And why had Marcus really become a thief? No one could explain it, least of all the psychiatrist who had spent hours in therapy with him. Why had a boy from a good, Catholic home, wanting nothing and with everything to live for, started to steal? He said life was too perfect, too well ordered, too safe. But other boys in situations similar to his didn't steal. They went on to university and academic glory and became partners in their fathers' successful practices; doctors, or lawyers, accountants or whatever. They married local girls with backgrounds similar to their own and procreated children like them. What weak link was there in the Thornton family that produced such a disappointment as Marcus?

Nothing much had ever been expected of Pauline, dear, sweet girl. She would marry a nice man, have a few children—there would be surely no problems about contraception there, given that James wasn't a Catholic and Pauline certainly not a very devout one. Had she, Clare, sacrificed her marriage and happiness on the altar of obedience to some archaic laws formed by men in the Church with no experience of marriage themselves? Had she been unfair to Andrew? Was this what drove him to take on more work than he could cope with?

Had he, perhaps, a mistress? Someone else? She closed her eyes. The idea didn't bear thinking about. Besides he went devoutly to Holy Communion with her every Sunday and, surely, he couldn't do this in a state of mortal sin, which having a mistress would be. No. Andrew was too honest, too dignified, too afraid of Divine Wrath to attempt such a deception. Besides, she couldn't imagine Andrew with a mistress. She was sure he was incapable of such duplicity.

On the other hand, the way he threw himself into public affairs was surely indicative of *something*? They hardly ever had a holiday. They seldom discussed personal or intimate matters with each other. In fact, Clare wondered what she and Andrew had in common, besides the scale and extent of their voluntary work, the number of committees they were on, the organisations that looked to them for support. And what would they have to say to each other if they did go on holiday together? Could they survive three weeks, let alone six months? If she was honest she was aware that for a long time now there had been a very slow, almost imperceptible sense of growing apart.

They were no longer the people who had shared those first happy years of marriage together, full of promise and hope.

Clare got out of bed and on bended knees began to pray. 'Dear God let this chalice be lifted from me . . . Not my will, but Thine be done.'

She waited for a few moments but still the heaviness, the burden was there. There was no lightening of her load. In her life she had received much consolation from her faith; but, was it enough?

# CHAPTER ELEVEN

## JUNE 1991

On the whole Lewis Gould had a good life. He'd given up trying to be the great novelist of the twentieth century and concentrated instead on enjoying himself and, where he could, needling Eleanor to whom he owed practically all his comforts, and, indeed, his not insubstantial allowance. Every morning, after a leisurely breakfast, he would saunter along to one of the pubs in the area—The Steels in Haverstock Hill or The Washington in England's Lane—and read the paper over a pint or two of lager. He was most likely to encounter some cronies with whom he exchanged the time of day. They were mainly like himself: disappointed, disaffected members of a society which they felt, for one reason or another, owed them a living. They milked the benefits system for all they were worth while living in the comparative comfort of Swiss Cottage, Belsize Park or Hampstead. They would have a good natter about the deficiencies of the Government, the unfairness of the benefits system, their various ailments and the tragedies of others, and then disperse.

Sometimes Lewis ate at the pub—a ploughman's or a pork pie, with another pint of lager. Sometimes he went home and made a sandwich or ate bacon and egg accompanied by a whisky or two. Then he lolled in front of the TV, or in the garden if it was warm, and had a nap.

Later he might go for a walk on Hampstead Heath or in Regent's Park, or just stroll around the streets where he liked to imagine he was observing human nature for a possible novel that he was always working on in his head, though he seldom put pen to paper or, more accurately, sat down in front of his typewriter.

Occasionally he sortied into Soho for a drink at the Groucho if he could find anyone to buy him one, though he was never short of money. He had no agent and no publisher, so the literary world was almost closed to him, though he still had a fcw literary friends, mostly in the same situation as himself, and they would rail against the iniquities of publishers and the greed and arrogance of agents and bemoan the good times that were no more.

When the pubs opened in the evening he'd have a few more drinks, then go home for another night of baiting Eleanor for her undeserved success which she owed entirely to him.

Lewis had had one of his usual vaguely pleasant idle days doing nothing much, drinking a few lagers, walking on the Heath, going to Hampstead High Street to get a new strap for his watch. As he got home at about seven after calling in at the pub, the telephone was ringing.

It would be Eleanor to say she was late again, and he'd give her a blast just to get it off his chest though he didn't really care except that his meal would be late. It would never have occurred to him to get it himself. No, Eleanor would rush in, apologise for being late, throw things on the kitchen table and set to, producing something delicious in the time it took Lewis to have a couple of whiskies and watch the evening news on TV.

'Yes?' he barked.

Silence. Then: 'Is that Eleanor Hamilton's residence?'

'It is.'

'Oh!' Pause again. 'Is she there?'

'No.' Lewis did his best to be discourteous to Eleanor's friends to discourage them from ringing again.

'Do you know when she'll be back?'

'No.'

'I see.' The voice sounded exasperated, which was the intended effect. 'I'll call again.'

The caller, a man, replaced the phone and Lewis, feeling pleased with himself, turned on the TV.

Eleanor's programme. He had clean forgotten about it and, of course, that was why she was late. It went out on a Tuesday, live at seven-thirty.

The subject was Yugoslavia and the very real risk of civil war. Slovenia and Croatia had both declared independence and Serbia, determined to prevent the break-up of the country, had sent warplanes to attack Slovenia.

'Shoot the bastards down,' Lewis muttered as some graphic newsreel footage of bombs falling from the air interrupted the discussion. Eleanor sat at a table surrounded by people who were mortal enemies: Slovenians, Croats and Serbs, glaring at one another, and two international journalists who favoured one side or the other. With her usual skill Eleanor did her best to be neutral and tried to steer the discussion along productive lines. It was a near impossible task. At one time it nearly turned to violence as the Serb lunged for the Croat who was accusing his country of genocide.

Eleanor did a creditable job, cool, knowledgeable, above all, the charm. That and good dressing, always. You had to admire her. Lewis sat back and stared at her, feeling, despite himself, some pride. He had really made her what she was. But for him she would be a provincial hack in Southend. One could say that he had given her a leg up and she had done the rest but . . . well, the leg up was the all important thing.

*And* he had made her pay for it.

The fact was that Eleanor was one of those women who hadn't quite jettisoned their old

258

innate suspicion that the male was, indeed, a superior being, or abandoned their age-old habit of subservience, despite their undoubted abilities, their capacity to handle high-powered, well-paid jobs, their independence of mind. It was as though men were half-gods and half-children and, whichever it was, they had to be looked after, cared for, their food cooked, their clothes washed and ironed. It was the very helplessness of men that, paradoxically, made them such powerful creatures.

Eleanor was forty-five, a dangerous age, on the brink of the menopause, worried about her figure, her looks, her capacity to keep her job. That self-confidence, so finely honed by her mid-thirties, had blunted a little, which was understandable given the modern emphasis on youth and youthful achievements. Maybe she'd overdone the blonde streaks in her hair. She drank, perhaps a bit more than she should and lived on her nerves, yet she was superb at her job. She wrote her weekly column, she presented this tough current affairs programme, took part in late-night shows and was generally highly thought of and numbered among the great and good.

She was also a terrific cook and, despite their general lack of rapport, good in bed. She enjoyed sex, and in fact this was the one true moment when they seemed to come together, to fuse, metaphorically as well as literally.

It was a bond that united them, one that would be hard to break.

Lewis supposed he loved her, or was it simply that he needed her? He would certainly be lost without her.

'Thank you, everybody, for watching and goodnight.' Eleanor, her smile a little forced, and her aggressive companions faded from the screen as the credits rolled.

Lewis got himself another drink and opened the *Evening Standard* while waiting for her to come home and get his supper.

But that night was not quite as other nights. Eleanor arrived in a temper, banged the door shut behind her, scowled at Lewis, who was refreshing his glass with ice from the fridge, and threw her shopping down on the kitchen table.

'You're terribly late,' he snarled, looking at the clock on the wall. 'I'm hungry.'

'Then *why* didn't you get your dinner yourself?' Hands on hips she glared at him. 'Really, Lewis, you are *so* bloody lazy.'

'I was watching your programme, my darling,' his voice heavy with sarcasm, 'wondering which of those dagos would biff you first.'

'Please *don't* use that word, Lewis. It's horrible.'

'But it's true. Look at them, all fighting one another. They're all bloody savages. I'd bang their heads together.'

260

'Please, Lewis. I have had quite enough for today. In fact a fight did break out in the studio after the programme and some damage was done. The producer didn't want to call the police but there is going to be an enquiry. People might say I should have foreseen and prevented it, that I can't handle my job.'

'Oh, that's ridiculous. What's for dinner?'

Eleanor had a stiff gin, ordered Lewis out of the kitchen, where he always got in the way, and in a quarter of an hour had produced a prawn mousse starter from Marks and Spencer, two nicely grilled sirloin steaks and a green salad tossed in a home-made vinaigrette.

She called Lewis back into the kitchen and they began their meal in silence. Lewis opened a bottle of red wine and poured.

'Sorry about your bad day.'

'That's OK. Sorry I was in a temper.'

'You don't *seriously* think your job is on the line?'

'Well not seriously,' she broke into a fresh bread roll. 'But you never know. If they think I can't handle it.'

'*I* thought you handled it very well. A less skilled interviewer would have blasted them all to hell.'

'Frankly, that's what I felt like doing. I never dreamed it would be so explosive. Sorry again.' She smiled placatingly at him. Always trying to placate Lewis, gain his favour, his approval . . . Contemptible, weak of her she knew, but there it was. Modern woman she might be, but that was only theory. She didn't know that younger women fared much better.

She really couldn't fathom the hold Lewis had over her or why, unless it was guilt. Guilt that she was successful and he wasn't. Pity too. Guilt and pity were such an awful combination. She guessed she and Lewis were bound together for life. She had the money, she paid the mortgage and bought the food, paid for the holidays, saw he was well-dressed and shod. What state benefits he got he spent on visits to the pub. It was pitifully small anyway, barely enough to keep a man in a week's supply of booze.

You couldn't chuck anybody out into the street who was so dependent on you, even if you no longer felt you loved them. There had been other men who wanted her; but there was always Lewis. And as long as there was Lewis she said 'no'.

Eleanor rose and began to stack the dishes into the dishwasher. She would be glad of an early night.

'Oh by the way, some bloke rang you.' Lewis sounded deliberately offhand, which was normal. She turned.

'Oh? Who?'

'Didn't leave a name. Said he'd ring later. One of your admirers I guess.'

'I haven't any admirers.'

'That's what you say.'

'Would you blame me if I had?'

'I don't see what you're complaining about, Eleanor. I got you the job in the first place.'

'*And* don't I know it.'

They were interrupted by the persistent buzz of the phone.

'That will be him again. I'll get it.' Lewis made for the door.

'No,' she said, walking past him. 'I'll get it. I know how off-putting you can be and if it's something to do with work it makes a bad impression. Hello?' she said, putting her ear to the receiver.

Pause. Someone trying to speak. Maybe one of those calls. She was ex-directory but somehow people managed to find her number.

'Is that Eleanor Hamilton?'

'Yes.'

'This is Simon.'

'Simon who?' Polite, detached.

'Don't you have a son called Simon?'

Eleanor dropped the phone, it dangled on the end of the wire backwards and forwards like a pendulum. She picked it up quickly.

'Simon . . . are you still there?'

'Yes.'

'I had a shock. I'm sorry. I dropped the phone.'

'That's OK. I didn't quite know how to contact you, whether to write . . .'

'It's quite OK. I mean really . . .'

'Was that your husband?'

263

'Sort of.'

'Would you like to meet up?'

'Of course I would. Simon, you may not believe this but I have thought of you every day since . . .'

'Since you gave me away,' he said, not bitterly, matter-of-factly.

'Had to,' she murmured. 'Please believe it. You don't know how much I long to see you.'

They arranged to meet next day at the Arts Club in Albemarle Street.

'Don't be late.'

'I won't.'

She stood for a long time by the phone, head bowed in thought, almost paralysed by the powerful, overwhelming nature of her emotions.

After a while Lewis called from the sitting room.

'Who was it?'

Eleanor walked slowly into the room.

'Simon.'

'Who is Simon?'

'My son.'

'Your *son*?' Lewis put down the paper and looked at her with incredulity.

'Simon, the baby I had.'

'Go on, I don't believe it. Someone's having you on.'

'Why should someone have me on?'

'Well it seems funny to me after all these years. Why should he try and find you now?'

'Maybe he is curious.'

'More like he wants money.'

'Maybe.' She sat opposite Lewis and looked at him. 'Why are you so nasty, Lewis?'

'I'm not nasty, I'm just trying to protect you. I think it very peculiar that a man rings out of the blue and claims he is your son.'

'If he is will you be pleased for me?'

'Not particularly. You've never wanted to see him before.'

'I have, always.'

'Well you never mentioned that to me.'

'Maybe I thought you wouldn't understand.'

Lewis sniffed unbelievingly.

'Besides, I gave him another life. Anyway it is up to the child to find the parent. I don't think you can do it the other way round. I wouldn't have had the nerve. The authorities don't make it too easy. I signed away my rights when I gave him up for adoption.'

'I always thought the adoption authorities had to get in touch with you first,' Lewis said. 'If you ask me he's an imposter. He's seen you on the telly and he's trying it on. He's probably on the sponge.'

Eleanor looked at him witheringly but resisted the obvious retort. Instead she said: 'Besides, how would he know about Simon?'

Unusually for Lewis he had no answer.

\*     \*     \*

He didn't look at all like Ted. In fact Eleanor thought he looked a lot like her. He had been born nearly twenty-four years ago and then she had only known him for a week. Now here he was sitting opposite her and they were both looking at each other rather warily, a little timid, a bit afraid. There was a lot to be afraid about: all those years they had spent away from each other, mother and son. They were meeting like strangers yet between them there was an essential bond.

He had a frank, open face, her colour eyes, her hair. She would have said he was good-looking. Like her, he was tall. He had nice teeth, hers were so so. He wore jeans and a blue shirt, he looked tanned as though he'd lived abroad or spent much time in the sun. They'd greeted each other shyly, recognising each other immediately. He told her that he'd seen her on the television and his instant recognition of her, the way he came towards her in the vestibule, helped her to know who he was.

Simon, her son.

'Such a lot to talk about,' she said. She could hardly take her eyes off him. They had been given a table by the garden and the place was full, so no one took much notice of them. Just another man and another woman in a crowded room. 'What made you get in touch?'

'A strong desire to know who my mother and father were.' He looked at her directly.

266

'Who was my father?'

'He was called Ted. Ted McGuinness. I mean he *is* called Ted. I've no reason to think he's dead. He was a journalist, my boss. He was married and I was only twenty when I became pregnant. Not deliberately, out of ignorance.' She lowered her eyes. 'At the time, I felt terribly ashamed of what I'd done.'

'You had no need to be.' His voice was curiously tender. 'You could have had an abortion.'

Eleanor shook her head.

'No I couldn't. I was a Catholic. An abortion was quite out of the question but,' she raised her head again, 'I did think the very best thing for you was to have you adopted. To give you a start in life. My parents knew nothing about the pregnancy. I was twenty-one when you were born. It seemed at the time out of the question. Today it wouldn't be so difficult. But in 1967 it was a very different matter.'

Simon gazed thoughtfully at the tablecloth. 'But did you *want* to keep me, I mean, if it had been possible?'

'Oh yes. Yes. With all my heart, and I never ceased to regret what I did. I always felt, had I tried, I could have got round it. Not a day has gone by, as I told you, but I thought of you, and when I heard your voice . . . I nearly fainted. I dropped the phone!'

'And what about Ted in all this?' His tone was laconic.

267

'Well, as I said, Ted was married. He had four children and he didn't want to know. I came to London and did temporary work. I'm not very proud of what happened.'

'Why shouldn't you be? It must have been very hard for you,' Simon said, and his hand closed over hers.

*       *       *

They ate very little, Eleanor scarcely noticed what was on her plate, and then they walked out into Albemarle Street and, still talking, wandered across Piccadilly, down Lower Regent Street and into St James's Park. It was a beautiful day and they sat by the pond watching the birds. Eleanor knew she would never forget that day, every precious minute, when she at last found her son. He could have been bitter, but he wasn't. Why?

'And what about you?' she asked him at last. He waited for a long time before replying, gazing into the water as if carefully choosing his words. He was rather a solemn young man, rather sad. She knew that, besides loving him, she liked him as an individual.

Simon flung his arm over the back of the bench on which they were sitting.

'My adoptive parents never really accepted me. I don't know why they adopted me in the first place. They were called Hastings.' He looked at Eleanor. 'I was given the name

Michael. That is my name: Michael Hastings. My mother, who was told she would never have children, then had a child of her own when I was six. I think it unsettled me and I became a very naughty boy. When I was eleven they put me in care.'

'Oh *Simon*!' Eleanor clasped his hand. 'I was told they were such good, caring people.'

'Well they weren't. I'm completely out of touch with them now. You see,' he looked at her earnestly, 'I never really felt I was loved by anyone, and then when it became possible to trace one's parents I decided to try and find mine.

'When I did find you and discovered that you were a celebrity I felt I had so little to offer you, that you might be ashamed of me. I've watched your programmes, read your column trying to get to know you. I have been a failure . . . Mother . . . Eleanor . . . I don't quite know what to call you.'

'"Mother" sounds nice, but give it time,' Eleanor said soothingly. 'I'm devastated to hear about the Hastings couple. It makes me feel more guilty than ever.'

'It wasn't *your* fault. It was mine. I was a silly bugger. I came back home eventually. My "sister" was very nice. Very practical, still is. She's called Mandy and we keep in touch. She urged me to try and find you. She knew quite well that my adoptive mother couldn't give me any affection, and didn't, in fact, give her much. I went to the agency that helps you trace your parents. When they identified you they were supposed to contact you; but I wasn't sure it was what I wanted. I said I'd think about it. I did think about it for a long time. Years.'

'*Years!*' Eleanor gasped.

'About three years, plucking up courage. It was a big step. You might have rejected me too. I got your telephone number through your programme.'

'They're not supposed to give our private numbers, but I'm glad they did.'

'I told them I was your son. I don't think they believed anyone would make that up.'

'What did Mr Hastings do?'

'He was a store manager. A senior position with one of the big multiples. Had a very good job. Nice house in Eastbourne. He was alright, actually, but he was a cold fish too.'

'So what have you done?'

'I wanted to go on the stage, but I had no qualifications. I got two O levels. Couldn't get to drama school. I thought I might get in through the back door, stage management, and sometimes I get jobs, but mostly I'm on benefit. Not much to be proud of, I'm afraid.'

It did sound depressingly a bit like Lewis, but Eleanor hurriedly put the idea out of her mind. Simon was only twenty-three and he was her flesh and blood. That was the difference.

Now she would help him all she could to

make up for the mistake she'd made, the act of rejection twenty-three years before.

*       *       *

*October 1991*

'Please come this way,' the nun who opened the door told Clare. 'Sister Mary Frances is expecting you.'

Clare stepped inside the dark corridor of the convent in central London and, even when the door was shut, the noises from the busy road outside seemed obtrusive.

It reminded her of the early days of St Catherine's when she and Pippa were both schoolgirls, so many years ago.

The polished parquet floors, the lamps burning in front of the religious statues in alcoves along the walls, the mystery. But above all the silence here in this enclosed Order of nuns was very different from the noisy hustle of girls at St Catherine's, taking care not to be seen sliding along the floor.

The nun showed Clare into a parlour not unlike the one at St Catherine's. It faced on to a pleasant lawn with trees, though this was bounded by a high wall and not a beautiful meadow leading down to a lake.

Pippa was waiting for Clare by the open door and flung her arms around her. The two women clung together while the sister portress

271

discreetly shut the door, leaving them alone. They gazed at each other for a long time, hugged again, then Pippa led Clare to a chair and sat opposite her, pulling her seat up so that they were close, knees almost touching.

'It is so *good* to see you.'

'And you.' Clare reached out to squeeze her hand. Pippa's appearance rather shocked her. She knew her to be her age—forty-five, but she looked well over sixty. Her face was wrinkled and worn and her hair was almost snow white.

'You look so well, Clare . . .' Pippa hesitated as she saw Clare's expression. 'I know you can't say the same about me.'

'Well . . .' Clare groped for words. Clare, as usual for her trips to the Metropolis, was smartly turned out in a woollen dress, belted, and with a polo neck over which she wore a beige cashmere coat. She had on high brown calf boots and carried a matching bag. Her dark curls were stylishly cut, only flecked a little with white, and her make-up, carefully applied, concealed what tiny facial blemishes, what minute lines and wrinkles she might have had. She wore large gold earrings which seemed to add just the right finishing touch to her ensemble. The impression was of a wealthy attractive woman in her middle years.

Pippa held up a hand as if divining Clare's dilemma, her slowness to respond.

'I know I know, don't say it. I was extremely

ill after they brought me here. Do you know I had a shadow on my lungs, the beginnings of TB, a disease I thought they'd eliminated? The nuns were very good and after I had a spell in hospital they took me home—I think of it as home—and nursed me. Believe me, if you'd seen me a year ago you would never have expected me to survive. You know I spent several years on the streets. It did me no good at all, except in a spiritual sense.'

'How do you mean "spiritual"?' Clare frowned.

'It drew me close to God and enabled me to bring souls to Him. I learned a lot about human nature. I was very ignorant. Years spent in convents for the education of well brought up young ladies is a poor preparation for life.

'I realise now I was living a ridiculous life. I was spoiled, I was capricious, I could do as I liked. I lived a life of ease—painting, mixing with interesting, cultured people. I was not really a nun at all, not Christ-like. *He* brought me back to reality.'

'What happened?' Clare asked gently.

Pippa left out nothing and told her the story of Maria Tardini and the paintings.

'Of course I see how stupid and naïve it was now,' she finished. 'I mean, I knew nothing about homosexuality. To be accused of intimacy with a pupil was horrifying, degrading. To me she was a beautiful subject, as she would have been to any other artist. But

273

I was naïve and I was punished.'

Pippa sat back and sighed. She wore a black dress with black stockings, black shoes and a black half veil. The nun who had let Clare in wore the graceful, old fashioned habit of the Order, and this was not it.

'I was punished, but I was also rewarded. I was rewarded by the people I met on the streets. When I left I missed them, but I would have died had Father Casey not found me. My legs were ulcerated, and my lungs hardly functioned. They had to remove half of a lung through disease. I have spent nearly two years now among these good nuns and I owe them my life.'

She looked searchingly at her old friend.

'And you, Clare, what of you? Did life turn out well for you? I remember that splendid wedding. How is Andrew?' Her expression was kindly, head on one side, and Clare knew it would be difficult, if not impossible, to tell this saintly woman who, despite what she said about her experience on the streets, was still not quite of this world, how a happy marriage could deteriorate into routine where one partner went one way and the other another.

'Andrew is well,' she said brightly. 'He is now leader of the council. Tory of course. He was a strong supporter of Margaret Thatcher. Shattered by what happened to her. We all were.'

Pippa gave her a vague smile as if she hadn't

the slightest notion of what she was talking about.

'We don't see television or read the papers here I'm afraid, but I do know there is a new Prime Minister. We see *The Catholic Herald* from time to time, but, as you know, it is largely about religious matters.'

'I . . . I keep very busy. There are so many voluntary causes I support and guess *what*?' She leaned forward and put a hand on Pippa's knee. 'I am *still* the Secretary of the Old Girls' Association! I've been trying to give it up for nearly *twenty-five* years.'

'They'll give you a medal.' Pippa suddenly laughed and Clare had an acute vision of the sixteen-year-old lying in the long grass on a summer's day sketching away: dreamy, gentle, other-worldly Pippa. It was almost impossible to imagine what her life on the streets must have been like. No wonder she hardly survived it. In a way she was a religious crank; but in the modern world wasn't holiness a little crazy?

'My daughter Pauline is married. We like her husband James. He's a soldier. Unfortunately he isn't a Catholic, but they're happy, a baby on the way. Unfortunately, too, he's being sent abroad, probably to Germany, not too far and not, thank God, Northern Ireland, but it will be a wrench. He expects to be stationed there for about five years. Marcus, well,' Clare lowered her eyes, 'a *little* disappointing. He didn't quite fulfil the

275

promise he showed at school, and works on a sheep farm in Australia. I don't think he'll ever come back to this country.'

'You must go and see him,' Pippa said encouragingly.

'Oh yes we will. One day we will, when Andrew is less busy. He may well resign one of these days. He doesn't like John Major and would have preferred Heseltine, even though he helped get rid of Thatcher . . .' She stopped, realising that again Pippa was not quite with it. She wondered if John Major's name ever appeared in *The Catholic Herald*?

'It's just Andrew and me really,' Clare said with a downward turn of her mouth. 'Rather sad when you think that we wanted a large family.'

For a moment the women looked at each other, aware of so much that had, in a short time, to be left unsaid.

'I don't suppose you can come out for tea?' she enquired of Pippa. 'Or can you?'

Pippa shook her head.

'I can, but I won't. You see, my dear, Clare, I have decided to enter the Order. There has been a dispensation from Rome releasing me from my vows as a nun of St Catherine's Society. I am officially a lay person now, but I am to enter one of our remoter houses in central Wales in a few months' time. We choose a house for life and never leave it. We are not moved around. This one's very beautiful in the Welsh mountains. I shall feel very close to God.' At that moment she looked joyful like a bride: the bride of Christ.

'I am drawn to the contemplative way of life. The Order is devoted to perpetual veneration of the Blessed Sacrament. We do not go out in the world, we maintain strict silence, we fast and we pray ceaselessly for the salvation of souls. For a time my health was an issue before they would accept me. Was I strong enough for the rigours and discipline of the strict monastic life? I think I am. I hope I am. I think now that after many a misdirection God has guided me finally into my real destiny which is to remain shut away from the world and to pray, pray.

'At last I have found my true vocation, a life of silence.'

'And your painting?'

Pippa shook her head.

'Oh, don't talk of that! It was nearly my downfall. I was too vain. The Devil, I'm sure tempting me. I never touch palette and paint and never will again. All that is quite behind me.'

'Don't you miss it?'

'I regard it as a sacrifice for the love of God. We are, after all, told to put aside all earthly things and follow Him.' She looked rather briskly at the clock on the mantelpiece in the small, sparsely furnished room. 'I think it is time for you to go, my dear . . . by the way, do

277

you ever hear from Eleanor?'

Clare shook her head. 'She has become a celebrity.'

'Oh really?' Pippa only looked vaguely interested.

'She's very famous, a very controversial journalist on television and in *The Examiner* newspaper. Always has something interesting, challenging and acerbic to say.'

'Dear me.' Pippa seemed bewildered. 'And you're not in touch?'

Again Clare shook her head.

'I should imagine she's abandoned the faith by now,' Pippa said sadly. 'I never felt it was very strong, but I remember her every day in my prayers.' She rose and looked fondly down at her old school friend. 'And you, dear Clare. I remember you and your family and I always will, for God knows it is possible, even likely, that we shall never see each other again.'

Gently she took Clare's arm and led her through the door, along the gleaming corridor where the lamps burned before the statues of Our Lady, St Joseph and the Sacred Heart.

Clare paused, once again absorbing the atmosphere, feeling it under her skin. There was nothing quite like it; the smell of polish and burning candlewax, the guttering lights on the plaster faces of the statues.

She embraced Pippa, pressed her hand and watched her as she turned away, to disappear, possibly forever, into that great silence which she had chosen or which, perhaps, had chosen her.

Clare had a curious feeling of emptiness and loneliness, almost of disorientation as she stepped out once again on to the busy street, knowing that, indeed, she probably never would see Pippa again.

Nevertheless as she hailed a cab en route for a shopping spree in Knightsbridge she was very glad that God had not called her to the religious life.

# CHAPTER TWELVE

## JANUARY 1992

Eleanor remained very still in bed. She didn't like to think that Simon could hear them making love. Lewis lay beside her, panting. She wished he'd do so more quietly. He'd made a terrible racket when he came. She felt as stiff as a board. She hadn't had an orgasm, but it was very easy to fake, at least she thought it was.

Maybe Lewis realised that it was all up between them. Forcing yourself to have sex with a man you didn't love, scarcely liked, wasn't much fun. It was a huge effort. But it had become a habit, as was everything else about their life together. Then Simon came to live with them and everything changed.

After a while the panting subsided and Lewis lay still. A moment later he said: 'What's the matter?'

'Nothing,' Eleanor replied.

'Go on, you haven't come for ages. You just pretend.' He turned on to his back, sighing deeply. 'I wish you'd get that bloke out of the house, he's spoilt our life together.'

'We never had much of a life, not for years.'

'Oh that's not true, Eleanor.' He looked at her sharply. 'We had a good life, until that bastard arrived.'

'*Please* don't use that word, Lewis.'

'But it's true, isn't it? If he is your son—I say a very big "if"—then he is a bastard. You weren't married.' Lewis gazed at the ceiling. 'Frankly, I'm not even sure he's your son.'

'Of course he's my son!'

'Did you see the birth certificate?'

'No.'

'Did you ask to see it?'

'No. How stupid can you get?'

'Very, by all accounts.'

'But no matter how stupid you think *I* am the adoption authorities will have seen it. *They're* not stupid and they'd hardly put him on to me if I wasn't his real mother.'

'Just the same, I think it's all made up.' Getting into his stride, Lewis sat up in bed and lit a cigarette. 'He saw you on the telly. He was on his beam ends. He thinks: "She looks wealthy, looks like a sucker". He gets your number and within weeks he has moved into the house. Clever bugger.

'From that moment on you cared more about him than me, and we've been together twenty years.'

'You forget you never wanted to marry or have children. You can only blame yourself if it's all gone wrong.'

'Eleanor, I don't think it has gone wrong. I think we were happy, are happy.'

'I'll get the certificate.' Eleanor had a

281

sinking feeling in her heart. 'Then will you feel satisfied?'

'What if he isn't?'

Eleanor didn't reply, but lay thinking. What if he wasn't? But she knew in her bones that he was.

\*　　　　\*　　　　\*

Simon was very good in the house, domesticated, self-effacing, tidy, all the things Lewis wasn't. Lewis made as much mess as he could for Simon to clear up, but Simon did it willingly. He was also a good cook and spared his mother the chore of getting a meal every night.

That Simon felt contempt for Lewis was beyond doubt, but he tried not to show it.

He wanted very much for Eleanor to approve of him, to deserve her love. They called him Simon though he always felt he was Michael. It took some time to get used to the name. He was still Michael Hastings inside, but he wanted to please Eleanor.

Lewis resented Simon. Lewis hated him. He often felt murder in his heart for this person who had interrupted his easy style of life. He really believed he could have run him over, pushed him down the stairs, if he had the chance, as long as no one saw.

\*　　　　\*　　　　\*

After Eleanor had gone to work Lewis had a bath, shaved, dressed with his usual care and went downstairs to find Simon busy emptying the dishwasher from the night before.

'Morning, Lewis,' he said cheerfully. Lewis didn't reply but stared at the table.

'Where's my breakfast?'

'Coming up,' Simon said. 'Mum just had cornflakes.'

'I don't know why you have to call her "mum", a man of your age.'

'She likes it and I like it.' Simon re-laid the breakfast table and put a bowl of cornflakes in front of Lewis. 'I've never had a proper mother.'

'If she is your mother I wonder you don't resent her.'

'What do you mean: "If she is my mother"?'

'Personally I've got doubts. I think you're on the make, young man, on the scrounge. I think you saw her on the telly and . . .'

Simon very deliberately broke an egg into the frying pan and felt as though he would like to crack it over Lewis's head. 'I've got my birth certificate upstairs if you'd like to see it.'

Lewis looked surprised.

'Do you carry it around with you?'

'No, but it's very precious. I can show it to you now.' He took the frying pan off the ring and went upstairs where he opened a drawer in which he kept the few things that were

283

important to him. One of them was the certified copy of his birth certificate, registered in St Pancras in the London Borough of Camden on the 21 August 1967. The father was given as Edward McGuinness, occupation journalist, and the mother Eleanor Hamilton, occupation not required.

Simon ran down the stairs and thrust the document into Lewis's hands. Lewis, a cynical expression on his face, studied it.

'I see,' he said, flinging it down. 'You better show it to Eleanor.'

'Why? Surely she doesn't doubt I'm her son?'

'Well,' Lewis scratched his head. 'It's been very nice and cushy for you here, after a life in the sticks.'

'I was not in the sticks. Mother . . . Eleanor asked me to move in. You know she did. And I am actively looking for work.'

'I thought you were going to try and go to college?'

'Yes, after I've taken some O levels.'

'And your "mother" will have to pay?'

'I hope I'll get a grant.'

'You "hope".'

Simon tried to ignore what he knew was a deliberate attempt to inflame him. He finished frying Lewis's bacon and egg and handed his plate to him.

'You can make your own toast and coffee,' he said. 'Frankly, I'm fed up with you.'

'And *I'm* fed up with you,' Lewis roared, dying for the chance to let off steam. 'Eleanor and I were very happy until you put your nose through the door. You have completely unsettled us. You have unsettled Eleanor. She's very nervy, edgy. Frankly I don't know why you wanted to find her. She gave you away, didn't she? Didn't want you. Had you adopted and, apparently, it wasn't a great success. You have not had a very happy life, you poor bugger, and you have her to thank for it. I wonder you don't hate her, or maybe you do and you just feel that she owes you and you will take all you can get from her. You'll probably bleed her for the rest of her life.'

*　　　*　　　*

Eleanor got home earlier than usual because she wanted to change for an evening function. She was astonished to find luggage in the hallway, and then Simon appeared at the top of the stairs, a rucksack slung over his shoulders.

'Where . . . what on earth?' She sank on to one of the bags.

'I'm going, Eleanor.'

*'Going?'*

'I can't stand it here any more with Lewis. I could have killed him this morning. I had visions of hitting him over the head with the frying pan as I was cooking his breakfast. It

285

was awful.'

Eleanor rose slowly from the suitcase and went across to Simon who had reached the bottom of the staircase. She put her arms around him, hugging him very tightly.

'I don't want you to go.'

'I simply can't stand Lewis. He baits me at every opportunity. He was implying this morning that I wasn't your son, so I showed him my birth certificate.'

'Oh!' Relief flooded her heart. 'You have it?'

'Of course, and I wonder you never asked to see it.'

'I knew you were my son.' She tucked her arm through his and they strolled together into the sitting room. 'I didn't need a certificate.' She sat down on the sofa, pulling Simon down next to her.

'I am not in love with Lewis and haven't been for a very long time.'

'He said that you were both very happy until I came.'

'It's not true. *He* might have been happy, but he has a very nice life. No reason why he shouldn't be.'

'I thought he treated you abominably, but I didn't like to say anything. I mean,' Simon coloured slightly, 'I know you . . . sleep with him.'

'Yes, I think the neighbours also know about it too. He likes to broadcast his virility to all and sundry. Maybe it makes him feel big. But you don't have to love someone to make love to them, and for a very long time now this aspect has become mechanical. It is also very one-sided.'

Simon looked embarrassed. 'I'm sorry I mentioned it.'

'No, I'm glad you did. It clears the air. I want you to know the truth.'

'I really can't think how you stayed with him so long. He's awful. He's lazy, he's rude and he drinks too much. He drinks practically all day, never horribly drunk, just keeping himself topped up, and then he comes back and expects you to cook him dinner.'

'I can't throw him out.' Eleanor agitatedly twisted her hands in her lap. 'He's so dependent on me.'

'But *why* did you let him get like this?'

'It happened. When we first met it was the other way round. He was a successful writer and I was a not very successful provincial journalist. He was a very attractive man and I loved him. For a time we were very happy.

'Through Lewis I got a job on *The Examiner* and some years after that Lewis's publishers told him they could no longer publish his books. He then went into a steep decline. It was inevitable I suppose. It was a shattering blow to his pride. By that time I was becoming more and more successful. I tried to hide it, or at least share it with Lewis, but his bitterness increased. Even today he reminds me that I got the job on *The Examiner* through him.'

She put her hand on Simon's knee. 'Lewis is a very sad, almost tragic figure. I want you to remember that. Now that he knows you really are my son maybe he will stop baiting both of us, and we can get on with our lives.

'As for the other thing you mention, sex, I did intend for us to have separate bedrooms. I've meant to do that for some time and I have made it clear to Lewis how I feel.'

'He'll hate me even more.' Simon gnawed a fingernail. 'Mum, I do think I should find some accommodation elsewhere . . .'

'It's *ridiculous* when we have this great big house.'

'He'll always find something to goad me about. This morning he said he wondered I didn't hate you because you had me adopted.'

'He is a shit,' Eleanor said with some violence. 'A real, complete shit.'

*     *     *

Matthew Clements was a fashionable and stylish producer of some of the best plays in the West End. As Eleanor knew everybody who was anybody, and not just in the political world, naturally she knew Matthew. They'd worked together on a programme on government funding of the arts, and kept on meeting at parties.

Now she sat facing him across a table at The Ivy, a favourite eating place in Covent Garden. For a while they discussed generalities including the possibilities of an election later in the year. Could John Major, who had had a difficult time with Thatcher's cronies, make it on his own?

Matthew thought he could. Eleanor was not so sure.

They ordered lunch, stuck to mineral water, as was the fashion these days, and then Eleanor said: 'Matthew, apart from the pleasure of seeing you, I have asked you here for a specific purpose.'

'Oh?' Matthew, urbane, slim, elegant, a lover of men rather than women, looked at her curiously.

'I'd like you to help my son.'

Matthew appeared surprised. 'I didn't know you had a son, Eleanor.'

'Well I have. I had him adopted when he was a baby. I won't go into all that because it was a tragic period in my life. I was very young and it was not at all what I wanted.'

'I'm sure,' Matthew murmured sympathetically.

'Anyway, about six months ago he contacted me, and I love him.' She beamed widely at her guest, who said:

'I can see that. You are like a woman in love. I wondered who it was, but didn't suspect a son.'

'He is such a nice person. I don't deserve him. But he has had rather a hard life and only got two O levels. He loves the stage and has worked in stage management and done some acting . . .'

Matthew knew what was coming and spread his fingers deprecatingly. 'Eleanor, I can't really . . .' he demurred, realising, not for the first time, that there was no such thing as a free lunch.

'I'm not asking you to put him in a play or give him a job. I just want to know if he has talent, and if he has I'm prepared to pay for him to go to drama school. If he hasn't we should tell him and I'll persuade him to get some other qualification. More O levels for a start, then maybe an A or two. He may even go on to university.'

'How old is he?'

'Twenty-four.'

'Mmmmm!' Matthew didn't sound impressed. 'Look, I'll tell you what I'll do. Because I'm your friend I don't want to let you down. I'd like to help you and your son . . . what's his name?'

'Simon.'

'I'd like to help Simon. I'll get one of my directors, maybe an actor or two, to give him a reading and they will tell you the honest truth. You don't have to waste your money, Eleanor, even for love. There are too many out of work actors about.'

'You *are* a darling,' she said and reached out to squeeze his hand. It really was such a pity he was gay.

*     *     *

'I hope you're satisfied, Lewis, now that you've seen the birth certificate and know what I've always known.'

'I still think he's a sponger.'

'He thinks *you're* a sponger.' The conversation took place in bed where she'd joined Lewis, rather late, after a broadcast.

'He's got a bloody nerve. All he wants from you is what he can get out of you.'

'Sounds rather like you. At least he's my son, my blood relation.'

'Now I suppose you're going to spend a fortune to keep him in drama school.'

'Only if he's good enough. I think he will be.'

'Why didn't he go to drama school before?'

'He didn't have the money. You can't get a grant for drama. Anyway, he didn't have enough O levels.'

'Well, he still hasn't.'

'I'm not talking RADA or the Central School. I'm talking a drama school which, hopefully, if he is good enough, Matthew Clements will recommend.'

'You're making a rod for your back.'

Lewis slipped his hand under her nightie

and began to stroke her thigh, his lips touched her cheek. Eleanor felt such revulsion for him that she could have been physically sick. She got out of bed, reached for her gown and tied the cord tightly round her waist.

'I'm going to sleep in the spare room,' she said. 'And tomorrow I'm going to make it into *my* room. Permanently.'

'Go and fuck yourself,' Lewis shouted and, turning on his stomach, banged the pillow with pent-up rage.

*    *    *

Matthew Clements said: 'He's not Antony Sher or Alec Clunes but, apparently, he's very good.'

Eleanor's heart skipped over several times.

'He read some Sheakespeare . . .'

'I know,' she felt quite breathless, silly mother that she was, 'I heard him rehearsing in his room . . .'

'Some Pinter, and then something he'd written himself.'

'Well I didn't know that. He kept that from me.'

'I had Gerald Livingstone, one of my best directors, and Kathleen Seymour audition him. . .'

'Kathleen *Seymour*, that's very good of her.' Seymour was currently the darling of the London stage.

'Yes, lucky old Simon, but I thought he should have the best, also, for your sake, the most critical. Anyway, they liked him and they took him out to lunch. They would never have done that if they thought your son was a dud. They will give you some advice about schools. There are one or two quite good small schools of drama where Gerald at least has influence.'

Eleanor blew him a kiss down the phone, too close to tears to speak.

\*      \*      \*

*March 1992*

Pippa wrapped her coat very tightly round her, secured the woollen scarf over her head and stepped out into the night. There was a biting wind, a hint of snow, and she was reluctant to leave the comparative warmth and comfort of the convent, although the central heating was always turned off at night and even when it was on it was never very warm. But it had to be tonight. In a few days she was embarking on her new life. There would, hopefully, be no return in her lifetime to London; no chance to visit again her old haunts. Nostalgia drew her back; nostalgia, memories, a lot of them bad, some of them fearful, many regrets.

She wondered if she would recognise any of her former companions in misery, or if they would recognise her.

She walked along Marylebone Road, Regent's Park on one side, but she wouldn't go there at night. She'd always kept away from the parks when she was living rough because they were patrolled by police. No dossers were welcome in the Royal parks.

She passed the church where she'd been received and where Father Casey had found her two years ago. She remembered the rather bleak little ceremony of her reception by a priest whose name she no longer remembered, with Eleanor sitting nearby for support. She could recall going to see Eleanor in hospital and she wondered what had become of the baby. He'd be a grown man by now.

The last memory of Eleanor was when she made her final vows. She'd thought even then that she might never see her again.

Fancy Eleanor being famous! It wasn't too much of a surprise because Eleanor had always been ambitious, not ruthless, but she had wanted to succeed.

Pippa found herself thinking a lot about Eleanor as she turned off Marylebone Road and walked down Portland Place, past the grand houses, the embassies and the BBC building and into Oxford Street.

It was amazing how the number of people sleeping rough had increased, even in recent years. There was a crumpled figure in almost every doorway, or a cardboard box with a person inside, and sometimes a dog as well.

From Regent Street she turned into Soho. One of her regular places had been over the heating vents of the Regent Palace hotel. Tonight, because it was so cold, it was crowded, bodies jostled for a good position. In the light of the streetlamp she tried to peer at the faces, but they were either hidden or they were people she didn't know. Many were very young.

She crossed into Piccadilly, went down the Haymarket and across Trafalgar Square, then continued down by Charing Cross station and on the Embankment.

Here the territory was very familiar. This was where she and the people of the streets used to gather and huddle together to keep warm, separating out during the day in order to beg. Here the junkies would give themselves a fix and the alcoholics would roll over into the gutter until they were hauled back by the brethren because of the traffic.

The brethren. Yes they were the brethren, the children of God, unwanted, unloved, imperfect specimens of humanity, yet made in His image.

The image and likeness of God.

Pippa felt a strong surge of yearning for the old life. She would sit on the Embankment refusing a puff on a joint or a cigarette, or a swig of cheap booze or meths, yet retaining their respect and affection because she did it with good humour and politeness. Many of them were not used to either. She often gave them her food, especially in Lent or on fast days. She thought that was one of the reasons she eventually became ill, not enough nourishment.

When it grew dark she would sit looking at the lights of the Festival Hall reflected in the water of the Thames, and imagine the lovely music and the audience listening and then maybe dining out before returning home in their warm cars to their comfortable beds. But she personally never missed that because it wasn't a life she was familiar with, though she knew about it from the wealthy parents of her ex-pupils. They all liked to patronise the arts and be seen at fashionable events: the opera, the symphony, the National Theatre, also just across the river.

No, she had never known that life because she had been a nun for so many years.

She walked slowly along the Embankment, beginning to feel tired. Her legs ached. Eventually she came to the arches close by the Savoy. These offered a shelter from the wind and the rain and it was a very popular spot. She walked along by the bodies lying there, peering as close as she could, when a voice said: 'Pippa!' and she turned to confront a bundle of rags with a mangy dog by its side. She recognised the dog and then she knew who it was.

'Sally!' she cried, stooping towards the

bundle, as a wan face appeared in the half-light. A mile away the clock of St Paul's began to chime midnight.

'Pippa, what *happened* to you? We were worried!'

'I got very ill,' Pippa said, putting her hand on the head of the mongrel who, if she remembered, was called Scruff, and looked it. 'I've been in hospital.'

'And are you back now?' Sally, pleased to see an old chum, happily edged along to make room for her, invitingly patting the pavement beside her. 'It's a terribly cold night.'

It was. Pippa looked at the helpless creature next to her, who was younger than she was, a hopeless heroin addict and an alcoholic. She had never been at all interested in hearing about Jesus Christ, but a bond had sprung up between the two women, because Sally was educated, had even been to university, but dropped out before she could take her degree. She'd started on drugs young.

'I missed you a lot,' Pippa said, dropping down beside her. 'How's Scruff?'

'I think Scruff has rheumatism. Sometimes I think I should take him to the dogs' home.'

'I'm sure he'd rather be with you.' Pippa's eyes glistened as she looked at her friend. 'Live with you and die with you . . . in time. If you took him to the dogs' home they'd put him down.'

'I would never let them do that,' Sally said

indignantly. 'He's my only friend since you left.' Timidly she touched Pippa's arm. 'I'm glad you're back, though you must look after your health.'

Pippa didn't have the heart to tell her she wasn't staying.

*      *      *

Just before daylight Pippa stirred and sat up. Sally had had her usual fix the night before together with a quantity of alcohol and was fast asleep. Scruff was relieving himself against the wall. Shortly he would disappear and scavenge for food, an enterprise he seemed to perform with singular success because he was never thin and scraggy like some of the dossers' animals. Anyway, he knew he wouldn't get fed until Sally surfaced at about ten in the morning, maybe not even then. He probably made off for Covent Garden, which was full of scraps left in bags on street corners which had been broken open by foxes or the birds, or loitered at the back doors of the Strand Palace or the Savoy. One day, Pippa felt, he would never come back. He would be caught by a dog warden or killed in the heavy traffic that plied along the Strand.

Anyway today, after his pee, he wandered off without a backward glance. Independent old dog. In her heart Pippa wished him luck.

She stood up, bones creaking a bit, glad she

wasn't going to have to sleep another night on the pavement, and looked at her friend snoring away. She wished she had some money to leave her but she had nothing. She would like to have kissed her, but others were stirring and gazing at her curiously because her face was washed and her clothes, though dowdy, were clean. Surreptitiously Pippa gave Sally her blessing. 'God bless you,' she whispered in her heart, touching the bag lady's shoulder, 'and keep you safe.'

She walked past the flotsam and jetsam of humanity arranged on the pavement, giving them in turn a little half-smile. They stared up at her apathetically. She was really of no interest, not wealthy enough to give them money, not poor enough to share their lot. She no longer looked like one of them.

She no longer was one of them.

*     *     *

Pippa sat in the train that was taking her from Cardiff to the station nearest to her convent. The single-track line was one of the few left in Wales and it was an experience, running through some beautiful scenery: towering mountains, some snow-capped, some covered in cloud; gentle, undulating valleys full of fat white sheep; a river, little streams, small villages tucked into the hills, a croft or two clinging to the mountain sides.

299

She sat back and closed her eyes savouring the peace, the sense of fulfilment, now that she felt her life had come full circle.

She had been a nun teaching in fashionable convents, enjoying a life of ease. It was almost pagan, when you came to think about it. Nothing really godly about it at all.

She had come nearer to Christ as a bag lady on the streets. She had lived as He would have lived, she had brought Him to a few souls, not many.

'I was a stranger, and ye took me in. Naked and ye clothed me.'

The Bible, the good book, had just the right phrase for everything.

Now the third and, she thought, final stage of her life was upon her. She had been close to Christ, but now she would be closer still. She would submerge herself in Him, think of Him constantly present in the Blessed Sacrament. She would devote her life to prayer, fasting and acts of self-denial.

She would pray for all the people on the streets, all the refugees in battle-scarred lands, the teeming poor of India and the Far East, all the people she had known at school, particularly Clare and Eleanor. She would pray for Father Casey, through whom God had guided her on her way.

The train halted abruptly and her eyes, which had closed during her reverie, opened wide. The unpronounceable name of the station was written on a board in front of her. She seized her little bag and hurried along the coach, stepping out on to the platform just as the guard raised his whistle to his lips. He gave her a kindly smile and, banging the door shut behind her, jumped on to the train as it moved off.

Pippa was alone. No one on the platform to greet her. No sinister-looking women waiting to take her away.

It was about five miles to the convent, but she would walk. She would enjoy it. Her bag was light because she had so few possessions, and what she had were about to be surrendered.

As she left the station she saw a rather ancient-looking car parked in the forecourt, with a man at the wheel.

'Sister Mary Frances?' the driver enquired, and as she nodded he got out and opened the door for her. 'Reverend Mother sent me. Hop in.'

'How *kind*,' Pippa murmured gratefully as she sank back against the battered headrest.

It was a lovely day. Cold but sunny. The road through the valley narrowed until it became a mere track; but obviously the driver was familiar with it because he tackled it with ease. On either side the hills rose gently towards the craggy mountain tops. The grass was a luscious green and the sky a vitriol blue, with little wispy clouds scudding by. She would love to paint it, but she knew she never would. Painting was temptation, and she had put all that behind her to concentrate on God.

A few birds flew about because spring was upon them and they would be thinking of nesting. Spring was a lovely time, a time of renewal and hope, and the liturgy was so wonderful: the Pascal Candle, the singing of the Lamentations, the reading of the Gospels, the joy of Easter day welcoming the Risen Christ when the bells rang out.

In the distance now, beyond the driver's head, she saw the walls of the convent, which completely enclosed the buildings, hiding them from the curious, and the only way in, or out, was through a single wooden door before which, a moment later, the driver stopped.

'This is as far as we go, Sister,' he said, getting out to open the door for her. She reached in her purse, but he shook his head.

'The convent pays. They have an account.'

'Oh I see. Thanks very much,' she said, and gave him her brilliant smile.

'Good luck, Sister.'

'Thank you. Thank you *very* much.'

The door opened as she turned and a little old nun in the grey habit of the Order came out to take her bag.

'Sister Mary Frances?' she asked with a twinkly smile.

'Yes.'

'Did you have a good journey?'

'Yes.'

'Reverend Mother is waiting for you. I expect you'll be hungry.'

The nun stood back to allow Pippa to pass but, for a second, Pippa hesitated and looked back the way she had just come. The nun watched her. Did she have any doubts, a moment's qualm, perhaps? the face seemed to say.

No. No doubts. No qualms. None at all. As Pippa crossed the threshold, the door closed behind her, shutting out the world, and her old life, forever.

# CHAPTER THIRTEEN

## JUNE 1994

*'All the world's a stage,*
*And all the men and women merely players:*
*They have their exits and their entrances;*
*And one man in his time plays many parts,*
*His acts being seven ages.'*

The melancholy, lugubrious figure of Jaques—thoughtful, contemplative, cheek resting on the palm of his hand—stood to the front of the stage delivering those famous lines about the seven ages of man.

*'At first the infant,*
*Mewling and puking in the nurse's arms.*
*And then the whining schoolboy, with his satchel,*
*And shining morning face, creeping like snail*
   *unwillingly to school.'*

The narrator continued his perfect delivery until:

*'Last scene of all,*
*That ends this strange eventful history,*
*Is second childishness, and mere oblivion,*
*Sans teeth, sans eyes, sans taste, sans*
   *everything.'*

There was a burst of applause, the woman in the front of the stalls clapping more frantically than anyone else, the tears in her eyes unnoticed because of the darkened theatre.

Orlando re-entered carrying Adam. Duke Senior bade him be set down and the play continued.

There was no doubt that Jaques was outstanding, even to the rest of the audience. As the cast took curtain after curtain at the end, he continued to be pushed to the front of the stage by his peers but refused to take a solo bow. He glanced down at Eleanor, momentarily catching her eye, in that instant acknowledging her part in his success.

Of course they were all proud parents in the audience for the end-of-year play at the Artemis School of Drama in north London where Simon had done two years' intensive training for the stage. He had been awarded the silver medal for the year. He had worked hard and Eleanor was very, very proud of him.

In a sense they were all privileged youngsters, Simon by no means the oldest, whose parents or relatives had paid for them to have places denied to those who couldn't afford them. But everyone had to make sacrifices, and many students had.

For Eleanor the seven ages speech seemed to sum up everything she felt about her son:

305

his goodness, his wisdom, and a lot of it was delivered from the heart, as though he knew how much of it applied to him.

Watching him she felt so proud. He was billed as Simon Hamilton, having changed his name by deed poll in the course of the year. It was a comparatively trivial matter, but Eleanor felt that sharing the same name made their bond even closer. Even if he hadn't made her proud she would have loved him. Even if he'd been a hopeless case she would have tried to understand. All these years she'd missed the joy of motherhood and for that she blamed not only Lewis but herself too.

But now Simon was there and he was hers, and whether or not he succeeded on the stage she loved him.

She joined other members of the audience crowding backstage. People were milling around but Simon, taller than all the rest, was looking for her. He held out his arms as she came up to him and hugged her.

'You were marvellous,' she whispered.

'Thanks to you,' he whispered back. Behind him stood the girl who had played Rosalind. She was beautiful: tall, fair-skinned, lissome with long blonde hair and a mellifluous voice.

'Mum, this is Jessica,'

'You were wonderful too,' Eleanor said, shaking hands.

'Of course I know who you are,' Jessica smiled. 'My mother was quite excited to know

306

that your son was at the school.'

Simon put an arm round Jessica drawing her closer, and Eleanor gave him a tacit nod of approval and then said she must be going as she had a programme to record.

Simon and Jessica saw her to the stage door.

'I might not be home tonight, Mum,' Simon said, winking at her, 'we're having a bit of a party.'

'I'll see you when I see you,' she said and kissed him, shaking hands again with Jessica.

It had been an afternoon performance and she took a taxi to the studio to record her programme. The recession was biting and interest rates were sky high. The Chancellor was not a popular man and the Prime Minister had made an ass of himself by saying that if it wasn't hurting it wasn't working. Try telling that to all the thousands of people whose homes were being repossessed.

She was pleased with her contribution, which would go out later that night, and got a cab home, letting out a sigh as she inevitably did these days when she opened the door. Lewis had managed to make himself a sandwich. He must have been starving. It was past eight and he was sitting morosely at the kitchen table looking at the TV.

'You're terribly late,' he said.

'I'm sorry.' Eleanor felt her stomach muscles tense up. 'It was Simon's play today and I had to go to the studio afterwards to record my views on the economic situation for the late night programme.'

Lewis bit thoughtfully into his sandwich. 'And how was the budding Olivier?'

'Don't be so sarcastic.'

'Offered a part, no doubt, at the National, or is it the Royal Shakespeare, both anxious to sign him on?'

'Lewis, I asked you, *please* stop. Simon, as a matter of fact, was excellent.'

'Of course. That's his doting mother talking. I can't believe he's really any good. They're all trying to please you—Matthew Clements, the school, the lot. They think you're a person of some importance and any favour done to you will need one in return.'

Eleanor poured herself a glass of wine and leaned against the kitchen table.

'Lewis, I don't want to live with you any more. I'm asking you to leave this house.'

Lewis, in the act of raising his sandwich to his mouth, paused, looking at her in amazement. 'It is not *your* house.'

'It is. I bought it and it is in my name. I made quite sure of that.'

'Well *I'm* sure I have a right . . .'

'I will fight you in court, Lewis, if need be. I'm warning you.'

'This is all to do with that sodding Simon.' Lewis threw the sandwich untouched back on his plate. 'That little bastard . . .'

'You can't blame Simon. Blame yourself. I

have lived with you for over twenty years, and for at least half of that time I have wanted to leave you. Your rudeness, selfishness and chauvinism are at times intolerable.'

'Then why didn't you leave?'

'God knows. I suppose I felt responsible for you. I was sorry for you. But that pity changed to resentment, which has grown over the years. I don't think you realise the effect you have, or how unpleasant you can be. Until Simon came I reckoned this was the way some people lived, and they put up with one another.

'A lot of women live with partners they don't really like because they're afraid of being lonely. I suppose that I was like the rest, but no longer.

'No man is better than a man like you. I feel tense every time I come through the door.'

'You're just doing this for Simon,' Lewis said furiously.

'No I'm not. In fact I met a very pretty girl today and I suspect something is going on. Who knows, they may move in together? Anyway, if he does get a job it will hardly be in London. Simon has really very little to do with this decision. It's you and the way you are. Maybe he makes me feel a little bit stronger.'

'You can't just throw me out. I do have rights . . .'

'You also have a cottage. Your very own property. Well you can go and live there. I don't ever want to see you here again. I'll give you an allowance, a small one, and you must manage the best way you can.'

'I think you're brutal. You don't know how much you've changed—for the worse.' His rage had turned to petulance. She could see he was seriously upset and disturbed.

She sat down opposite him. 'It was your decision not to marry, Lewis. You said you didn't want to be tied down and you didn't want children. Consequently, we are as free as air to do as we like. But I do take account of the years we have been living together and I shan't just throw you out. But you can't linger on here either. It's got to be within the next week or two. No wriggling, please, or there'll be no allowance.'

'I could make hell for you,' Lewis said maliciously. 'If I wanted to I could go to the papers and tell them . . .'

'I don't think you would, or that if you did they would be particularly interested. I'm not a film star or a pop idol. I don't know what you'd tell them anyway. We are not young enough to be interesting. No other man is involved, you have a very reasonable dwelling, plus money. Frankly, as a journalist, I don't think it's a story.'

'When you think of what *I* did for you . . .'

Eleanor held up a hand. '*And* another thing. All you did was give me an introduction for which I was not ungrateful but I didn't expect it would be rammed down my throat for the rest of my life as it has been. Every time something happens you remind me that you introduced me to *The Examiner*. I don't tell you, or haven't until now, that while I've been making the best of my opportunities you've been mooning about, doing sod all when you could easily have been at least trying to write something that people do want to read, and which I think you're quite capable of.'

'I'd like to strangle Simon . . .'

'And I'm sure he feels the same about you. You could have been a friend to Simon. He was hopelessly insecure. Instead, you taunted him and were rude to him and rubbished me in front of him. We could actually have been the family I'd always wanted. You'd think you'd be delighted that Simon had a gift. He *can* act. There's no doubt of it. He may not get very far, but it's a start.

'I think Simon is one of the nicest young men I've ever known. Not just because he's my son. He's kind and thoughtful. He did his best to be nice to you, yet you accused him of trying to worm his way into your affections, so he didn't try any more. You could have been a father to him, but you haven't. I, who have been denied all these years the pleasures of children and a secure marriage, have had to put up with your laziness, your self-pity, your sexual demands, all the drivel you talk, and now I'm taking charge of my life.'

Sister Martha had been the superior of the convent for ten years. She was an erudite, pleasant woman, liked by most people. She could be stern, however, and some preferred her when they became ex-students.

She always circulated freely on Association Days, an event which she seemed to enjoy.

This year they were particularly lucky with the weather. The sun had shone from a cloudless sky all morning, and umbrellas were put up to provide shelter for those sitting at the little tables on the lawn. Now they were all occupied, with the overflow sitting on the grass or the steps, balancing cups and saucers and little cakes and prattling away to friends they had probably not seen for a year, at least. The women wore pretty dresses, many of them hats. Once again there seemed more old girls than ever. There were the usual enthusiasts on the tennis courts and the younger members fooling about with the boat. Nothing ever changed, Clare thought, as she watched the headmistress mount the steps leading to the house and put up her hand for silence.

But this year something would. It would change it forever.

Once Sister Martha had the attention of her audience she began. She could do nothing about the noise coming from below, from the lake and the tennis courts, but the voices were

312

not obtrusive.

'I want to welcome you once again to our Association Day, the tenth year I have had the pleasure of doing so. I feel I know you all so well, even those who left the school long before I came.

'Now I am sorry that I have something very sad to say to you.' Sister paused and a murmur of concern went round the assembly.

'St Catherine's is to close . . .' The murmur grew to a crescendo and she raised her hand once more. 'Please let me finish. We have known for some time that this was a possibility, but the economic situation and the effects of the dreadful recession we have all been experiencing has made this inevitable. We have fewer girls coming to the school as boarders. Parents can't afford the fees and every year we have to increase them. Our scholarship fund is exhausted and we can offer no more assistance to those in need of help with fees. Also, costs have risen. Fuel is very expensive, books are prohibitive. We have always had such high standards in the convents of the Society and we feel we cannot allow these to decline. We shall gradually phase out the school, but it will certainly close in a year's time. There will be no intake next year. We are in discussion with the authorities of the new university of Wolversleigh that they might buy our convent with its beautiful grounds for one of the colleges. We might even be able to

313

continue to use it for Association Days, if that is the case; but at the moment I can't promise anything. We will certainly lose our lovely chapel, but well,' she looked around and when she spoke again her voice was full of emotion, 'God is everywhere, and we can have Benediction out of doors as we have for the Corpus Christi processions.

'So,' she continued trying hard to smile, 'it is not all gloom, but I am very, very sorry to give you this news and those of you who have children at the school will receive a letter from me outlining the situation in full in due course.'

Sister Martha was about to get down, and then changed her mind and again held up her hand for the buzz of conversation to cease. 'Before I go I must pay tribute to all who have helped run our Association Days and, of course, in particular to Clare Thornton, who has shouldered the burden of the secretaryship for over twenty years, I believe, Clare?' She looked across at Clare who nodded. 'She has been a wonderful secretary, a wonderful supporter of the school. I know she wants to give this up, as she has so many demands on her time, but I hope she can be persuaded to continue for the time being, at least until we find a worthy successor.

'Clare will be a very hard act to follow.'

'Hear! Hear!' There was a burst of enthusiastic applause and heads turned to look at Clare who had been standing at the back.

'Speech! Speech!' everyone cried, but Clare shook her head. She didn't trust herself to speak.

She was immediately surrounded, as was Sister Martha as she descended the steps. Everyone started to talk at once. Clare held her hands to her head.

'Please, *please*.'

'Did you know?' Mary Barlow had several of her many children at the school, and it was true they were struggling to pay the fees.

'Yes, I've known for some time.'

'Why didn't you *say*,' Lucy Walsh said reproachfully.

'Nothing definite was decided until a few days ago. Sister Martha wanted a decision from Mother General so that we could announce it today. We have tried desperately to save the school. Done *everything* we could but,' she shook her head, 'it was not to be.'

'Maybe even *now* something could be done?'

'I don't think so. It is not the only school in the Society to close. There are others too. Things are not what they were. Times are changing.'

'Well I'm not going to send my child to a comprehensive school!'

'Wait until you get Sister's letter,' Clare appealed to the anguished parents, 'she may have other suggestions.'

At that moment, fortuitously perhaps, the bell rang and all those on the lawn rose and began to troop into the building for Benediction.

Once again Clare knelt at the back. The windows were wide open because the day was so hot, and the trees seemed taller than ever. She was sure they'd grown several feet since she first came to the school. The priest processed down the aisle in his golden cope preceded by two altar boys swinging their thurifers. They reached the steps of the altar, bowed and the choir began the beautiful Latin hymn:

> 'Tantum ergo sacramentum
> Veneremour cernui . . .'

Clare was forty-eight and had been associated with the school since she was nine. She remembered the day she was brought there by her parents and given a respectful welcome because Dr Pearson was such an important man.

Her father had died the previous year and life was not quite the same without him. Her mother was now in her seventies and looking for a smaller house.

There were so many changes. They were all horrible. Pauline and James continued to live abroad. They liked it and hoped they could stay there. Pauline was learning to teach

English as a foreign language and her German was increasingly fluent. They had a little girl and another baby was on the way.

Clare and Andrew had been several times to see them and they came over twice a year, but it wasn't the same. They hardly ever heard from Marcus. He was a bad correspondent and they could seldom get him on the telephone.

So there was just Andrew and her . . . and, well, life which had once seemed so full of promise, full of hope, turned out to be not quite so rosy after all.

Benediction was over. The blessing had been given. Clare realised she hadn't really been concentrating. Everyone trooped out of the chapel, chatting immediately began outside. Clare stayed in her pew until they had all gone and then she went slowly along the side aisle, closing the windows, pausing before each one to stand and look out on to those grounds that she loved so much, so beautiful in high summer; the smell of flowering currant seemed to rise from the grounds and mingle with the scent of incense in the chapel.

One by one she closed the windows. It was a little like closing a chapter of one's life.

\*     \*     \*

*October 1994*

St Catherine's Convent wasn't the only

institution in trouble. The women's refuge might have to close. Clare sat in her tiny unheated office, wrestling with the accounts. If only Andrew could have been of more help, but he said he had no time. Anyway he wasn't very sympathetic towards women who, in his opinion, were silly enough to let themselves be beaten up and turned out of their homes. He really didn't think they deserved much help.

And did they? Clare raised her head towards the window high up in the wall and pondered. Maybe Andrew was right. Most of them went back to their aggressive spouses, had another baby and then returned with an extra mouth to feed. Some of them really were stupid, or seemed to be. They were like sheep, and it was quite easy to imagine a man getting cross with them. But beating them? No.

And for every sheep there were a lot of good, stout-hearted goats who wouldn't let their men bash them and tried to make a new life for themselves.

No, she would go on. She would find the money, but where? The place was badly in need of renovating. The local authority had threatened to withdraw the licence unless improvements were made. The central heating was on in the main rooms, the bedrooms, but off in the offices where it was bitterly cold, and workers were meant to have heat too. It was the law. The plumbing needed attention, and rewiring the whole place was becoming a matter of urgency. The furniture was deplorable and . . . oh there was no end to it. Clare threw her pen down on the table and buried her face in her hands.

That horrible feeling of despair and emptiness once again was creeping up on her. She was overdoing things. She should take a break.

'Hi!' Chrissy put her head round the door.

'Oh hi!' Clare looked up with a smile.

'Thought I might find you here.'

'Struggling with the accounts.' Clare pointed to a chair. 'I literally do not know how we're going to make ends meet. I thought if you and I put our heads together . . . we could organise some events, you know dinners, receptions, concerts, in aid of the Refuge . . .'

'Clare . . .' Chrissy interrupted her. Clare realised now that Chrissy looked agitated and, most unusual for her, she wore no make-up. She still looked pretty but, like Clare, she was over forty too.

'Anything the matter?' Clare asked. 'Sorry. I'm so preoccupied . . .'

'Clare, I don't quite know how to tell you this. I hoped I'd find you here so that we can talk, but . . . I can't stay on the committee any more.'

'What? Why?' Clare's face crumpled. 'You can't let me down, Chrissy, not *you*.'

'Clare, I'm leaving Mark. I'm going to move out of the area . . .'

'You're leaving Mark? What do you mean you're leaving Mark?'

'I'm in love with somebody else. Have been for ages. You don't know him, but I've been deceiving Mark for years. I wanted to wait until the children grew up, and now I think they're old enough to understand.' She lowered her head, bit her lip. 'But they haven't taken it very well. A natural reaction I suppose.'

'And when did all this happen?'

'Yesterday, last night. I told Mark and I told the children. I'm staying at the Royal Oak. Harris—my boyfriend—is making arrangements for us to go abroad for a while. I've got to put all this behind me.'

'And leave chaos, I suppose?' Clare looked at her witheringly. 'Chrissy, this is *the* most shocking news. I can't tell you how upset I am.'

'I'm upset too, don't think I'm not; but I have held on for years. I think I owe it to myself, and Harris, to have a few happy years. Life with Mark has been hell.'

'But,' Clare spluttered, 'Mark is the nicest, kindest, most *considerate* person.' She paused, as if to get her breath.

'Besides, I thought you were so ambitious for him? You fought like mad to change the name of the firm so as to acknowledge the part played by Mark. You were always on about his career, as if it meant so much to you. As if *he* meant so much to you.'

'He does mean a lot to me.' Chrissy raised her head defiantly. 'Of course he does. You can't undo the past. I respect him. He's the father of my children but,' she gave a gesture of helplessness, 'it's time to move on. I love somebody else and, let's face it, Mark is a dear but he is a very dull and boring man, so set in his ways. In fact, to put it bluntly, he's a typical Pearson.'

'I do resent that. You couldn't call our father, rest his soul, dull and boring,' Clare said heatedly. 'And I don't think Mark is either.'

'No, but your father was very dogmatic and opiniated and so is Mark. He has no imagination, no insight. He is a typical dull, boring accountant and I've had enough.'

'And what does this Harris do?'

A flush stole up Chrissy's cheeks. 'Well, Harris is an accountant as well. That's how I met him, several years ago, at a convention. But he's not like Mark. I can't explain it. He's different. He's been asking me for a long time to go away with him. He's divorced his wife for me and now he has given me an ultimatum. Mark or him. Naturally I chose him. I've got the rest of my life to think of.'

Clare got up from her rickety chair and began to pace the room. 'I think it's contemptible. I think it's utterly *wrong*. To break up a family, to leave a good man like Mark for . . . merely selfish ends. I suppose

Mark's happiness isn't important? Or the children's? What about your wedding vows? In the Catholic Church divorce is not permitted.'

'My happiness is important too. And please don't bring up religion. I have never really been interested in the Church, but I think I have been a good wife and mother and I'm sure Mark will find someone else. He's got plenty of money—so has Harris, so I shan't be asking for a huge pay-off when we get divorced.'

'Has he agreed to divorce you?'

'Not yet, but he'll have to, eventually.'

'I don't know what Andrew will say.'

'Does it *matter* what Andrew says?'

'Of course it matters.'

'I had the feeling you two weren't very happy,' Chrissy said slyly.

'Of course we're happy. What do you mean? I know that Andrew would never leave me, however dull and boring I was. He is a good Catholic man. In our Church, fidelity is everything. It matters to us. Andrew takes the wedding vows seriously and so should you,' she said, pointing her finger at Chrissy.

'I see . . .' Chrissy hesitated. Then she went on rather breathlessly, 'I suppose I shouldn't be saying this but seeing that you are so sanctimonious I will. Well . . .' she paused again, 'Andrew patronises a well-known house of ill repute in the town. I believe he's been doing so for years.'

'House . . .'

'A brothel,' Chrissy said crisply. 'He's been frequenting prostitutes. I didn't think *that* was approved of by the Church either.' Chrissy lowered her voice. 'Or is that alright as long as it's within marriage?'

Clare sat down again at her desk. 'I simply don't believe you.'

'Well ask him.' Chrissy's tone changed. 'I'm sorry, Clare. I thought maybe you knew, or suspected. Everyone else does, including members of the Labour opposition on the council. I have heard—I hope not, for your sake—that it may be made public to stop him being re-elected as leader of the council. Some journalists are baying for his blood.'

Clare had a feeling of disembodiment, that she was looking down on herself.

'*Andrew* going to prostitutes?'

'I think a lot of them do. Mark, for all I know. I don't really care and nor should you. If you don't sleep with him you won't catch anything.'

'I think that's a disgusting thing to say. I can't believe it of Andrew. He receives Holy Communion every Sunday.'

'Ask him. Go on, ask him. You can't blame him. A man needs his bit of nooky. The silly laws of the Church don't mean as much to other people today as they do to you, Clare. You're living in the past. If you deny Andrew sex, as we know you have for years, you can't

323

blame him.'

'*How* do you know? I've never said . . .'

'Andrew told Mark ages ago. I think Mark has warned him that the leadership is in jeopardy.' Feeling she'd done enough harm, feeling perhaps a little guilty, Chrissy picked up her bag. 'I'm sorry, Clare. It was pretty brutal, but I thought you knew, in your heart. *Must* have known.'

'I'd rather he had a mistress,' Clare said woodenly. 'That way it would be clean.'

'Oh I think they're very clean. I mean these days, with AIDS you've got to be so careful. I think a brothel is better than a mistress. That way you don't get involved. I'm sure he did it out of respect for you. I'm sure he loves you. But I'm sorry now that I told you. It is a ghastly shock I suppose, but you did needle me. You provoked me. However, if it is on the verge of becoming public you really should know.' She stooped and kissed her quickly on the cheek. 'Best of luck.'

*    *    *

Clare sat for a very long time after Chrissy had gone. A great chasm seemed to open and grow wider in front of her. The phone rang and she didn't answer it. Dusk fell and she didn't put on the light. She could hear noises elsewhere in the building, but she took no notice of them. Finally she put on her coat, and without saying goodbye to anyone left by a side entrance and got into her car, reversing rather erratically before turning by the gate and into the busy main road.

Andrew going to prostitutes. For how long? Twenty years? More? They had been married for twenty-six years. Last year had been their twenty-fifth wedding anniversary and they'd had a huge party. It was before her father died, and Pauline and James had come over from Germany.

She had thought then how lucky they were to have stayed together for twenty-five years, and Andrew was so sweet and bought her a beautiful pearl necklace. She gave him a diamond tiepin.

How could she possibly *face* Andrew after this? What could she say? A good Catholic man who received the Sacrament every Sunday, a pillar of the Church and the Establishment, had been visiting a brothel. It was unbelievable. What on earth would happen if it got into the newspapers? People loved a scandal—sex and politics, irresistible to everyone. The Pearsons and Thorntons had been prominent families for years. There'd never been a breath of scandal attaching to *any* of them.

It would be practically impossible to live this down. She thought of the faces of the old girls at Association Day, the stares, the snide remarks. 'Poor Clare' they'd say, 'How terrible for Clare.'

What horrible, sordid places brothels must be and how desperate a man must be to visit one.

She realised then that she shut her eyes to a lot of things. She always had. She was rigid in her views, in her faith. A bit unbending. Maybe she was dull and boring like her brother Mark. She always did the right thing. She always wanted to, except that, for most of her married life, she had denied her husband sex, and he had got it elsewhere. It was very naïve and stupid of her to expect anything else. But she had high standards and she thought Andrew had too. Look how upset he'd been over Marcus.

She shuddered. Still, it was so despicable, so dirty.

Clare realised she was driving very fast and a car passing on the other side hooted at her. It was at that twilight hour when cars were beginning to switch on their headlights, and everywhere was shadowy. Maybe the blast of the horn meant that she should put on her lights. They should have been on already. She forgot where the switch was and fumbled for it. She thought, in a way, she was in such a state she ought not to be driving at all.

She should have phoned Andrew and asked him to come and get her. But how could she? How could she *ever* speak to him again? What would she say?

A car passed her again and hooted. The driver of a car in the next lane waved frantically at her. She'd forgotten something. She looked around and then realised that she had put on the rear windscreen wiper instead of the lights.

She fumbled for the switch again. The car swerved. It was getting dark and to drive without lights was against the law. There was an awful lot of noise about. Maybe there had been an accident somewhere.

She looked ahead and a car right in front of her flashed its lights and then left the beam full on. More cars were hooting all around her.

Something was terribly wrong.

# JUNE 1998

I reached the top of the steep path which was shaded from the terrace by trees and stood on the edge of the group looking nervously around. The lawn was swarming with people, all of them unknown to me. If only Clare or Pippa would emerge and rescue me. Would we recognise one another? Of course we would.

One or two people looked at me curiously and turned away. It's odd, I thought, how people can behave at reunions, as if they would prefer not to know who you were. But then a woman with a pleasant expression of anticipation on her face detached herself from a group and came towards me. 'Eleanor Hamilton?'

'Yes.'

She put out her hand. 'I'm Christina Handley, the Secretary of the Association. I wrote to you inviting you to attend. It's very good of you to find the time.'

'I'm delighted,' I replied, looking round. 'I haven't been back since I left the school.'

'You'll find many changes.'

'Yes indeed.' I smiled at the woman many years my junior. 'I feel a bit nervous.'

'Oh I can't believe that. Lots of people are

dying to meet you. Now, who would you know here?'

We looked about us. There were tables and chairs on the lawn and some optimist had put up umbrellas that could be unfurled if there was too much sun. It had been a rotten summer and it was only by the merest good chance that we had a fine day. There was a festive air with flags and balloons, and a huge birthday cake on a trestle in front of the main steps. Over the portico was a giant banner with the words: 'ST CATHERINE'S CENTENARY' emblazoned on it. The point was, I thought, that St Catherine's hadn't quite made it. The nuns, who were the successors of those hardy pioneers, had left three years before.

An older woman in a suit and blouse turned to my escort who said: 'Sister, this is Eleanor Hamilton, the well-known broadcaster. She's an old girl of the school. Eleanor, this is Sister Martha, the last headmistress.'

'How very nice to meet you.'

'And you.' We shook hands.

'When were you here?'

'I left in 1964. I must be one of the oldest "old girls" present.'

'Oh no!' Sister Martha laughed. 'There is one lady of eighty and plenty in their sixties and seventies.'

'Did you know Pippa Sidgwick?' I asked her.

The nun shook her head. 'I don't think so.'

'She was a contemporary of mine. She

330

entered your Order. We lost touch. And then there was. . .' I was about to mention Clare but she shook her head.

'No, I'm afraid I don't. You don't happen to know what name she took in religion do you?'

'Sister Mary Frances.'

'Ah . . . I think. . .' she seemed on the verge of some recollection when an excited voice broke in: 'Eleanor!' I turned. A plump woman with a smiling face beamed at me. 'I bet you don't remember me.'

'Margaret Potter.'

'Of course.' I bent to kiss her recalling that I hadn't seen her since Clare's wedding.

'And me,' a tall, stately woman proffered her cheek. 'Jennifer Cuthbert, as was.'

'Jennifer!' I clasped her hand. 'It's *so* nice to see you.' I felt myself slowly unwinding, less nervous.

'We're awfully proud of you,' Jennifer said. 'My husband wanted to come himself when he heard you were going to be here. He's a great fan of yours.'

'Do you know what happened to Pippa Sidgwick?'

'Pippa became a nun.'

'Yes I know. Where is she now?'

'She's in a convent in Wales. She left St Catherine's Society to enter a strict contemplative order.'

Sister Martha nodded as if something had clicked into place in her mind.

'Before that she spent several years as a bag lady on the streets of London. She's had a most extraordinary life.'

Pippa a *bag* lady? Impossible. I might even have passed her in the street, if that was the case.

Someone else was waiting with a mysterious smile for me to recognise her.

'Mary Barlow,' I obliged. 'You've hardly changed at all.'

'I must have changed a bit,' Mary said. 'I've had ten children.'

Ten children. I was impressed. Ten Mary Barlows, or their male equivalents, must have been a sight to behold.

'Have you children, Eleanor?' Jennifer asked.

By now a crowd had gathered round us, listening with interest to the conversation.

'I've a son called Simon,' I replied. 'He's thirty-one this year. He's an actor.'

'Has he been on telly?'

I laughed. 'Not yet, but he's hopeful. He's doing rep in the Midlands at the moment.'

'And your husband . . .'

'Oh he faded away,' I said diplomatically, thinking of poor old Lewis probably drinking himself to death at his cottage in Essex. At that moment I became aware of a young woman standing close to my elbow whose features were familiar.

'Hello?' I said encouragingly.

'I think you were a friend of my mother.' She smiled at me and I immediately saw Clare's smile. I took her hand.

'You must be Clare's girl.'

'Yes, Pauline.'

'Pauline—how *is* your mother?' I asked excitedly. 'I'm longing to see her. I do hope she's here.'

A sudden silence fell upon the group who had been twittering like birds in an aviary.

'I'm sorry. I didn't realise you didn't know.' Pauline paused. 'I'm afraid Mummy's dead.'

I closed my eyes with shock.

The group tactfully dispersed leaving Pauline and me alone.

'She was killed in a car crash four years ago.'

'That's ghastly.' I didn't know what else to say.

'She was driving without lights on the wrong side of the road in front of the oncoming traffic. It was twilight. Rush hour. All the cars were hooting and trying to stop her, but she carried on as though she didn't know what she was doing. She was hit by a juggernaut and went into a tree. She died instantly.'

'This is a terrible shock for me, Pauline. We were such great friends.'

'I know. Mummy used to talk about you and we watched you on TV. She wanted to get in touch, but she never did.'

'I wish she had.'

'Mummy was such a careful driver normally.

She was never reckless. But from time to time she did suffer from depression. She had a bad breakdown in the seventies and occasionally she wasn't well. There was an open verdict.'

Clare, the star of the school, clever, beautiful, good at games, suffering from depression? I could hardly believe it.

'The Coroner said there wasn't enough evidence about her state of mind at the time. She saw my Aunt Chrissy, Uncle Mark's wife, just before it happened, and Aunt Chrissy felt guilty because she'd just told Mummy she was leaving my uncle. Mummy was very upset and Aunt Chrissy thought she should never have left her alone.'

'How did your father take it?'

'Terribly badly. He resigned both as leader of the town council and from the council altogether. He's better now and has resumed his interest in the family business. He and Uncle Mark are like a couple of old bachelors, having dinner from time to time and taking holidays together.'

'Do give him my best wishes.' I pressed Pauline's arm because the crowd was beginning to gather round us again.

'I know Daddy would love to hear from you.'

I nodded, but I knew I wouldn't, not without Clare.

Pauline moved away and my eyes followed her sadly.

334

The others re-joined me. 'It was a terrible business.' Jennifer lowered her voice. 'We couldn't believe it.'

'I didn't realise she suffered from depression.' Then I said the unthinkable. 'Was there any suggestion that it was deliberate?'

Jennifer appeared to hesitate. 'Yes there was. She had a miscarriage in the seventies and it affected her deeply. She wasn't able to have any more children. She seemed to recover completely, but I think there were a lot of off days, though she threw herself into every activity going. She was secretary of the Old Girls' Association for twenty-five years. We all loved Clare.' Jennifer sighed sadly. 'And no one will ever know the truth. But when Andrew resigned from the council some people said it was to avoid a scandal. We often wondered if that had something to do with it. Something that Clare knew.'

Mary Barlow, who had I remembered enjoyed a reputation as the school gossip, added her little bit. Her voice sank almost to a whisper, her head nearly touching mine: 'As a matter of fact I think I know what the scandal was—my husband is a town councillor too— but I'd rather not say, except that, if true, it was quite shocking for a man in his position.'

'*If* true,' I thought, knowing Mary. I decided not to give her the satisfaction of probing any further.

'Clare was so religious, so true to the faith.

She would never have committed suicide.' Margaret Potter's voice was firm. 'I'm convinced it was an accident. Dear Clare, so good, so thoughtful about others, would never have killed herself. But it was an awful way to die.'

An awful way to die. I thought of our life together as children; her laughter, her brilliance, her splendid wedding. It was an end one could never have predicted.

\*　　\*　　\*

A bell tinkled and Sister Martha, flanked by what I presumed to be the committee of the Association, mounted the dais on which rested the birthday cake whose candles were now about to be lit. The balloons and flags waving about in the bright sunshine created a festive air that momentarily cheered me.

Sister Martha called for silence, and then began to speak: 'I'd like to welcome you all here today which is a special day as it marks the one-hundredth anniversary of that day in 1898, though I believe it was winter and bitterly cold, when some brave and intrepid members of our Society first occupied the house and subsequently started a school. That school, alas, is no more, but so many of you here today, and many who are not, are witnesses to the advantages of the sort of education that St Catherine's gave its girls.'

336

She looked at the committee member carefully lighting the candles. 'Now, before I cut the cake—and before all the candles blow out—I have another announcement. Regretfully this is the last Association Day that will be held in these grounds. The authorities of the new university are going to make extensive alterations and it really isn't convenient for them to have us here any more.

'However,' she gave a cheerful smile, 'let's face it. It hasn't been the same since the school closed, has it? We miss the chapel and they have shamefully neglected the grounds which were always kept so beautifully. Frankly, I shan't be sorry to meet elsewhere and you will be notified well in advance about the new venue. Now the cake is ready and your committee have generously provided sparkling wine with which to toast the centenary. When you've all got a drink, please will you raise your glasses to a hundred years of St Catherine's.'

And so we did.

'A hundred years of St Catherine's . . .'

Well, almost.

By now I was surrounded by familiar faces which, like mine, showed their years: Joan Dixon, Georgina Fox, Kathleen Lonsdale, Ruth Brown, Mary Barlow, Margaret Potter . . . some I couldn't put a name to. Others I didn't know at all. But no Pippa, no Clare.

People recognised me and introduced

themselves. I talked my head off, relishing my performance as a minor celebrity. I had scarcely time to drink my wine or eat my cake. Eventually two altar boys in white surplices appeared and began getting the dais ready for Benediction.

I didn't feel I wanted to stay for it. I hadn't practised as a Catholic for thirty years and it would show. Also, too, I was full of nostalgia. I was sorry I had not attended class reunions before, and I had not kept in touch.

But I would not come again to the new venue. I said no 'goodbyes'. As everyone turned to face the altar I slunk away to the path between the trees and walked down to the tennis courts, now overgrown with weeds, past the lake with no swans, and the wall bare of Dog roses, and up the other path where only a few stray rhododendron bushes remained. Soon, I suspected, they too would be gone.

The strain of 'Tantum Ergo', the Benediction hymn, drifted towards me. I remembered the Corpus Christi processions—the event of the year—the school plays in which I played a prominent part, the exams in which I did so badly, high jinks in the dormitory after lights out, cold mornings running round the lake and expeditions to the town in well-ordered crocodiles.

The sound of voices grew fainter as I reached the gates and I turned and looked, possibly for the last time, at the place where I had spent those vital, formative years of my youth.

I thought of the musketeers: of Clare on that last dreadful journey, and Pippa entering a life of silence which was also a kind of death because she had cut herself off from the world.

\*      \*      \*

They say the past is another country. Sometimes, perhaps, it is best left unvisited.

B